'In *Charity*, Dewhurst examines patterns of guilt, recognition, shame and agency. A taut, fraught and stylish novel about notions of the culpable and the complicit, drawing upon the facts and fictions of an oft-neglected moment in history'
Eley Williams

'A shocking, expertly plotted story about family and betrayal, which keeps you guessing until the end. Much more than a page-turner, it shines a light on a brutal period of history, asking important questions about justice and revenge. A dazzling array of voices that brilliantly merges the past and the present'
Emily Bullock

'By turns humorous and heart-wrenching, impeccably researched and beautifully written throughout, this is a haunting and original debut that demands to be read'
Lianne Dillsworth

'The authenticity of its human relationships makes this hugely enjoyable tale of cultural and generational friction truly stand out. Madeline Dewhurst subtly subverts our understanding of her characters as layers of plot naturally reveal themselves. Assured and impressive, it's hard to believe *Charity* is a first novel'
Tony Saint

'An accomplished storyteller, Dewhurst takes the reader on a suspenseful journey, exposing dark family secrets. A brilliant debut that shines a light on our colonial past and its haunting effect on the present'
Julia Barrett

CHARITY

MADELINE DEWHURST

Lightning Books

Published in 2021
by Lightning Books Ltd
Imprint of Eye Books Ltd
29A Barrow Street
Much Wenlock
Shropshire
TF13 6EN

www.lightning-books.com

ISBN: 9781785632303

Cover by Ifan Bates
Typeset in Adobe Garamond Pro

British Library Cataloguing in Publication Data
A catalogue record for this book is available from the British Library.

Printed by CPI Group (UK) Ltd, Croydon CR0 4YY

For Colin, Oisín and Lily

'In December 1954 the daily average number of Mau Mau detainees and convicts held in the colony reached a peak figure of 71,346, among them some 8,000 women...many other individuals passed through the system who were not counted...a conservative estimate is that at least one in four Kikuyu adult males were imprisoned or detained by the British colonial administration at some time between 1952 and 1958... Violence was not exceptional but intrinsic to the system.

...only thirty-two European civilians were killed in Kenya as a result of Mau Mau attacks, with another twenty-six being wounded. More Europeans would die in road traffic accidents between 1952 and 1960 than were killed by Mau Mau'

David Anderson, *Histories of the Hanged*

LAUREN

I DIDN'T LIKE THE HOUSE at first. I literally felt like it was looking down and judging me. It and all the other houses in the square – all of them exactly the same, with their shiny blank windows, glossy black front doors and spotless grey brickwork, no gaps, no cracks – all of them lined up against me.

'All right mate,' I thought. 'You might be high and mighty, looking like you belong on Downing Street or something, but we'll see who's going to end up the winner here.'

That was the other thing about the house. Right from the beginning I found myself talking to it like it was a person.

Even the pavement was clean. No litter or ground-in gum. Nothing. Just this old-fashioned bike with a basket, chained to the railings. It was so quiet there, you couldn't even hear any traffic. Just some birds chattering in the bushes.

The park in the middle was lovely though – full of big old trees. A woman was sitting on a bench in the sun eating a sandwich and reading a magazine. She looked like she was enjoying her lunch break. I wished I could swap places with her.

It took ages for Mrs Forbes to open the front door. I thought maybe the bell wasn't working, or she might be deaf and not hear it. I lifted the brass knocker and gave a little rap. I didn't want to come across as rude or impatient. The longer I waited the more jittery I got. My palms were all sweaty from nerves, I wiped them on my skirt in case she shook my hand.

I could just walk away now, before it was too late. Forget the whole crazy scheme. I didn't really want to meet Edith Forbes – didn't want anything to do with her.

I had to give myself a little pep talk. This wasn't just about me, I was doing it for Nan. And it wasn't like I had any other options. I couldn't stay at Sam's much longer – she needed her bedroom back to herself. I could tell her parents were getting pissed off with me being there. Her mum kept asking if I'd found somewhere else yet. Like I could afford anywhere in London.

I looked up at the house towering above me. I'd be mad to pass up the chance to live here. It was bang in between two tube stations instead of miles from anywhere, like Mum's was. Think of the fares I'd save getting into work, and it would be easier to get up to Colindale for my courses. No more having to spend an hour on the bus from Southgate.

I'd never be able to look myself in the face again if I didn't go through with this. I'd feel like a complete waste of space.

I knocked again, louder this time.

She was kind of how I expected – short silver hair set in waves, tweed skirt and pink round-neck cardigan, very M&S Tory lady. She waited for me to introduce myself before letting me in, checking me over with her light blue eyes. She was thin and a bit twitchy; seemed very with it. I'd have to watch my mouth around her.

'I've made tea,' she said, expecting me to just follow her as she thumped away down the hall with her walking-frame.

A tray was all set up in the kitchen, with cups and saucers, a milk jug and a teapot. It was the Barker Brothers Art Deco tea set, hand-painted with red and gold cherries, but of course I didn't know that then. She'd even bought these fancy chocolate biscuits. Florentines. I think she was trying to show the kind of standards she expected from the start. Her hands shook as she poured boiling water into the teapot. Half of it splashed onto the biscuits, melting the chocolate. At least she let me carry the tray through to the front room. Well, ordered me, more like.

It was a massive room with a real marble fireplace, very old-fashioned. It had that furry wallpaper, like the Taj Mahal restaurant me and Mum used to go to for a treat, only in grey, which seemed a bit of a weird colour choice for a living room.

She made me sit on a wooden chair in the middle of the room, like I was in a gangland interrogation or something, only with tea and biscuits balanced on my lap. Talk about trying to disadvantage me.

A framed black-and-white photo hung on the wall. I guessed it was Colonel Forbes – he was wearing his uniform, medals and all. I tried not to look at it, to focus on her instead, but it was like a magnet pulling at my eyes.

She noticed. 'Handsome chap, my husband.' She sounded proud.

I just nodded. Couldn't handle thinking about him right now.

Still, we hit it off straightaway, without me having to try too hard even. She'd been an actress when she was young, before she got married. She had that way of talking, you know, like Judi Dench or the duchess off of *Downton*.

'Why'd you stop?' I asked her.

'Graham didn't approve. I grew up in Kenya. The Europeans

in Kenya may have had a reputation for louche behaviour, but I married an Englishman. Military – straight as a die. He had certain expectations of his wife.'

She had a funny way of pronouncing Kenya – 'Keenya' – very posh.

I told her how I was a beautician, I'd almost got my level two diploma and was training for a level three in advanced nail technology. That impressed her. She didn't even know there was such a thing as nail technology. She said she had arthritis in her hands, could hardly move her fingers, so I offered to give them a massage. I know where the reflexology pressure points are, to stimulate blood flow and improve overall health.

I had some hand cream in my bag and I worked it gently into her hands – the loose flesh, the backs all blotchy with freckles, her knobbly fingers, her flaky nails. Old people don't bother me. She still wore her wedding and engagement rings, yellow and white gold, the wedding ring set with round-cut diamonds and three blue sapphires, the engagement ring with a single solitaire diamond. I guess Forbes had chosen them, or maybe they picked them out together. Her fingers were a bit swollen so I had to leave them on.

I moved in a week later. Didn't have much stuff, just Ubered it over from Sam's. It was amazing to have my own room again – top of the house, at the back. 'So here I am,' I said to the house. 'Queen of the castle and nothing you can do about it.' I could see over the whole manor – nicely kept gardens, all tasteful shrubs and shaped lawns. Blue and white flowers, bit on the cold side. None of the bright orange or pink flowers my nan used to love. Only one house had a trampoline, a huge one with a net around it. Bet the neighbours hated that. Not that I ever saw any kids on it. Amber and Leo would've loved it. They were always asking Mum for a trampoline.

The house backing onto Edith's had a conservatory built out from the kitchen. Sometimes you could see people moving about in there, glasses of wine in their hands. The couple that lived there – you could tell they loved each other from the way he kissed her on the cheek when he topped up her glass. Sometimes they just stood together looking out at the garden. When it was hot they ate outside at a long table they'd cover with a white cloth and set with all these different coloured bowls and plates and napkins – turquoise and emerald and terracotta, like something off Instagram. Then they had friends over, or their kids would be there. I guess they were students home from uni – looked the type. You could just hear the murmur of their voices and their laughter, but it never got too wild.

It was quiet there, at the back of the house. I'd leave my window open and all these amazing smells would drift up from the gardens below. Better than a Glade. Better than the smell of diesel. Apart from the odd siren, I hardly knew I was in London.

I'd told Mrs Forbes I didn't smoke. I'd been meaning to give up anyway, there's nothing worse than getting a facial off someone with fingers stinking of fags. I was surprised how easy it was in that house, not to smoke. It was like I was stepping into a new personality. I wish I could say I was leaving all the bad bits behind, becoming a better person, but it wasn't like that. It couldn't be.

Sometimes I felt homesick, seeing that family eating together, but homesick for what? What home? Mike was a dickhead, either bossing me around or ignoring me and making a big show of Amber and Leo. Mum still hadn't forgiven me for that party.

When I said I wasn't staying on at school they said fine, you think you're so grown-up, you can pay your own way. You'd think they'd give me a chance to get trained up. It's not like I could work full-time. I told Mum I could end up on Harley Street. You should see the prices those aesthetic therapists charge. It's a growing industry.

'But you did so well in your GCSEs. Your English teacher said you were university material.'

God knows why Miss Grey wanted me to stay on. She was always telling me off in class. Either I was talking too much or too little. It was probably just for some Ofsted form or something – make the school stats look good.

Anyway, I like doing something practical. I love messing around with all the bottles and colours, making women feel good about themselves. Some of them treat you like shit of course, but there's others that are really nice. This lady came into the store the other day, said she'd never dared wear make-up, her husband was abusive, used to beat her up. She had a scar on her cheek from where he'd hit her. I did a full make-over for her. Took ages. But by the end you couldn't even see the scar. She was over the moon, said I'd made her feel confident about herself again. She said I should get a job as a make-up artist on films or TV. Maybe I will – use my creative side. That's the thing – just because I'm training in beauty therapy doesn't mean I have to spend my life doing it.

I'm going to live like those people in the house opposite. I'm going to have the sort of home people want to visit – all warm and golden and glowing. Anyone with troubles, they'll know they can just drop in and I'll put on the kettle or open a bottle of something. We'll sit around the kitchen table, or out in the garden under the trees and they'll tell me all about it. There'll always be a bed made up in the spare room. My husband won't mind. He'll be the understanding, laid-back type.

Mrs Forbes' room was at the front of the house, on the first floor. She kept saying she'd have to move downstairs, but

I told her we'd get a stair-lift. She didn't want to give up her bedroom. It was a beautiful room. Two long windows, nearly floor to ceiling, looking out on the square. And her bed was a massive old thing with a carved headboard – we'd never of got that downstairs. Plus, she had a double wardrobe and a dressing table. It was like something out of one of those old black and white films with Katherine Hepburn or Greta Garbo I used to watch in the afternoons with Nan. Sometimes I watched them with Mrs Forbes. Her TV was crap though. I kept telling her we should get a new one – big one, with a sound bar so she could actually hear it. She said she'd think about it, which meant 'No' as far as Mrs Forbes was concerned.

I did offer to pay some rent – felt like I had to really – but she said she'd rather I paid her 'in kind'.

'I'll train you up to be a first-rate housekeeper,' she said.

That was OK. She could think that for now. One day I'd tell her the truth. Then she'd know I ain't nobody's fucking servant.

EDITH

'WHERE ARE YOU FROM?'

I looked up from my list of questions intending to look stern, but my hand betrayed me, shaking visibly as I removed my reading-glasses. It was the arthritis, but I didn't get a chance to explain that.

'London.'

'I thought a Londoner would be better placed to find their own accommodation. What about your family?'

The girl gave a slight shrug. 'No space. My brother and sister are getting too old to share a bedroom, and well, to be honest, me and my step-dad don't exactly get along.' She sounded apologetic rather than self-pitying.

'You come from a broken home? Or is your father deceased?'

'Dead? Don't think so. Haven't seen him since I was little. He could be anywhere.' She glanced out of the window, as though she might spot him suddenly on the street outside.

'Your mother remarried?'

'She was never married to my dad in the first place, but she is married now, yeah, and I've got a half-brother and half-sister.'

'I suppose that makes one full sibling.'

Lauren smiled at my attempted witticism and I warmed to her. She had a delightful smile, open and spontaneous. I didn't think someone with a smile like that would be capable of much dishonesty, however unfortunate their circumstances. I could see that she was nervous. She sat perched on the edge of her chair, holding onto her cup and saucer throughout our interview without, as far as I could see, taking one sip of tea.

'Why don't you share a flat with someone? A friend or colleague, say.'

Paul had assured me that, on paper, she was the best candidate by far, but I wasn't taking any chances with someone I was bringing into my home. I hadn't had servants since we left Africa. Things are different there of course, but still, I'd had enough bad experiences to be cautious.

'London rents are mad, there's just no way I can afford them, even sharing a flat.' She jerked her hand and some tea slopped out of her cup and into the saucer. 'Most of my friends are still living at home. I can only work part-time while I do my Level 2 Diploma in beauty therapy. I've nearly finished it. Eventually I aim to run my own salon.' She nodded proudly.

I glanced down at my notes. The letters looped across the page in indecipherable waves. Couldn't see where I'd put my glasses now.

'I was really looking for someone with nursing experience.'

'I've done a first-aid course, and I'm used to handling bodies. I've already got a Level 3 award in intimate waxing.'

'Intimate?' I held my hand up and she closed her mouth. I'd read about this fashion for the complete removal of body hair.

It had something to do with pornography. I hoped she wasn't involved in anything like that, though she didn't look buxom enough for a stripper; she was a skinny little thing with knobbly knees.

'I just meant, you know, you get to see it all in my job. Plus, I'm quite strong, physically. You have to stand for hours working at a beauty counter. You're not allowed to sit down and they make you wear heels. So if you need help getting up and down the stairs, to the bathroom – that kind of thing – that's no problem for me.'

'I'm not incontinent yet, thank you very much.'

Though I had to admit, things weren't as watertight as they used to be. She offered to give me a pedicure, but I declined. I wasn't about to remove my shoes in the middle of an interview.

'A hand massage then?'

Why was she so keen on physical contact?

'Can you cook?' Someone that thin was unlikely to have much appreciation of food. She'd hardly taken a bite out of the biscuits I'd bought.

'Yes, I'm quite a good cook actually. I got an A* in food technology at GCSE.'

'That doesn't sound very appetising. What has technology got to do with food?'

'We learnt all about nutrition, so I can make sure your meals are balanced and healthy, plus,' she held up one finger, 'the design side. Not just the appearance but the sensory experience as well.'

'Goodness, it all sounds very space-age.'

'This is a beautiful room, Mrs Forbes.'

The girl swivelled round in her chair, taking in the sitting room with her large eyes. They were an unusual colour, almost golden when they caught the light, with flecks of green.

'So big, and I love the wallpaper. Very vintage. I've never seen that type of wallpaper in those sorts of colours before.'

I followed her gaze. 'Flock wallpaper; blue-grey. The pattern is traditional damask.'

Apart from a bit of re-painting, this room hadn't been changed since I first decorated it, back in the Seventies. It's funny to think of it now, but when Graham suggested moving to Islington I'd been horrified. It was what you might call a ghetto back in those days – full of immigrants; West-Indians mostly. Graham pointed out that Barnsbury was different: it had been turned into a conservation area with no through traffic and you could pick up a three-storey Georgian for a steal. The council tenants had all been moved on to more suitable places, like Holloway. I still think of myself as living in Barnsbury rather than Islington; old habits die hard.

'Flock is very hard-wearing. I don't think elegance ever dates, does it?'

She leant towards me eagerly. 'That's exactly it. It's that classic look; timeless elegance – same as with clothes.'

I had been hoping for a medical student, but none had answered my advertisement. Lauren was my best option, despite her young age. At least at only eighteen she shouldn't have acquired too many bad habits. She seemed harmless enough, submissive, well-intentioned, not terribly intelligent, but bright and bubbly enough to make pleasant company. And she was fairly well-spoken. She said that was her grandmother's influence. Apparently she was a real stickler about grammar, which was quite reassuring to hear. We agreed to a trial period of six weeks.

I wasn't sure I had the energy to really train her up, but if she was the best of the bunch, well, she'd just have to do. I couldn't afford live-in help from a professional and I couldn't bear to be stuck in a nursing home, being patronised, or worse, maltreated, by foreigners with hardly a word of English. The house was too large for one person, and, I have to admit, I found living on my own quite lonely. I never had, before Graham died. But I had promised myself, the only way I was going to leave that house was to be carried out feet first.

LAUREN

'I AIN'T BEING FUNNY, but does it smell?' Stacey asked. 'Bit
depressing innit? Like living in a old people's home.'

'What you talking about?' Ash sprayed a shot of eau de
cologne in Stacey's direction. 'She's living in that big old house
rent-free, what's not to like? Why don't you invite us round,
have a party?' Ash laughed.

He knew I wouldn't do that. Edith didn't like guests. It was
one of the rules. No guests. That was all right. It's fine to have
rules if they're set down from the start and you both agree to
them. It's when people introduce new rules, out of the blue –
that's when you get problems.

'Wish I could move out of my mum's. She doing my head in.'
Stacey sighed. 'Dunno how I'll ever save enough money for a
deposit though. Even fifty pound a month. I can't even save that.
Just getting here costs a fortune, d'you know what I mean? Then
there's lunch. I buy, like, salmon, tuna and fucking avocado. It

all adds up don't it?'

'You should bring in a packed lunch, some grains, a bit of salad, fruit.' Ash mimed, fitting his imaginary lunch into the compartments of a box. Not that he'd be caught dead with anything so fresh off the boat as a plastic lunchbox.

Stacey snorted. 'I don't have time for all that. Takes me an hour just do my hair every morning, then it's over an hour to get here, innit?' Stacey lived miles out, in Hertfordshire or somewhere like that. 'Least I can do my make-up on the train.'

Ash nodded. 'Crowded this morning, was it? Somebody jog your arm?'

I couldn't help laughing. I swear to God, sometimes Stacey looks like she puts her make-up on in the dark. She doesn't even blend her foundation over her jawline – and she works on a beauty counter. Mind you, some customers like the fake-tan look. And don't get me started on the square eyebrows.

Only takes ten minutes on the tube to Oxford Circus from Highbury Corner, and the Victoria line's always packed, so I do my make-up before I leave the house. There's a lot of products to apply, but I like taking my time, using all the proper brushes I've got now, trying out different shades and contouring. Putting my face on, Edith calls it. I guess it is like my social face. Makes me feel good, and it's definitely not 'warpaint' like Mum says.

Stacey put a hand up to her mouth, looking at me like a thought had just popped into her head. 'Oh, babe, do you have to wipe her bum?'

'Whose bum?'

'Your old lady's!'

Stacey could be a right idiot sometimes.

'I just do her shopping, cook her dinner and clean the house. Things I'd be doing anyway if it was just me.'

I checked the foundations were lined up in the right order,

from Ivory to Cappuccino. There was nothing in the range for skin darker than milky brown.

'Fair exchange,' Ash said, fanning himself with perfume tester cards. 'Maybe I should find myself some rich old lady, marry her before she dies and inherit the lot.' He raised his eyebrows at a woman in a Burberry trench coat checking out the lipsticks on the Bobbi Brown counter.

'I thought you was gay?' Even though Stacey's brunette, she acts so blonde.

'Maybe I'm bi,' Ash said.

'Ooh, are you?' Stacey squished her collagen-filled lips into a pout.

She was punching well over her weight there. Ash looks like Zayn Malik from 1D, right? He wants to be a make-up artist for celebrities – proper A-listers like Rihanna and Beyoncé. I reckon he'll definitely make it. I can just see him with his own TV show. Customers come in specially to get him to do their make-up. I've learnt more off him than my tutor at college.

'What d'you reckon, Lauren, what're my chances with your old lady?'

'Don't be grim. Anyway, Edith's got a daughter.'

'Why don't her daughter look after her then?' Stacey said, eyeballing Burberry woman, who'd started giving us dirty looks.

'They don't speak no more.' I swapped the Warm Beige and Sand Dune over to their correct places.

'I wish my mum would stop fucking talking to me for a while.' Stacey swivelled round. She was sitting on the chair meant for customers. She never even tried to look busy. 'To be fair though babe, she could pay someone to take care of her mum, d'you know what I mean?'

'Edith doesn't want a carer. She calls me her housemate.'

'Nice,' Ash said. 'Sir, would you like to try the new Acqua di

Palma unisex fragrance?' He strolled off after a man in a Paul Smith suit.

I wished I'd never said anything about Edith's daughter; made me feel anxious. Out of sight and out of mind, that's where I needed her to stay.

'Can I help you?' I forced myself to smile at Burberry woman smearing the wrong shade of concealer over her under-eye shadows.

'That ain't even a tester.' Stacey was muttering behind me. 'And she's using her fingers.'

EDITH

LAST NIGHT MARY came to me. Not as she had been the last
time I saw her, but as she was when we were children and played
together. She ran around my bed giggling and tugging at my
bedclothes, glancing at me mischievously out of the corners of
her eyes. I could hear the swift pat pat of her bare feet passing
back and forth; her legs hidden by the bed. Her head was smooth
as an egg, with just its soft tuft of black hair at the crown. Her
teeth shone like pearls in her laughing mouth and her beads
rattled like teeth in the cold of an English winter. The room was
filled with the musty scent of pyrethrum flowers drying in the
sun.

The footsteps paused as she stopped to look at me. I feared
she was going to climb up onto the bed and I huddled in the
centre, clutching at the sheets. But she just kept running, back
and forth, chanting, 'Edie, Edie, what you hiding there for? I
can see you!' It was making me sick with dizziness, watching her
run, when suddenly she slammed the palms of her hands down

on the mattress, pressing so heavily on the side of the bed I felt myself rolling toward her.

'I can see you!'

She had stopped laughing, her plump cheeks had hollowed out and lost their dimples. Her skin was ashy grey and her eyes were like caves in her face, full of shadows. I felt her breath as her mouth opened above me, a black pit sucking me in. I screamed but my voice was trapped in my throat. I tried to move but my limbs were paralysed.

'It's just a nightmare, Edith. You go back to sleep.' Lauren was standing over me and the room was filled with light.

Just a nightmare. How many times had I said those words to my child? And what a ridiculous contradiction. Who wanted to sleep when nightmares lay in wait?

'What are you doing here?'

'I heard you shouting so I came to see if you were OK.' She straightened out the sheets, tucking me back in. 'I'll get you a glass of water, or how about some hot milk with sugar? That's very soothing. My mum used to make it for me when I was little.'

'Just water.' I was so disorientated I'd forgotten Lauren had moved in. 'Thank you.'

I spent the rest of the night propped upright with the light beside me on. I hadn't thought of Mary in years. What was she doing, trespassing on my dreams?

'Are you Jewish?'

I had to ask. Her origins had been puzzling me. She has pale skin and large hazel eyes, with a smattering of freckles over her nose, but her hair is not exactly European. Lauren was carrying in the tea tray. She always looked as if she was about to drop the whole thing.

'Your hair. It's quite frizzy. A lot of Jewish people have hair like that.'

Lauren laughed. 'Never been asked that before.' She held out a plate. 'Have a biscuit. I made them this morning.'

'Goodness, and you've put them on the best china.'

I wondered how she'd found it. I thought I kept it locked away. It gave me quite a shock, seeing it again. I hadn't used it since the early days of my marriage.

Lauren looked upset. She wasn't much more than a child really and always eager to please. 'They're shortbread; I made them specially. You said it was your favourite.'

'It is, of course. That was very thoughtful of you.' The biscuits were cut into uneven rectangles and looked horribly dry and pale.

'And I made the tea just like you said, in a pot, leaves not bags.'

She certainly tries hard. 'I noticed the strainer.' I nodded at the silver tea strainer sitting in its ornamental stand. She had gone to the trouble of polishing it at least, though she ought to have asked before using it.

As if she had read my mind she said, 'There's no point having things if you don't use them. The sideboard was open and I thought, that's a pretty tea-set, we should get it out. Shame to leave it in the dark, gathering dust.'

Which was odd because I was sure it had been packed away in the attic, but she can't have gone up there. You needed a ladder to get into the attic.

'Do you like the biscuits?'

I tried to eat one, but it disintegrated onto my lap in a shower of crumbs.

'I must've cooked them too long. It's that oven. Burns everything.'

Lauren has a bad habit of always blaming her failings on someone or something else. It's part of our litigious culture now, I suppose, to evade responsibility. I try to correct this tendency in her.

'Perhaps you didn't use enough butter. They're a bit on the dry side.'

'I followed the recipe exactly.' Lauren got up. 'I'll get the Hoover.'

'It's a Dyson. But wait until we've finished our tea.' I couldn't face the noise and disruption of the vacuum cleaner.

'What you need is a dog. A dog would make those crumbs disappear in no time.'

The thought horrified me. A smelly, drooling creature shedding hairs and snuffling up the crumbs in my lap.

'We had dogs in Kenya, but I wouldn't keep one in London. It isn't fair to the animal, to keep it in a city.'

The dogs we had in Kenya were hardly pets either.

'I could walk it for you. It'd be company, when I'm out at work. I can just see you with a little dog – a Bichon Frise, say, or a Cockapoo!'

'A what?'

'They're so cute, I'll find a picture of one on my phone.' She tapped on her mobile phone and a photograph of a dog appeared. 'They're a cross between a poodle and a cocker spaniel.' She showed me some small, curly-haired dogs that looked as though they had once been white, but had been dipped in tea.

'So where does it come from, the curl?'

'I'm not a dog breeder, I don't know.' She rolled her eyes.

'Not the dogs'. *Your* curls.'

'Oh, that.' Lauren laughed again.

She has a delightful throaty chuckle, no high-pitched giggling thank goodness, and good teeth, white and even. I expect she wore a brace as a child. Everyone does now – like the Americans.

'Well, my grandad was Irish.'

'Was he?' That would explain it. Celtic locks. 'Where in Ireland was he from? Ulster or Éire?'

'Airer?'

'Northern Ireland or the Irish Republic?'

'I don't know. He died when I was little. Do you want more tea?' Lauren poured herself another cup and then topped up mine before I had a chance to decline.

'Graham was stationed in Northern Ireland for a while. We stayed in a house in Enniskillen one summer. Quite scenic countryside there, like a minor Lake District, but I could never get used to the weather. So grey and cold all year round.'

The people had that Presbyterian dourness too and I thought the accent horribly ugly, but I didn't say that to Lauren.

'Growing up in Africa, it must've been hard getting used to the climate over here. I bet you still miss the sun, don't you? And the heat. I would.'

'Oh it was a dreadful shock when I was first sent to boarding school in England. My mother had told me all about the wonders of the seasons in Britain; the beauty of the spring with its blossom and birdsong, the rich red colours of autumn. There are only two seasons in Africa you know; dry and wet. I was expecting balmy evenings walking under the russet-coloured trees. Instead, all there seemed to be was endless icy, grey dampness. I used to huddle under my thin blanket, shivering in bed all night, crying into my pillow. And then I remember drawing the curtains in the morning to find frost patterns on the inside of the windows. So pretty, but so painfully cold.' I pulled my cardigan round me. 'Still, what doesn't break you makes you stronger.'

I think that's where it began, what Joanna used to call my 'emotional repression'. Of course self-restraint is a thing of the past, people just fall over themselves to bare their chests nowadays, both literally and metaphorically. The Seventies spawned a generation of spoilt children. I tried not to spoil mine, but apparently I failed miserably as a parent.

'Didn't you ever want to move back? As an adult I mean.'

'It's all changed so much now. Kenya is not the country I grew up in.' I don't like to dwell on what has happened to Africa. 'We had this tea-set in Kenya you know. It was my mother's. Our house-boy used to serve tea on the veranda. He always wore white gloves…'

Lauren interrupted me. 'Barack Obama's dad was Kenyan.'

'Yes, I know. The press made a great deal of it.'

I do keep up with the papers, despite my advanced age. I've been trying to get Lauren to read the *Telegraph* to me, but she is, I fear, a sad indictment of our education system. Her ability to concentrate is minimal; she's always breaking off mid-article to make irrelevant comments. I don't really think she grasps what she's reading. Perhaps it's the Irish genes. She is a sweet little thing who hasn't had many opportunities in life. She is doing her best to make something of herself and that is to be applauded.

I took a sip of tea. 'Have you met Paul? Our downstairs lodger?'

Lauren looked surprised and shook her head.

'Ever such a nice chap; lives in the basement flat. He's been renting it for about a year now. I do like to have a man about the place. Even if the flat is separate, just knowing he's downstairs makes me feel safer. And he's a great help in the garden.'

I shifted in my chair, the pain in my hips was spreading down into my thighs and my left foot had gone numb. 'He's a huge improvement on the sitting-tenant we got stuck with when we first bought this house.'

Mrs Abrahams. Such a miserable old hypochondriac; there was always something wrong with her yet she kept on going well into her nineties.

'Graham always wanted to turn the house back into one. The basement was going to be his study and den, but by the time Mrs Abrahams finally died it was too late for Graham. I couldn't face dealing with all the trouble and expense of knocking through to the basement now.'

Lauren waved her arm to take in the sitting-room. 'What would you do with the extra space anyway?'

We used to have drinks parties in this room, before Graham retired. I always insisted on a real Christmas tree, the largest he could get, placed between the two windows. How enchanting it used to look. I'd decorate it entirely in blue and silver, to match the wallpaper. Sometimes Joanna tried to help. I had to remove her handmade decorations once she was in bed. She never noticed.

'I did think my daughter might move in. I thought, after her father died, she might want to come home and keep me company. She's no husband or children to look after. But Joanna is too busy pursuing her dreams to care for her mother.'

'Did you say Joanna lives in Italy?'

'That's right. She runs some sort of farm, yoga retreat place in Tuscany. They sound like a bunch of hippies to me. Goodness knows how they earn a living, let alone run a business. Apparently, it's a 'collective'. Graham did not approve.'

That was putting it lightly. I shuddered slightly, remembering their last angry exchange. Graham had thrown an empty bottle of Scotch at Joanna, just missing her head and leaving a dent in the wall behind her. Typical Graham: he would never have thrown a full bottle.

'Must be nice though, living in Italy. Have you been out to visit her?'

'Good God no. She sent me some pictures once. It looked quite squalid.'

'Do you think she'll want to spend the rest of her life there? In Italy?'

'As far as Joanna is concerned I don't like to count on anything.' My daughter has a capricious nature. I don't know where she gets it from. 'We tried for so long to have a child, Graham and I, that when she finally came along I spoiled her. We always hoped to have more, but it wasn't to be.'

I smiled at Lauren, I didn't want her to think me self-pitying. She shows such an interest in my life I find myself telling her things I'd never, as a rule, reveal to anyone.

'Nowadays you could have IVF or something. Doesn't always work though. My manager at work's had three rounds of IVF and still no baby.'

'It doesn't look as if I'll be getting any grandchildren either.'

All my old friends and acquaintances seemed to have acquired grandchildren. Like poor Heather who died a few years ago; she'd devoted her life to hers. They must miss her now. I really ought to give Bob a call; check how he was coping without her. He'd been very kind to me after Graham died. Graham had hoped for grandsons, to take to cricket matches, to enter his regiment. It had always been his dearest wish, to have a son to carry his name and continue in his footsteps.

'Paul was in Graham's regiment. He said Graham had been – how did he put it? A mentor, no, a role-model to him.'

Lauren was looking at me with concern. Perhaps she noticed my physical discomfort. My joints make such awful cracking noises every time I move, I'm afraid bits of me will start snapping off.

'So Paul was in the army then?' she asked.

'Yes, but he works for a military charity now. That's how I met him; he invited me to a charity event. I think he was hoping Graham might become a patron. He didn't know Graham had passed away.'

I looked up at the framed photograph of Graham in uniform that hung on the wall. His jaw was firm and his cheekbones pronounced; not a speck of stubble on his chin. His nose was straight and slender. His lips were closed in that enigmatic half-smile. Better to remember him like that and forget the slobbering, bulbous-nosed old man snoring in the chair where Lauren now sat.

'I think Graham would have been better with sons. He would have been the perfect father for a boy.'

Lauren got up and started fidgeting with one of the curtains. It was still light out; there was no need to draw them. Her generation have short attention spans. It's all the videos they watch on their telephones. Instant entertainment.

'I'm not suggesting Graham was inadequate as a father.' I didn't want to give the wrong impression, to demean Graham's memory. 'He was the most responsible, hardworking father and husband anyone could wish for. He was awarded an MBE for his work in Kenya, you know. He was absolutely brilliant at dealing with the natives; knew just how to handle them.'

Lauren evened out the pleats in the curtain and fastened it back into place, pulling sharply on its tie-back. She'd have to do the other one now, so that they were symmetrical.

'What was the right way to handle the natives?'

There was an edge to her voice I didn't care for.

'One had to be firm. I know that sort of thing isn't considered politically correct now, when former terrorists like Nelson Mandela are fêted as heroes, but really, Graham had to deal with the worst of the worst. Terrorists who murdered women and children. All this guilt about the colonies – it's completely misplaced. Just look at the situation in the Middle East. If we had let the Mau Mau win, if we hadn't stood our ground and taken tough measures, Kenya would have descended into all-out civil war.'

'So, what sort of tough measures did we take?'

I'd forgotten to ask Lauren about her political leanings when I interviewed her. It was one of the first things Graham would have wanted to know, but she hadn't appeared to have any strong views either way.

'Graham said his men never did anything worse than you'd see in a rugger scrum in some of the best schools in England. People have become very soft, Lauren, and it just doesn't do. Look at the state of the world, for goodness sake.'

'You're right there, you don't want to be too soft.'

'That's why, when I finally decided to rent the basement out again, it was such a relief to me that Paul said he'd take it on. You hear such terrible stories, and knowing he's just downstairs if I need him – a soldier trained by my own husband, someone I can trust – it's very reassuring. You're lovely dear, but I don't think you'd be able to fight off an intruder, would you?'

When I thought of Paul my chest felt lighter. I could breathe more easily. I really didn't know how I would have got through the last year without him.

'I always meant to take up martial arts.'

Lauren began putting the tea things onto the tray. She seemed to have calmed down, her tone had become friendly again. Sometimes all that's needed is a little flattery.

'Like more tea?' she asked.

'Oh no, dear, I've had more than enough, thank you.'

I'd stopped having afternoon tea before Lauren came, but

I make a point of having it now whenever she isn't working. Especially on Tuesdays and Thursdays before she goes off to her evening classes. It's a good custom, punctuates the day, stops the afternoon from drifting on endlessly.

I wished Lauren hadn't got me onto the subject of the Mau Mau. It upsets me to recall those times; I prefer not to think about it. I hoped I hadn't been ranting on, but really I'd only said what needed saying. I don't think I said anything Graham would have disapproved of.

Could she have heard the news reports or seen that horrible interview on *Newsnight*? They'd lulled Graham into a false sense of security by acknowledging his achievements, his work for the UN and the Ministry of Defence. Which only made it worse when they stuck the knife in, dredging up those awful accusations. The depths to which some people will sink. They had destroyed Graham when he was too old and frail to defend himself. It was the lawyers I blamed most. Vultures. Lauren wouldn't have seen them. She was too young, and besides, she has no interest in the news.

Lauren went out that evening. She was going to the cinema with friends. She left me a ham salad for my supper, but I wasn't feeling hungry. I just had a brandy and a sleeping tablet. Then I was so drowsy the next morning, I completely forgot to tell her about Joanna's phone call.

LAUREN

I WAS GLAD EDITH brought up that stuff about Kenya and the British needing to be tough. I'd been starting to go soft myself.

Edith wasn't exactly how I'd imagined. She was stuck-up in some ways and she definitely had a mean streak, but then she could be really friendly. She'd tell me stories about her life, the places she'd been, all the animals she'd seen in Africa, and personal stuff too, like how she'd wanted more kids. Then I'd feel so bad. I'm not a sneaky sort of person, I like everything to be upfront. It's got me into trouble in the past. People never thank you for it – they like it better if you fake it and tell them what they want to hear.

OK, so I was lifting things here and there, which I never planned on doing, but they practically begged me to take them. It didn't feel like stealing – more like house clearance. This might sound crazy, but every time I sold something I felt like the house let out a big sigh of relief. Like the weight of all that stuff was being lifted off its beams. Most of the stuff was stuck up in the attic, giving the poor old house a headache.

You see, me and the house had reached a sort of agreement. We were equals now, even if we didn't always like each other. I put up with its creaks and groans and bad history and it put up with me, the cuckoo in the nest. A house can't help who owns it, know what I mean?

Paul left the stepladder on the landing outside my bedroom after he fixed the smoke alarm. It was pointing directly up at the square hatch in the ceiling, like an arrow showing the way.

I opened up the ladder and gave it a shake. It felt pretty sturdy. I've always been good with heights – even joined the after-school climbing club in Year Seven. I had to stand right on the top step to reach. Keeping my feet as wide apart as I could on the metal rung, I clenched all the muscles in my legs and belly to help balance me and pushed at the hatch. It wasn't moving. I shoved again and nearly fell backwards.

'So you don't want me going up there,' I said. 'Well that only makes me more determined to see what you've got hidden away.'

Leaning forward so I wouldn't topple off the ladder I punched at the hatch with both fists. Edith never came up to the top of the house and she was deaf as a post, so I didn't have to worry about her. Finally the hatch gave way and I could push it to one side. I stuck my hands in, scrunching up my eyes and holding my breath in case I touched something disgusting. Just a wooden floor, no squeaking or scampering, nothing biting my fingers, thank God.

A few scenes from horror films played through my mind, but I quickly switched them off, telling myself to get a grip. It was bad enough I was talking to a building. I didn't want to lose it completely.

I hauled myself up through the doorway. I could just make

out a light cord hanging from the ceiling. I pulled on it, half-expecting it to come away in my hand, but a bare bulb lit up the attic. It was all really neat, under the dust and the cobwebs. I suppose that was Forbes, keeping it all ship-shape, or whatever they do in the army. There were suitcases, big bags full of golf clubs, tennis rackets, an old doll's house and stacks of crates and cardboard boxes. It would take me a few visits to get through it all.

I had a peek in a couple of boxes. Most of it seemed to be papers, old bank statements, tax forms – boring stuff like that – nothing personal. No handwritten letters or diaries.

The crates had the china and silverware wrapped up in old newspaper. The silver had gone black, but some of the china was really pretty – delicate cups and saucers with gold borders and tiny painted birds peeking out behind pink and red flowers. There was some cheesy stuff too – plates with women in olden-day dresses acting like they was scared of a naked baby pointing his bow and arrow at them. Must've been for Valentine's or something. And a couple of vases with fat pastel-coloured peaches and plums shaped just like Kim Kardashian's arse. Looked expensive though; the colours were lovely. I gave them a wipe on my t-shirt and they came up as vibrant as any top-quality nail lacquer. Names were written on the base. I'd have to check them out online.

The thing that got me started didn't come from the attic though, and I figured it was fair enough me trading it since no one else seemed to want it. It was a gold snake necklace with ruby eyes Edith kept in a box on her dressing-table. She said it'd been a present from Forbes on her thirtieth birthday, but she'd only worn it to please him. She didn't like snakes. She'd offered it to her daughter after Forbes died and Joanna had laughed in her face. Said she'd never wear anything so hideous, which I thought

was a bit harsh, till I tried it on. It was an evil-looking thing –
ribbed with a fat tail and a mean little pointed face. Its ruby eyes
glittered like they was watching you.

When Edith opened the red leather box and poured the snake
out into my hands I literally jumped back in fright. The gold was
heavy and slippery against my skin. The necklace slithered from
one palm to another. I seriously thought a forked tongue might
whip out of its mouth and sting me.

'Whatever's the matter with you? It's just a piece of jewellery.'
Edith leant back in her chair. 'Put it on. Model it for me.'

I fumbled about with it, trying to do up the fastening, but I
couldn't see how it worked. In the end I had to kneel down in
front of her so she could clip its mouth onto its tail.

'That's it,' she said. 'Now go and stand in front of the window
so I can see you properly.'

I could feel the cold weight of the metal against my collar
bones. It's just a bit of jewellery, I repeated to myself, and
probably worth a bit too. Maybe she wants to give it to me. I
stretched out my neck. Edith was making me feel stupid, the
way she was staring at me and nodding, like she was a judge on
a talent show and I was one of the contestants.

'Move your head from one side to the other. That's it, slowly,
left and then right.'

The more I turned my neck the tighter the necklace got.
It felt like the snake was coiling round my throat, wanting to
choke me. I pulled at it, but that only made it tighter. The gold
scales dug sharply into my skin. My mouth filled with spit, but
I couldn't swallow. I started to cough. My cheeks were burning.
Sweat was pooling in my armpits, trickling down my sides. I
tried to call out to Edith to help, but I couldn't catch my breath.
The room was spinning, everything was going misty. I could
hear the blood thumping in my ears. Grabbing the chain with

both hands, I yanked as hard as I could. I didn't care if I broke it, I just needed to breathe. Why wasn't Edith helping me?

At last the catch opened and it fell to the floor. I swear I saw it move, like it was wriggling towards me across the carpet. I let out a hoarse scream.

Edith laughed – a thin, mean sort of laugh. Called me a silly girl for making such a fuss. I swear she'd enjoyed the whole thing. She just sat there, holding out a tissue. It was like she'd known that necklace would choke me and wanted to see how I'd react. Maybe her and Forbes were into S&M. Wouldn't surprise me.

She hadn't even been planning on giving it to me. After all that, she told me to take it down her bank for safe keeping. Would've been only too happy to see the back of the fucking thing, but then the manager said they'd closed all their safe deposit boxes. You have to go to an independent provider now. UK banks have withdrawn from safe custody, apparently.

I walked slowly back from the bank with the snake coiled in my bag. What was the point in giving it back to Edith? She'd only get all flustered and anxious about it. Didn't take much to set her off. And who else was she going to leave it to? I might as well sell it to someone who was into that kind of thing and make some money out of it. You can't take it with you, as my nan used to say. Not that she meant it in that way exactly, but you know, I had as much right to profit from it as anybody else and it's not like Edith needed the money.

I'd just get on with being nice to Edith for now. I wasn't going to model any more jewellery for her though – or anything else for that matter. I kept seeing her face as she watched me – the greedy look in her eyes, then the disrespect. Like I was supposed to act out some part for her and I'd failed.

OCTOBER 1959, KENYA

EDITH FELT LIKE A BOTTLE of lemonade that has been given a good shake; sweet, effervescent joy was fizzing up out of her, scattering bubbles of affection over everyone at the Muthaiga Club, but most especially over her fellow actors from the Nairobi Players. She'd never felt such a sense of camaraderie or belonging before. Everyone had been so kind after the curtain came down, hugging her and telling her what a little star she was.

As soon as she'd stepped on stage her terror had melted away and her lines had tripped as naturally out of her mouth as though they were her own words. For two hours she was Sorel Bliss, a nineteen-year-old English girl without a real care in the world.

She hadn't told anyone yet, but her ambition was to become a proper actress, on screen as well as stage. She even had fantasies about becoming the next Audrey Hepburn or Grace Kelly. How she longed to escape the constant tension of Nairobi, to travel to sophisticated, cultured cities like London, Paris and Rome. Now she began to think it really was possible, she might even make it to Hollywood.

Afterwards Edith couldn't put her finger on what it was that made her look up from the animated conversations taking place around her, but when she did, there was a tall man in uniform standing on the other side of the table, watching her over the heads of the other actors. He raised his eyebrows, pointing the bottle of champagne he was carrying in her direction. Stretching across the table, she lifted her empty glass; holding it up for him to refill like a supplicant before a priest. In her memory, it was as if everyone else around the table melted away into the shadows and there was only this stranger, his dark blue eyes staring with hypnotic intensity into hers.

'Supermac does it again,' he said.

She'd momentarily forgotten about the election, though the Tory victory had been another reason for their celebrations at the Muthaiga.

'Thank God,' she said. Her parents had been fretting for weeks, terrified the Labour party might win and abandon Kenya to the Africans. Macmillan would never give up Kenya.

The corners of his mouth lifted, as if with wry amusement. 'Captain Graham Forbes. Pleased to meet you.' There was something compelling about his smile.

Squeezing round the table, she joined him where he stood. He was quite handsome: good bone structure, the sort of square jaw her mother would approve of.

She felt too tipsy for conversation so she was relieved when he took her hand and led her onto the dance floor. He was a competent dancer, if a bit on the formal side, holding her always at a firm distance. When another couple started smooching beside them, he whisked Edith round so she faced away. He was affable though; chatting easily with her companions, he stayed until the party broke up, then offered to drive Edith home.

She liked the way he drove with careless expertise, one hand on the wheel, the other holding a cigarette, his elbow resting on the open window as he casually flicked his ash out into the road. They travelled smoothly and swiftly through the deserted streets. Curfew kept the Africans safely indoors.

He parked outside the apartment she shared with two other girls, hopped out of the car and came round to open her door. She clambered out in as ladylike a way as she could manage after a night of drinking. When she finally located her keys at the bottom of her handbag, he took them from her and unlocked her front door. They stood for a moment pressed together in the hallway. She waited for him to make a pass, but he just nodded at the pistol in her bag.

'Be careful with that thing, won't you?' he said quietly.

She laughed. 'Don't worry, I've never had to use it.' She rolled her eyes. 'To be honest, I don't see the need, not any more, but I promised Mother I'd keep it by me at all times.' She patted her bag. 'You know, for protection against the Mau Mau.'

'It's not very feminine, all these women with holsters strapped round their waists, like cowboys in floral dresses.'

'That's why I keep mine in my handbag,' Edith said, doing her best Lady Bracknell impersonation.

Graham just frowned. Perhaps he'd never seen *The Importance of Being Earnest* and didn't get her little joke. 'Goodnight,' he said, reaching for the door.

'Still coming to the show tomorrow night?'

'Of course.' He smiled and gave her a little salute.

Well he was quite the gentleman; not like most of the chaps in Nairobi. She couldn't see why he objected to her gun though. It was such a pretty little thing, with a mother-of-pearl inlaid handle. Mother had given it to her on her fourteenth birthday and she slept with it under her pillow like all the other women she knew.

Edith decided Graham's reserve was very English and rather endearing. It wasn't that she wanted him to kiss her; it was only her pride, or perhaps her vanity, that wondered why he hadn't.

The following night, when Graham turned up backstage with the largest bouquet of roses she'd ever seen, Edith couldn't help but be flattered. Looking up at him under the bright glow of her dressing-room lights she noticed the grey at his temples and the lines on his forehead. He was older than she'd first thought.

He seemed happy to tag along to the Muthaiga Club with the Players again, but when Vivienne started dancing on the table he got up and left. Everyone had laughed. The Players liked to consider themselves terribly uninhibited, but Edith thought it was rather provocative of Vivienne to flash her knickers at him like that.

She was so caught up in the world of the theatre, she didn't give Graham another thought. She'd enjoyed his attention, but didn't consider him a love interest. Then a week later he rang up and invited her to dinner at the New Stanley Hotel. She could hardly say no; she'd only eaten there with her parents once before and, if nothing else, looked forward to a better meal than she'd had in ages.

It was such a treat to sit at a table spread with a thick white linen tablecloth, weighed down with silver cutlery and crystal glasses. The waiter handed her a menu with a slight bow. She studied the dishes carefully, her mouth watering. She wanted to make the most of this.

Graham turned to the waiter. 'We'll have the turtle soup to start and the braised lamb shank to follow.' He gave Edith an indulgent smile. 'And I expect the lady would like some trifle for dessert.'

Edith smiled back. It wasn't what she would have chosen, but since it was his treat she was hardly in a position to argue. He'd probably eaten here recently and knew what the best dishes were, she consoled herself. It all sounded yummy anyway.

Edith learnt a lot about Graham over that first dinner – at least about his recent history. He'd been stationed in Malaya for three years, fighting insurgents in the jungle, before being sent to Kenya. It all sounded terribly exciting, like something out of a *Boy's Own* adventure. Now he was a district officer, in charge of one of the prison camps and responsible for overseeing the rehabilitation of some of the most intractable detainees. It was a promotion for an army officer in his thirties and carried a great deal of responsibility. Edith began to see how debonair he was; the silver hairs above his ears only made him appear more distinguished. Really, he had something of Cary Grant about him.

By the time her dessert arrived, fortified by a martini and half a bottle of wine, Edith felt she ought to contribute something to the conversation. She wanted to prove to Graham she wasn't just some empty-headed actress, so, vaguely remembering an article she'd read in the *East African Standard*, she asked him if he minded all that hoo-ha in England, with politicians calling for an independent inquiry into the prisons in Kenya. Hadn't there been accusations of foul play at one of the camps? She'd forgotten the name of it. She didn't really follow the news, but she didn't want to admit that to him.

Graham just laughed. 'The Reds will stoop to anything to bring us down, but they were really scraping the barrel there, relying on the word of petty crooks and forgers.' He jabbed the cheese knife in her direction, like a teacher emphasising a point with a ruler. 'What people back in England don't understand is the level of savagery we are dealing with here. They have simply no idea. Think we can run prisons like holiday camps. What do they want? En-suite rooms and three-course meals for mass-murdering cannibals?'

He sounded like her parents. She could have told him it wasn't just the Africans who were capable of savagery, but instead she reached for her brandy glass. Graham's arm reached across the table, seizing her hand in his. Startled by the swiftness of his gesture she nearly knocked the glass over. He righted it carelessly with his spare hand, still maintaining his grip on her fingers.

'But I don't want to dwell on ugliness when dining with a pretty girl. If you married me, Edith, I'd ensure your life was filled only with beauty and pleasure. I would keep you safe from all the barbarity of the world.' His gaze fastened onto hers until she was forced to look away.

'It's a bit soon to be talking about marriage, isn't it?'

Sliding her hand out from under his, she fumbled in her purse for her cigarettes. She lit one from the candle, trying to maintain her cool but nearly setting fire to her hair in the process.

'I knew from the first moment I saw you I'd make you my wife.' He took the cigarette from her hand and placed it between his lips.

She forced out a light-hearted laugh. 'At the Muthiaga Club? I was half-cut. I'm sure I didn't appear at my best.'

He smiled. 'No Edith, at the theatre. I'd already seen you on stage earlier that first evening.'

So that was why he'd made a beeline for her. She was delighted he'd found her performance so captivating.

'Why ever didn't you say?'

'I didn't want to spoil that first moment, when the curtains opened and there you were, looking so ungainly, in a dress that was falling off you. You were cavorting about the stage like a little girl playing at dressing-up, with no self-consciousness at all.' He stubbed her cigarette out in his coffee cup. 'Don't look so hurt. I could never have fallen for a professional actress. It's precisely because you were dreadful that I found you so charming.'

Edith felt as though she'd been punched in the stomach. She couldn't speak, her vision clouded over with tears.

'Oh, Edith, really, it's a compliment. You're too good for all that.'

Graham pulled his handkerchief out of his top pocket and passed it to her. His initials were sewn onto the corner in crimson thread. She clenched it in one fist as she grabbed her bag and marched out of the hotel.

She told herself she wouldn't see him again after that, but he called on her the next day and persuaded her to come out for a drink. Well, she could hardly say no when he was standing right in front of her. He treated her like a princess. He wined her and dined her with no expense spared and no mean comments this time – only compliments. He asked her to forgive him for being such a cad. He said he'd spent too much time among brutes and had forgotten how to speak to a lady.

She was at a bit of a loose end since the show had finished. They'd hoped the run might be extended, but the theatre said they had another company booked in. The Nairobi Players were taking a break before setting up auditions for the Christmas panto. Edith didn't really think pantomime was her sort of thing. Everyone said Vivienne would get cast as Cinderella – she always got the leading lady role – and there weren't any other female parts.

Edith ended up seeing Graham every night of his leave. He'd appeared at just the right time really. Being part of the Nairobi Players was fun, but who was she kidding? She didn't have the looks or the talent to become a proper actress, let alone a film star.

A few days after Graham had gone back to work, she found his handkerchief in her jacket pocket. She spread it out across her lap. Tracing a finger over the curling, interlocked letters of his monogram, she realised their marriage was inevitable. Graham had laid claim to her and that was that. His will was so powerful he sapped all the resistance out of her. Turned her weak at the knees, one might say. There was something rather thrilling about his absolute self-assurance.

Being with Graham was like strapping oneself into a rollercoaster ride. All the trappings of authority were there to make one feel safe – the signs and the seat belts – but as the machine began to move, there was that lurch of excitement deep within the belly, as one relinquished control for exhilaration.

Edith went home to tell her parents. Father sent Thumbi, one of the farmworkers who knew how to drive, to pick her up. She felt rather sorry for him having to do a six-hour round trip on those winding bumpy roads to and from Nyeri. She slept most of the way home; opening her eyes just long enough to get a glimpse of the thick green forests of the Aberdare Mountains and only waking fully when they reached the rough murram track to the family farm.

The grevillea trees, planted to shade the coffee, were glowing with fuzzy amber flowers. The air hummed with the sounds of bees and sunbirds drawn to their nectar. Her heart couldn't help expanding as the stone bungalow, coated in cheery crimson bougainvillea, came into view. Despite all her conflicted feelings about it, some part of her would always think of the farm as home.

Father had always assumed she'd marry another settler, someone with land, but at least he was impressed when she told him about Graham's military background.

They were sitting on the veranda, sipping sundowners as they looked across the valley at the rows of coffee trees garlanded with red berries. The pyrethrum had been cut back, leaving tracts of bare soil waiting for the coming rains. The sun, a great crimson ball, was dropping behind lilac clouds, turning the whole sky vermillion.

'Do you think he'd like to take this on?' Father asked, waving at the landscape as if including the magnificent sunset in his bequest.

'For God's sake, Ralph.' Edith's mother set her empty glass down with a thud. 'You should be glad she's marrying an Englishman. At least he'll get her out of Kenya before the Africans take over and slaughter us all.'

It didn't take much for her parents to fall back into their ongoing argument about the future. As soon as there was talk of opening the White Highlands to African and Asian farmers her mother decided it was time to move to South Africa. Father, however, refused to leave the farm.

'You're overreacting, Irene.'

Edith could see the muscle in his neck twitching as he pressed his teeth together.

'Overreacting? They're releasing thousands of Mau Mau murderers and it won't be long before they let Kenyatta go. Just wait and see what happens when the Prince of Darkness is made president.' The fact that Jomo Kenyatta had left a white wife in England only made her mother detest him all the more. Now Irene's voice squeaked on the edge of hysteria. 'If you don't care about me, think of your daughter. Do you want to see her raped before they hack us limb from limb?'

'Mummy!' Edith squirmed as she cast a sidelong glance at Sammy, their houseboy. But his face remained as impassive as ever as he topped up her mother's glass from a jug of Tom Collins.

'You're forgetting I've been living in Nairobi. I was shopping on Victoria Street on Kenyatta Day and the demonstrators completely ignored me. They're more interested in boycotting European businesses than molesting European women.'

As the barefoot demonstrators swept past her towards Government House, singing *'twataka mashamba yetu. Hapa Kenya'*, Edith had caught sight of a young black woman about the same age as her and for a crazy second she had thought it was Mary. The girl had the same round, dimpled cheeks, the same determined energy; smiling as she raised a fist and called with gusto for Kenyatta to be freed. It was only for a second. Then a white man had grabbed her arm, pulling her out of the way before the police charged in, wielding their batons to clear the crowd. It was strange because Edith never thought about Mary – not even when she came home. She was very disciplined like that.

'Kenyatta Day,' her mother spat the words out. 'The man's a gang leader, a Mau Mau terrorist, and they talk about him as though he were a legitimate politician.'

'One of their placards said "the British are worse than the Russians". Edith and her father laughed. At least they shared a sense of humour. But this only enraged her mother further.

'If we stay here we'll be living under Communist dictatorship. You won't find that so funny.'

'The Mau Mau aren't released until they're properly rehabilitated anyway.' Edith said knowledgeably. 'That's what Graham's in charge of. He says any terrorists left alive are put through the rehabilitation pipeline. They don't get out of that unless they're changed men and women.' She took a sip of her drink, noting her parents' sceptical expressions. 'Honestly, he's had tremendous results. His re-education programme has turned die-hard gangsters into decent citizens.'

Not that Edith had any intention of staying in Kenya. She was about to become Mrs Graham Forbes, ready to embark on a life of globe-trotting on the arm of her dashing husband. Her parents might be stuck in Africa, but she couldn't wait to get away.

LAUREN

'LAURI, LAURI!' Amber and Leo came running down the hall. They threw their arms around me, squeezing me half to death.

'We haven't seen you in ages,' Amber said.

'It's not that long. I saw you last month.'

'That is long.' Amber jumped up and down. 'Have you got us a present?'

I'd got them each a magazine and some sweets, but I wasn't going to hand them over straightaway.

'Let me get in the door first.'

I'd never noticed the smell of the house before – Persil Bio and toast and something else I couldn't put my finger on. It was a friendly smell and it made me feel sad this wasn't my home any more.

'Where's Mum?'

The hall was very narrow after Edith's. I nearly tripped over the shoes and schoolbags dumped by the door.

'I'm in here, just putting a lasagne in the oven for you,' Mum called from the kitchen. 'Hi Lauren.' She shut the oven door and gave me a hug, but only a quick one. There wasn't much warmth in it, not like there used to be. 'It'll be ready at seven. You can all eat together. There's salad in the fridge – just needs washing and dressing. Leo has to do his homework – he's got maths and English – so no PlayStation until it's finished. They both need to be in bed by eight, lights out by eight-thirty. Amber's got a spelling test in the morning.'

'OK, I know the drill,' I said.

'So.' She looked me up and down. 'How have you been?'

'All right.'

'It's working out, your living arrangements?'

'Yeah, fine.'

'And Selfridges? And the beauty course?'

I shrugged. 'No complaints.'

'That's good.' She sighed. 'Do you want a cup of tea?'

Amber was tugging at my arm. 'I want to show her my hamster. Daddy got me a hamster, come and see!'

I let her pull me upstairs. The stripy orange and purple stair-carpet I'd helped Mum choose suddenly looked very bright. Edith had grey carpets throughout. They were a bit worn, but you could tell the quality. They were lovely and soft to walk on in bare feet.

'How come you got a pet? It's not your birthday.'

'Because I'm a very good girl.'

'Are you?' I grabbed her on the landing and tickled her tummy. She squealed and giggled, her strawberry-blonde hair coming loose from its bunches. Fine strands stuck to the nylon skirt I had to wear for work.

'It stinks.' Leo had followed us upstairs.

'And you have to share a room with it?'

'We've got our own rooms now.'

Leo pushed open the door to what used to be my bedroom. It had been redecorated. The walls were dark blue and the ceiling was covered with luminous stars and planets. He'd got a white bunk bed with a desk, shelves and drawers all attached underneath it. There were big cushions on the floor and a matching rug.

'Wow.'

Of course it was fair that he got his own room and he wouldn't've wanted to keep it the way I had it. But I thought Mum and Mike were supposed to be hard-up. What was wrong with my old bed? I'd never been bought new furniture.

'Can you see the constellations?' Leo had grown. His head came up to my shoulder now. 'There's the Plough, and the Milky Way. That's Pluto and that's Mars.' He pointed to the ceiling.

'What did you do with my postcards?' I'd had the whole wall covered in my postcard collection. Nan always sent me postcards when she went on one of her trips to the seaside – Margate, Brighton, Whitby. And my best mates from school sent me cool ones 'cos they knew I collected them.

'Mum took them down. She was really annoyed at you for using loads of Blu Tack and making a mess of the paint.'

I pointed to his Arsenal poster. 'And what's that stuck up with?'

Leo pulled a face. 'I dunno. Dad put it up for me.'

'I'm surprised he let you have the Gunners then.'

Mike was a Chelsea supporter. Leo laughed. At least I'd stopped him from going over to the dark side.

'See my room. It's all pink.' Amber hopped up and down, shaking her hands in the air.

'Pink – that your favourite colour now?'

'Come on, come and meet Hammy.'

'Hammy? Is that his name? Couldn't you think up something more original?'

'Mike calls it Hamburger.' Mum was standing behind me, brushing her hair.

It was reddish-blonde and straight like Amber and Leo's, only her colour wasn't entirely natural. She wore it quite long for someone her age, but it looked good on her. You'd never know she was nearly forty. The scent of Clinique Happy filled the landing. I couldn't tell you if I liked it or not – it was so familiar to me – the smell of Mum, of my childhood.

Amber screwed up her face. 'Silly Daddy.'

Mum just smiled at her. 'I've got to get changed. I'm meeting Mike at the restaurant.' She went off to her room.

Amber's bedroom had had a makeover too – looked like something off Pinterest, except the floor was covered in Barbies, Disney dolls and all their accessories.

'Be careful in my room!' Amber shouted at me as I stood on Cinderella's arm.

I went downstairs to wash the salad.

It was after midnight by the time they got back. I was annoyed because Mum promised she'd be home by eleven. She knew I had work in the morning.

'Cab's waiting for you,' Mike said as soon as they walked in. He plonked himself down on the sofa beside me and switched the TV over to the boxing.

At least I wouldn't have to wait for a bus. The train down to Highbury & Islington would've stopped running by now.

'Were the kids all right? Did Leo do his homework?' Mum stood in the doorway, swaying slightly.

'They were great.'

I didn't tell her they'd stayed up till after nine and then Amber kept coming downstairs because the Hamburger was making too much noise on his wheel.

Mum pulled two bin-bags out of the hall cupboard. 'I packed up the rest of your stuff,' she said, like she was doing me a favour. 'Thought you might want to take it with you.'

'Is that everything?'

'You'd already taken most of it, hadn't you? There wasn't much left really.' She kissed me on the cheek. 'Thanks for helping out tonight, love. It was a real treat for me. I haven't been out in ages.' She gave me a funny, lopsided smile. 'Cab's all paid for.'

'Thanks.'

'See you soon.'

I turned back to say goodbye, but she'd already closed the door.

I sat in the back of the cab, the bin-bags squashed onto the seat beside me. 'Like a fucking bag lady,' I thought. Mum must've thrown out a load of my stuff. There was no way this was everything. She was always threatening to give half my clothes away to charity. Said I had too many. She'd better not have got rid of my Christmas Elf onesie. Amber loved it when I wore that. And what about my orange platform sandals? One day I'd learn how to walk in them.

The cab had the sickly vanilla smell of air-freshener covering up something nasty. The driver was playing Love FM and the heating was turned up way too high. I opened the window and leant my face out, feeling the warm London air wash over me. The streetlights were turning the empty pavements a pissy yellow. We drove past the nail bars, hairdressers, charity and pound shops of Palmers Green. There was the ice-cream parlour me and Sam used to hang out in. Mr Georgiou, who ran it, gave us free ice creams sometimes. Sam said she hoped he didn't expect anything in return. I think he was just being nice. Mind you, Sam is one of those girls men go crazy for. She's not beautiful like, say, Gigi Hadid, but she always gets attention. Joel called her buff once. He used to try chirpsing her sometimes but she wasn't having any of it. She was loyal to me that way. I always knew I could trust her. Unlike Joel.

The cab got caught as always by the lights at the North Circular, across from the Turkish Food Centre, but before the Greek bakery. Those lights seemed programmed to turn red for whatever vehicle I was in. Finally we moved on, past the windows of Primark and JD Sports. I couldn't believe a trip to Wood Green used to be my shopping highlight. Only when I was little of course, before Mum finally took me down the West End.

We had to stop again by the Bagel Bakery. Sam's mum went all the way down there for her challah bread. Round Finsbury Park the lights from the all-night kebab shops and Cypriot mini-markets gave out a comforting glow. Joel made me get off the night bus once just for a kebab. It was, like, two in the morning. Then we had to wait nearly an hour for the next bus. It was all right for him, he could take a slash down an alley. I nearly pissed myself before we got back to mine. But I'd promised myself I wouldn't think about Joel, or any of the stupid shit he put me through, ever again.

North London's all right, but my favourite place will always be the flat in E1 me and Mum lived in, before Mike came on the scene. Up on the eighteenth floor. A good sunset turned the whole flat pink. Mum once caught me standing on the windowsill, my face pressed up against the glass, watching the clouds. I thought I could just step out onto one and it would carry me away like a flying carpet. It's the only time I've ever heard Mum scream. I was only little. The windows didn't open and the glass was reinforced, so I wasn't in any danger.

'Penthouse view,' Dad called it, when he was still visiting. 'Some people would pay a fortune for a view like that.' We'd look down on the world spread out below. 'Like a king and his princess'.

You could just make out children on the climbing frame in the playground and I'd pester him to take me there. Later I worried I'd pestered him too much, worn him out, and that was why he didn't come any more. He was a lot older than Mum – his hair was mostly grey.

'They wouldn't pay a fortune for broken lifts and pissy stairwells.'

Mum used to grumble, but the flat was spotless inside. She'd made it so cosy with plants and posters and brightly coloured rugs – our den. Sometimes me and Dad rolled up all the rugs and skated around the lino floors in our socks – only when Mum was out though. Most of the time it was just me and her. She was always into crafts. We'd bake cakes together and paint pictures, make little people and animals out of Plasticine.

As soon as she met Mike he was all she could think about – didn't have time for me any more. I really tried to like him. You know, tried to see him through Mum's eyes. I soon learnt I wasn't supposed to join in their conversations, gave up trying to be his friend, drawing him pictures, asking him to play with me. I was probably one of those really annoying only children who think they're another adult. Mike is the opposite of my dad in almost every way. I guess it was good for Mum to have someone dependable, someone who could provide for her. To give him his due, he does love her back – he hasn't let her down yet.

I was supposed to be happy when they got married – to be a bridesmaid, to move into his house, to have a garden and a nice bedroom, to live in a better area. But I missed being up on the eighteenth floor, I missed my friends and the playground down below. I missed my mum and all the things we used to share. At least I still had my nan to make a fuss of me. Now even she was gone.

The cab was driving up Upper Street. Another new restaurant had opened, next to the boutique toy shop that sold old-fashioned sweets and mad expensive 'retro' games. I'd thought of getting Amber and Leo something in there, but anything decent was out of my price range and I didn't think they'd be impressed by sherbet dib-dabs or wind-up music boxes.

'Just here?' The driver was turning into Gainsford Square.

'Over on the far side.'

Normally I'd walk across the square, but it would be locked now. I looked up at number 25. All the lights were off. The windows made me think of closed eyes. There was something shut off and lonely about the house that made it stand out from all the other houses in the square.

As I dragged the bags up the front steps I looked down at the basement flat. The lights were off down there too. Was Paul out, or in bed?

'Hey House,' I said. I'd make myself some hot chocolate and unpack the bin-bags. Maybe Mum had put my postcards in there. I'd stick them up in my room. 'What d'you think of that then, House? I'll make your walls feel all cosy, just like home.'

EDITH

AN INTENSE MIDDAY SUN was burning my eyelids. I wanted to open them, to move, but my limbs wouldn't obey me. Where were my sunglasses? Who had taken my hat? I lay paralysed, my eyes watering under their sealed red lids, listening out for the tide hissing up the beach, for the cry of predatory gulls, but there was only the quiet murmuring of voices in the distance and the occasional swoosh of car tyres on a wet road.

I hoped the voices were Graham and Joanna returning from a swim. Graham would lift me up, get me moving. Joanna would find my glasses. I tried burrowing my fingers into the sand, but I must have been lying on a towel, all I could feel was soft material beneath me. We couldn't stay here if it was raining; our things would get wet. How could the sun be so bright? Was it the rainy season? I must know where we were, but I couldn't focus my mind on the place or the time. Even Joanna's age eluded me.

I managed to force my eyes open. White light bore down on me from the ceiling. Rolling onto my side, I shielded my eyes with my hands. I must be on an operating table. I'd woken too early; the anaesthetic was wearing off. Where were the medical staff? I needed to explain, to stop them from cutting me open. I clutched at my stomach. Was it another miscarriage? I looked down at my body, curled up like a foetus. I was in my own nightdress, the pink sprigged poplin. I'd put it on the night before. There was no blood.

Pushing myself onto one elbow, I stared in fear around the room, expecting to see trolleys laid with rows of glinting scalpels, machines blinking and whirring, multiple lights bearing down on me, men in green masks ready to commence. But instead I saw my own dressing-table, the double wardrobe that had belonged to Graham's parents and the familiar gold velvet curtains drawn across the windows. I was at home, in my own bed and it was still dark out. No sunlight came peeking round the curtains, no morning traffic rumbled past, just this relentless artificial light illuminating everything so that each piece of furniture seemed to leap out at me accusingly.

Who had turned the light on?

'Lauren?' I called. But there was no one there.

The voices were coming from the radio. I leant over, squinting at the display: 2.30 am. But I hadn't been listening to the radio when I went to sleep; I had been reading. My book still lay open beside me on the bed. I often fell asleep halfway through a page. I like to have a book there, where Graham used to be. A talented writer can be just as good a companion as a person. I always return to Austen, even if I barely make it through a page these days, her novels are so familiar to me it doesn't really matter.

No sound came from the rest of the house. The light was so

intense my whole head ached. I couldn't have had such a high watt bulb in here before. Was it some sort of power surge? I swung my legs over the side of the bed, planting my feet on the floor. It was reassuring to feel the carpet beneath my toes. I sat for a moment, summoning the energy to move. Everything is such an effort nowadays.

The bathroom light seemed muted in comparison. I splashed water on my face, cooling my aching eyes. Who had put such a bright bulb in my room? I could never have fallen asleep with it on. Besides I never went to bed with the overhead light on. I always used my sidelight.

When I returned, my bedroom throbbed with an almost supernatural brightness. My skin prickled. I told myself not to be ridiculous, but I felt nervy, violated almost. Had an intruder come into my room in the night, playing tricks on me? I didn't believe in ghosts. Besides, if any ghosts were prowling that house, Graham's would be the first on patrol.

I switched off the light and the radio and went back to bed. The room became a murky grey; the furniture hulking shadows. I still felt heavy and drowsy from the sleeping tablets. I could feel them pulling me under again and my anxious thoughts couldn't resist their soporific effect. It was strangely jarring, as if my mind and my body were being pulled in two different directions at once.

If it had been a one-off it wouldn't have worried me, but the same thing happened every night, for at least a week.

'You must've turned them on in your sleep,' Lauren said, looking up at the light and then at the radio.

'That's nonsense. Those tablets knock me out for the count. I'd have to get up and cross the room to reach the light switch, by which time I'd be fully conscious.'

Lauren picked up the packet of sleeping tablets from my dressing table and began to read the leaflet that came with them. "'Possible side effects: believing something that is not true (delusions), rage, nightmares, seeing hearing or feeling things that are not there (hallucinations), disturbances in thinking." Oh my days! You sure you want to keep taking these?'

'My doctor prescribed them for me, after Graham passed away. She said they were the right sort and they've certainly been working fine up until now.'

'Well I'm here now.' Lauren smiled kindly at me. 'Maybe you should try going without them for a bit.'

I was tempted for a moment to ask her if she would sleep in my room with me. Not in my bed of course; there was plenty of room for a camp bed. It would just be nice to know there was another person there, to hear her breathing in the night. I hated sleeping alone.

When Graham was away, Joanna would come in with me. Graham disapproved – he thought I was being soft. He assumed it was Jo who was prone to night terrors, but I loved to have her little body close to mine, to listen to her breathing, to watch the rise and fall of her chest as she lay on her back in complete abandon, arms flung out above her head. I didn't mind her fidgeting, or taking up three-quarters of the space, I just liked to have her there, my baby, so precious and so long awaited. She'd still come in with me sometimes even when she was a teenager. We were very close back then, before she turned fifteen and didn't want anything to do with her parents any more.

Lauren inspected the windows. 'All locked. No one could get in there. And nothing's missing is it?'

'Oh no, I don't think so.' I had checked my jewellery box. Nothing in the room had been moved from its usual position.

'I'm quite shocked by how dusty everything is. I hadn't even noticed.'

'I'll get a cloth and give it all a good clean. You rest there and drink your tea.' Lauren bustled off. She was a good girl and a great comfort to me.

'I don't know what I'd do without you,' I called, but I don't think she heard me.

LAUREN

EDITH LEANT ON MY ARM as we made our way down the front steps to the basement flat. I could smell her perfume, Chanel No.5. There was a dusty old bottle on her dresser, but it was the first time she'd actually put any on. It was a bit sickly – maybe it'd gone stale. She'd put lipstick on too. The coral pink was bleeding into the lines around her mouth and there was a blob of it on her front tooth. Women of her age should always apply lipliner first.

Maybe I should start doing make-up tutorials online for older women. There were so many beauty blogs out there, I'd been trying to come up with something different. But then who'd watch that? Most old people didn't even know how to use the internet.

I could hear music coming from inside, sounded like '90s Garage. Edith literally insisted on introducing me to Paul, even though I said I could go by myself. I think she was just looking for an excuse to visit him. She was as excited as a little girl. I guess going down to the basement was a bit of an outing for her, seeing as she hardly ever left the house.

I have to admit, Paul looked like he'd just stepped out of that Diet Coke ad. Apart from the towel round his neck, all he was wearing was a pair of Adidas trackies. Beads of water studded his chest. He must've been working out regularly, more than just doing the gardening. I tried not to stare at his abs, but it was hard not to appreciate his flawless skin, especially for someone in their thirties. I wondered what body lotion he used. He smelt of cocoa butter and vanilla.

'Hi Lauren.' He took my hand in his and gave it a squeeze – just a quick, firm pump. Nothing dodgy. 'I was making coffee. Would you ladies like a cup?'

He had a proper coffee machine. It even foamed the milk. It was stainless steel and took up half the space on the kitchen counter. A Nutribullet stood next to it. He must live on liquids. I couldn't see anything to eat or to cook with. Maybe it was all packed away in the neat row of cupboards. It was a very clean kitchen, for a man. All the boys I knew were slobs.

The kitchen opened onto the sitting room. Paul didn't have much furniture, or anything else come to that – just one sofa, a table and two chairs. I looked around for photos, ornaments, anything like that, but there was nothing personal on display.

I parked Edith on the sofa. It was covered in dark grey felty material. Reminded me of a toy elephant I used to have. Edith was leaning forward. She looked like she could do with a bit of support, but there weren't any cushions.

Paul followed us in. He'd pulled on a plain white t-shirt. 'So, how are you two getting on then?'

He placed a cup of coffee in Edith's hands. She looked up at him like he'd just handed her a pot of gold. We both went to answer at the same time. I let her go first. I was relieved she said how well I was working out, but then she spoilt it by saying it was early days and there was still 'room for improvement'.

'You always tell me when I'm doing something wrong though don't you, Edith?'

She looked a bit miffed, so I added, 'Which is good, because it means I can get it right the next time.'

'Lauren goes out to work and to college and still manages to spend evenings with her friends.' Edith sighed. 'So I don't think I take up too much of her time.'

I wasn't letting her get away with that.

'I spend four nights a week in with Edith and I always make her dinner, and I have lunch and tea with her at the weekends.'

Paul just nodded his head thoughtfully, smiling to himself.

'You told me what a good listener I am, didn't you, Edith? Edith's been telling me all about her childhood in Kenya and her husband, Colonel Forbes, who won medals out there. She says you were in his regiment, in the army.' I tried to catch Paul's eye, but he'd moved over to the window.

You could see feet passing by on the pavement outside. The wheels of a buggy trundled past followed by tanned feet in a pair of silver Birkenstocks. It was dark in the flat. Paul had the light on even though it was a sunny morning. The room was painted a pale yellow so that you didn't notice how gloomy it was at first.

'Heard from any friends lately?' Paul asked Edith. 'Any visits or outings planned?'

Edith gave a little laugh. 'You know what a recluse I am, Paul. If it weren't for you and Lauren I wouldn't see a soul.'

Paul shook his head sadly. 'That's the trouble with the modern world. People are just too busy, too wrapped up in their own lives...'

'But Joanna called me the other day!' Edith interrupted.

'Was it Monday or Tuesday? Such a rare occurrence, I ought to remember. She didn't sound very happy. I think she might have split up with her boyfriend.' She put her hand to her forehead. 'Or was it a problem with the farm? Goodness I can't remember what it was she said. There was some sort of news.'

'She's staying in Italy though? I mean, you said she'd moved there permanently, didn't you?' I had to sit on my hands to stop myself from biting my nails. Why hadn't Edith said anything before about her daughter phoning? This had put me in a right panic.

'Maybe she's getting married?' Paul suggested.

'No, no. I'd remember that.' Edith shook her head.

A fat chocolate-brown Labrador stopped in front of the railings, raised one leg and began to piss. Paul banged on the window. The dog's lead went taut and a woman's legs moved quickly past, the dog dragged along slowly after them.

'Christ's sake,' Paul muttered.

'What's going on? Is there a problem?' Edith twisted round towards the window, but her neck was too stiff for her to turn her head fully.

'Nothing for you to worry about. Everything's under control, isn't it Lauren?'

Paul had this relaxed, confident way of speaking that made you feel safe just listening to him, but there was a hard edge to his voice when he said my name and I wasn't sure if it was a question or a warning.

Edith smiled. 'Is the flat all right for you, Paul? Do you need anything?'

If I hadn't been feeling a bit sick already, her adoration of Paul would definitely have made me puke.

Then, to make it worse, Paul held up his hands and said, 'How could I possibly want anything more than you two lovely ladies?'

I hoped he didn't expect me to suck up to her like that. I honestly didn't have it in me. I've never been an arse-licker. I scooped the last bit of sugary foam out of the bottom of my cup – comfort food.

'Well, I'm always here if either of you need me. I'll give you my mobile number, Lauren.' He raised his eyebrows at me.

'Sure.' I got out my phone.

'Great, so you can always text me if you need clarification on anything.'

'I've gone over everything with her. It isn't very complicated. If she has a problem she can come to me.' Edith patted her hair. She sounded a bit vexed, I don't think she liked the idea of me and Paul doing anything without her. 'Unless of course I have another funny turn, or there's an emergency, or something.'

'Understood. If you need me, Edith, I'll be there in an instant. You know you can count on me.'

Paul helped Edith up off the sofa. She leant on his arm till we got outside, then shifted her weight onto me. We stood for a minute, blinking in the sunlight.

She took the steps up one at a time, like a little kid, dragging on my elbow every time she paused. I heard Paul's door closing beneath us and my lungs contracted. I couldn't seem to get any air in through my nose. I stopped with Edith, opening my mouth to gulp down oxygen. I felt dizzy, like I might fall backwards onto the pavement taking Edith with me. I imagined the thud as her head hit the cement. Her skull would shatter like eggshell. An image of Nan flashed into my mind, lying on her kitchen floor, cold and alone, with no one even to call for an ambulance. I gripped a railing with my spare hand and felt the cool, twisted iron pressing into my palm. My eyes blurred over with tears. I felt like leaving Edith there on the doorstep and running off down the street.

'You've got the keys haven't you?' She was tugging on my sleeve.

'Yes, Edith, they're here.' I let go of the railing and felt for the keys in my pocket.

I'd attached them to a keyring Nan had given me for my last birthday. It was a terrier made out of felt – a bit of a joke, 'cos she knew I wanted a dog. I pushed the key into the lock. It slid round with an easy click and the door swung open. I stumbled into the hall, dragging Edith in behind me.

EDITH

'THAT'S BETTER, INNIT?' Lauren surveyed her handiwork with pride.

'*Isn't* it.' I nodded in assent.

I enjoyed watching Lauren polish the furniture. She lavished such care on it. Massaging away the dullness of the old walnut bureau and the mahogany dining-table until honey and amber tones glowed through the dark wood. The room took on the reassuringly familiar scent of lavender and beeswax.

Sometimes Lauren bought flowers. She would place them on the centre of the table in one of the vases I'd collected years ago. I suspected she was using my money to buy them, as they appeared whenever I sent her to the shops, but I appreciated the gesture. The lilies and irises in particular demonstrated a degree of good taste.

I tried directing her into the garden to pick roses, but she disliked the thorns and the aphids that accompanied them. She'd never make a gardener. She was proving to be a good housekeeper however. The house, during the daytime at least, had regained an atmosphere of order and calm under her ministrations. Graham would approve. He couldn't abide mess.

'We've got to get a new Dyson though, Edith. That one's spitting out more dirt than it sucks up.'

'Can't we get it fixed?'

The low interest rates must be crippling my savings and it wasn't as if I had any other means of support. My pension only covered the basics, council tax alone cost a fortune, and now I had Lauren to feed as well.

'It's totally knackered. You can't do without a vacuum cleaner. All that dust's bad for your lungs and the carpets get filthy.'

She had a point. 'I'll ask Paul to get one. I'm certainly not braving the crowds in Oxford Street.'

'We can do it online. Where's the iPad?'

Paul had bought me the iPad. He said it would be easy for me to use, with the arthritis in my hands. Lauren had taught me how to play patience on it, but apart from that I couldn't get to grips with the thing. I'm too old to take up the internet now. Lauren buys our weekly shop on it. I tell her what I want and a van comes round and delivers everything at no extra cost.

She pulled up a chair beside mine, the iPad on her lap.

'You want the same sort as before, yeah? They've probably got better models out now.'

'All right, but you'll have to ask Paul how to pay for it. He set up my John Lewis account. He knows how it all works.'

My memory isn't up to all these passwords and pin numbers required now. The last time I went to the shops myself I had the humiliating experience of forgetting the correct number for my Barclaycard.

It was the small supermarket on Upper Street – a Sainsbury's

I think. It took me such a long time to walk down there I was exhausted by the time I arrived. I'd only gone for some milk and bread, but I had to go up and down the aisles several times before I found them. They must have changed the arrangement again. Nothing was where I expected it to be.

And then at the till I discovered I didn't have any cash in my purse. I pressed my pin number into the machine three times and each time it was declined.

A queue formed behind me. I could feel their eyes on me, sense their impatience. A baby began to scream, its mother spoke urgently to it in a language I couldn't understand, Polish maybe. The man directly behind me kept edging forwards, talking over my head about the lack of staff, waving his bottle of wine in the air. I thought he was going to hit me with it.

The girl on the till insisted her machine was working properly. She asked me if I had another card, but I've only ever had one. In the end I had to leave my purchases and hobble out, past all those people thinking I was a bankrupt or a fraudster.

I've always used Graham's date of birth, but I must have been required to change the number. Paul said the banks insist on it periodically, but now they do everything by email I don't receive their communications. Banks don't care about their customers any more.

Since then I let Paul, and now Lauren, do all my shopping. I simply can't face it. Paul said he'd changed my card's pin number to Joanna's date of birth, or perhaps it was mine. I'm not going to risk getting it wrong again. Paul deals with the bank for me.

Lauren's brightly coloured fingernails were moving rapidly over the iPad. I was impressed by her dexterity, but hoped she wouldn't scratch the screen.

'We don't have to go John Lewis. What about Currys or Argos?'

'Cheap does not mean reliable. I'll ask Paul to do it. He'll find the best deal.'

Trying to look at that little screen gave me a headache. I leant on the left armrest. The ache in my right hip was radiating out across my thigh; it felt as though tiny burning arrows were being fired down my leg.

'Your hospital appointment should come through this week.' Lauren put the iPad down and lifted my feet onto the footstool.

When Graham became ill we used his private health insurance, but it turned out I wasn't covered so now I'm forced to rely on the NHS. I did feel cross about that. He'd promised he would always take care of me.

'I'm sure I'm the last of their priorities. If you want to get to the top of the queue you have to be a Muslim who doesn't speak any English, or a gay lesbian woman, then you'll get seen straightaway.'

'Oh, Edith, you crack me up, the things you come out with.' Lauren shook her head and laughed. 'I don't think people's religion or sexuality show up in X-rays.'

'You'd be surprised. They keep records of everything now.'

I may be old, but I know what's what.

Lauren sat cross-legged in Graham's old armchair, the iPad back on her lap. I'd got used to her sitting there, but Graham would be turning in his grave. Still, there wasn't much he could do about it now.

She looked up at me and smiled, clapping her hands together as if to signal a change in conversation.

'So, tonight, chicken Kiev with dauphinoise potatoes and green beans followed by chocolate and raspberry mousse. How does that sound?'

'Delicious.'

I know she doesn't cook these dishes from scratch. I've seen the boxes in the recycling bin, but they're more than I could manage now and they actually taste rather good, though I suppose I really ought to check how much they're costing me.

'Afterwards we could watch a film, now that we've got you the digital box.' Lauren nodded at the television.

'If there's anything worth watching on.'

'I'm sure we can find something.'

She scrolled through the channels with the remote control, flicking from one station to another so quickly I couldn't see what was on the screen. Before she moved in I just listened to Radio Four.

'*Out of Africa.* I've never seen it, have you?'

This amused me. Lauren is fascinated by what she thinks of as my exotic past. Anything to do with Africa she relates to me, even though it's over fifty years since I lived in Kenya.

'What about one of those David Attenborough nature programmes?'

'Yeah, all right.' She sounded disappointed.

'Graham was a great supporter of wildlife in Africa; elephants especially. He helped set up and fund an anti-poaching task force in Kenya. He flew out there several times to help them with their training.'

'What kind of training?'

I was pleased I'd caught Lauren's interest. The wildlife charity had been very dear to Graham's heart. 'How to hunt the hunters. Illegal poachers are dangerous men; it takes a team of rangers with military training and intelligence to stop them. They have videos you can watch on the internet.'

'On YouTube?' Lauren turned back to the iPad. 'What's this charity called?'

'Forbes Wildlife Trust.'

'Got it.' Lauren brought the iPad over to me, kneeling by my side as we watched.

'There you are. That's Kenya for you.' The film opened with the obligatory shots of Mount Kenya and acacia trees silhouetted against a golden sunset.

It was very impressive though. The charity had expanded; they had drones as well as aircraft now. It showed the rangers, armed with AK47s, tracking through the forest after poachers. Lauren seemed less taken with this than by the baby elephants being fed bottles of milk, but she's a sentimentalist. What is it they call them now? The snowflake generation?

KENYA, 1947

EDITH TIPTOED PAST her parents' bedroom. The door was ajar and she could see Mother propped up against the pillows, a silk scarf laid over her eyes. She must have one of her headaches. Edith headed on outside before she was caught and made to eat scrambled eggs for breakfast.

She checked the stables for Nero, Father's Friesian stallion. To her relief he was absent, which meant Father was out overseeing the squatters. According to Father, they were a lazy bunch and would lay down their tools as soon as his back was turned. He never went to the river where the children collected water though, so Edith knew she was safe there.

To her parents' bewildered disappointment, Edith was not a keen rider. She had a plump little pony called Mpenzi, which she was fond of, but she preferred sneaking down to the squatters' village to play with the children there. One girl in particular she considered her best friend.

She set off determinedly up the hillside, the sun heavy on her back despite the early hour. Little clouds of red dust rose up as her shoes hit the path. She'd get into trouble for scuffing them, but she didn't care. She'd had too many jiggers pulled out of her toes ever to go barefoot again. She clambered over rocks and boulders, her hands slippery with sweat, her eyes and ears on the alert for the sudden movement or rustling sound of a snake. She kept her mind on the reward of the cool water up ahead and the knowledge that, even if Mary wasn't there, she wouldn't have to wait long for her. It was the dry season and Mary's mother would send her out lots of times before they had all the water they'd need for the day.

Chattering voices rang out above her. Edith squeezed to one side of the narrow path as two girls came down, each with a large pot of water strapped to her back with the usual leather belt fastened across her forehead. They fell silent as they passed Edith, their eyes glazing over as they stared into the distance.

They were a couple of years older than she was, otherwise she was sure they'd have been more amiable. She was Mary's friend after all and Mary was very popular among the squatter children. Edith believed Mary was the prettiest, with her skin smooth and creamy as milk chocolate and dimples in her round cheeks. She was also the cleverest, outdoing Edith at every game they played, whether physical or mental. Mary's mind was so quick she easily grew bored, but Edith persisted in following her around. The two of them shared a love of make-believe which encouraged Mary to tolerate her as a playmate. Besides she seemed to find Edith entertaining.

One of Mary's half-brothers had taught her English and she was very good at it, insisting on speaking English to Edith, even though Edith had learnt enough Kikuyu to understand most of what the women and children said. The houseboys always spoke to her in Swahili, the language they used with her parents – not that either parent knew more than a few basic commands. Sometimes Edith tried to act as an interpreter for them, but her parents weren't really interested in what the houseboys had to say, only that their instructions were carried out.

As Edith reached the top of the path, the bushes cleared and she could feel the coolness of the running water rising up into the air. Mary was sitting on a rock, sucking on a piece of sugarcane, her water tin by her feet. Edith's heart swelled with happiness and relief.

'Hello slow coach,' Mary said.

'You learnt that name from me.' Edith flopped down beside her.

'I've been up and back three times already and you're tired after one.'

'Can you play now?'

Mary tugged at Edith's ponytail. 'Can I play? Only white children and babies play. My mother will be waiting for this water and then I have to weed my garden.'

'I can help you with that.'

All the Kikuyu children had their own little plots of land where they learnt to grow vegetables. Edith loved Mary's garden and had asked Mother if she could have a border in their garden to cultivate, but Mother kept changing her mind about where that should be. She didn't want her flowerbeds messed up and still hadn't let the *shamba* boy dig a plot for Edith.

'Hmmm.' Mary tilted her head to one side 'You are more trouble than help.'

'I know which are weeds now.'

Edith had accidentally pulled up a row of Mary's cherished beans. Mary had been disconsolate, but her mother had laughed, reminding Mary that was how she'd learnt to tell weeds from crops. They'd replanted the beans, but Edith didn't dare ask Mary if the wilting stems had revived.

'I guess Mama won't mind if I'm a little late.' Mary was her mother's only surviving child, which was why she spoiled Mary, letting her play with Edith instead of doing her chores. 'Let's go to the cave.' Stuffing her water tin into a bush, Mary went racing off higher up the steep path, leaving Edith to struggle after her.

Above the river was a waterfall and behind it a cave only Mary and Edith knew about. At least, they were the only ones who went there. Edith never thought to ask Mary how she had discovered it. To reach it they had to shuffle along a slippery ledge, backs pressed against the rocks to avoid getting wet or falling into the tumbling waters and being swept away. A couple of feet in, the cliff face suddenly gave way and they could step back into a shallow cave, screened off by the curtain of cascading water. The magic of it never ceased to thrill Edith.

They invented whole worlds in that cave, becoming princesses, warriors, spirits and demons, hyenas and lions, the roar of the water masking their hysterical shrieks and howls.

Knowing her parents were visiting neighbours that afternoon, Edith spent the whole day tagging along with Mary, fetching water and collecting firewood. Mary even allowed Edith into her garden, but Edith got fed up with Mary treating her like a baby and overseeing everything she did.

'Aren't they beautiful?' Edith pointed to her family's pyrethrum fields, admiring the rows of silvery foliage topped with white daisy-like flowers.

Mary rolled her eyes. 'The Kikuyu hate pyrethrum.'

'Why?' Edith's father was so proud of what he had achieved, clearing the wilderness to create a successful farm in the middle of nowhere. He said the market for pyrethrum was excellent – that's where the future lay: there and with coffee.

'That used to be our land,' Mary said slowly, as though Edith was stupid. 'Now this is all we have left.' She gestured to the little plots.

'My father bought our land from another European.' Edith knew this only too well as Father was always complaining about how much he'd paid for it.

'And that man stole it from my people.' Mary thrust a stick into the ground. 'It doesn't matter,' she sighed, rolling her eyes in imitation of a grown-up. 'As we say, no one lives forever. The Europeans will go home eventually.'

'This is my home,' Edith said stubbornly.

Mary smiled indulgently at her. 'Well, I'll let you stay if you learn how to garden properly.'

To Edith's delight, Mary's mother, Wacheera, welcomed her into their homestead, calling her *kairītu* and insisting she stay for supper.

Edith sat cross-legged on the ground with the other children. One little girl held her nose and pointed at Edith.

'She thinks you smell bad,' Mary told her, giggling as the girl scrambled away.

'But I have a bath every day,' Edith exclaimed indignantly.

Mother complained that the native women stank, but Edith liked the nutty smell of castor oil and tanned leather. She couldn't imagine what she smelt of, other than soap.

As the women cooked they encouraged the children to tell stories. Even the littlest were indulged as they tried to remember a well-known tale or made up some fantastical adventure. Edith wished she could join in, but was held back by self-consciousness in case her Kikuyu wasn't good enough.

When the food was ready, she joined the other children, scooping handfuls of *irio* topped with pumpkin leaves out of the cooking pot. She wished they could eat that way at home, instead of all the laborious slicing and spearing with unwieldy cutlery and always being told off for getting it wrong and having bad table manners.

Once they'd finished eating, everyone turned expectantly to Wacheera. Mary's mother was renowned in the village for her storytelling and Edith loved to listen to her as much as everyone else did.

Wacheera held her audience in the palm of her hand, sometimes teasing them by pretending she'd forgotten how a story ended so that everyone pleaded with her to continue, sometimes introducing a catchphrase they would chant back to her. She delivered her stories with such animation, her voice lifting and falling, her expressions changing with her tone, that Edith was always swept along, following the plot almost as well as if she were completely fluent in Kikuyu. Sometimes Mary leant in, whispering a translation, then Edith knew where Mary got her ideas for their imaginary games from.

Nothing matched the excitement of being terrified by tales of shape-shifting ogres and ravenous dragon snakes, all the while safely snuggled up next to Mary in a circle of similarly captivated adults and children. The pleasure of singing refrains in unison and laughing at the foolishness of hyenas, of being moved by the sorrow of a mother bird whose chicks were crushed by a careless elephant, and then satisfied with the revenge she enacted.

There was one story that made a particularly strong impression on Edith. Some young women were washing themselves in the river. They were splashing about, laughing and teasing one another, when they realised they were being watched. A handsome young man stood on the riverbank, leaning on his spear. His muscular body gleamed with oil and a sword hung in a leather scabbard at his side.

Reaching his left hand out to the girls, he called, 'Let me help you out of the river, for I have seen a snake close by.'

The girls hastily scrambled out of the water, looking around them for the snake. None of the girls, except one, took the man's hand.

'I have just filled a drum with the sweetest honey. Follow me and I will give you some,' the man continued.

The girls looked at each other and shrugged. There were eight of them and he was only one man. They saw no reason not to collect some honey, so they followed him into the forest. The girl who had taken his hand was the most eager, rushing to walk beside this handsome stranger.

They walked for some time along a narrow twisting path, the forest growing denser around them. The girls began to whisper uneasily to each other. Who was this man? He must have come from far away, since none of them had seen him at any of the festival dances. Flies were buzzing round the man's head and one of the girls thought she spied a tongue whipping out from the base of his skull to snatch a fly, before slipping back behind his hair.

The girls tugged each other's hands, slipping away in pairs as the handsome stranger walked on ahead, leading them deeper and deeper into the forest. Only the girl who had accepted his hand shrugged her friends off, her eyes fixed on the broad back and smooth skin of this fine-looking warrior.

Eventually she saw a collection of huts up ahead.

'Where is the honey?' she asked.

The stranger turned round, but to her horror the handsome young man had gone and in his place was a hideous ogre, his skin white and bumpy like the underbelly of a toad. Cavernous mouths spread open on either side of his head. A thin purple tongue, like a chameleon's, darted out to lick the side of her face. She tried to run, but the *irimu rieru* grabbed her round the waist and threw her over his shoulder.

'Look what I have caught,' he shouted triumphantly.

Other ogres came running out of their huts rubbing their hands with glee and smacking their drooling lips. 'We're hungry, let's eat her now,' they cried.

But the *irimu rieru*, squeezing the girl, told them she needed fattening up. He would keep her in his hut until she was ripe for eating. In truth he wanted to devour her all himself.

He threw her on the floor of his hut, where he left her, carefully barring the door behind him. Then he went to drink beer with his fellow ogres.

'There are plenty more girls,' he told them. 'Enough for one each. You just need to catch your own.'

The ogres began to argue over who had the right to this girl and when they should go to fetch more. As the girl lay in the hut, listening to the ogres' drunken dispute, she spotted a hole in the thatch. Climbing onto a stool, she managed to pull herself up and out of the hole, sliding down the roof onto the far side of the hut. As soon as her feet touched the ground she fled back into the forest.

Running in what she hoped was the direction of her village, she was overjoyed to meet her own relatives. For her friends had not abandoned her but rushed home to raise the alarm, whereupon their brothers and fathers lost no time in sharpening their swords and hastening into the forest.

The drunken ogres were easily defeated and the villagers saved from becoming the prey of these monstrous beasts, while the girl learnt to treat strangers with caution from then on.

Edith wished she could stay all night, curling up to sleep next to Mary, but the women called for one of Mary's older half-brothers to see her home.

'I think you'd like to be an African.' Kamau laughed, as she trotted along beside him.

Edith wasn't sure if he was making fun of her and was glad it was too dark for him to see her blushing. Kamau had fought in Burma. Mary said he was a hero who'd helped to win the war for the British. Now he was a journalist in Nairobi, writing for a Kikuyu newspaper called *Muigwithania*. Mary was always elated when he came home to visit, for not only did he bring her presents from the city, he also took the time to sit and talk to her, unlike her other brothers, who were always too busy with their own affairs to take much notice of a little girl.

Edith was glad to have him beside her now, as the night filled with the usual animal grunts and growls; the yelping of hyenas and the barking of a jackal calling for its mate. Wacheera's story of the forest ogre crept into Edith's mind and she reached out for the comfort of Kamau's hand. She wished she had an older brother like Kamau; a former soldier who now wore elegant linen jackets, rode a bicycle and brought her gifts.

An engine came roaring up behind them and the path was floodlit with the yellow glow of car headlights. Kamau pulled Edith aside, but the car screeched to a halt.

A man leapt out and came running towards them waving his revolver. 'What the hell are you doing with my daughter?' he bellowed.

Kamau held up his hands.

'He was just taking me home, Daddy,' Edith cried.

Her mother had also got out of the car and was gripping the door, watching them.

'Home? Where the blazes have you been?' Father demanded.

'I was in the village, at my friend Mary's, listening to stories. This is Mary's brother. He's a war hero. He fought in Burma.'

Father stared at Kamau. 'D'you work for me?'

Kamau looked her father square in the face as he explained

who he was, speaking without the usual deference the squatters showed him. Father didn't seem to know quite how to respond. Grabbing Edith by the shoulder, he marched her back to the car, bundling her onto the back seat. She was conscious for the first time of his rudeness, and an awful sense of embarrassment flooded over her.

'What were you thinking of, Edith?' Mother asked plaintively. 'You can't just go gallivanting off, especially not at night. This isn't England you know.'

Which seemed a pointless comment to Edith, who'd never set foot in England.

'You need to take proper control of the girl.' Father was hunched over the steering wheel, his gaze fixed on the bumpy road ahead. 'She's getting too old to be running around half-naked like one of the savages. God knows what rubbish that so-called journalist has been filling her head with.' Father lingered over the word 'journalist' with a sneer. 'I suppose he writes for one of those Commie rags, like *The Colonial Times*.'

'Isn't that an Indian newspaper?' Mother asked.

'Indian-owned, lets Africans write for it. Spews a load of seditious rubbish. "Give me liberty".' He muttered scornfully, swerving to miss a nightjar. It took off in front of the car with slow, heavy flaps of its wings. 'We should send Edith away to school.'

Edith held her breath. Father wielded the threat of sending her to boarding school with increasing frequency. The prospect of being banished to some institution, far from the life of the farm, filled her with dread.

'Not yet, Ralph, she's too young and she's the only baby I have.' Mother reached into the back of the car and squeezed Edith's knee.

Father harrumphed, but said nothing; they all knew this was

Mother's trump card. Like Mary, Edith was her mother's only surviving child.

'I'll take better charge of her lessons,' Mother continued, though her enthusiasm for tuition was usually short-lived. 'And I've been looking in the *Standard* for a governess. Perhaps we should advertise? It would probably work out cheaper than school fees.' This was another winning argument; family expenses were a source of great anxiety to Father.

For a while Mother kept a close eye on Edith, refusing to allow her beyond the garden without one of the houseboys. The next time Edith caught up with her friend, Mary refused to play with her and turned down her offers of being an under-gardener. Edith wondered if Father had said something to Mary's family. She hoped he hadn't threatened to evict them.

Sometimes Edith stood at the gate watching Mary and the other children as they passed by on the long walk to their school. The girls wore yellow gingham dresses. The boys tucked their beige shirts into their shorts. You could see how cheap the dresses were – the girls' brown legs were visible through the flimsy cotton. That didn't stop Edith from wanting one though. She was still having lessons at home with her mother and longed to go to school.

The children were always so animated: talking and laughing, kicking stones down the road, shoving each other playfully, sometimes holding hands and singing. She understood enough Kikuyu to know they sang about Jomo Kenyatta, 'the children's friend'. They sang about land and education and the 'foreign intruders'. It was just as well her parents didn't know any Kikuyu or there would have been trouble.

They seemed oblivious to Edith's presence and she wondered if they had been told to ignore her. Once she tried calling out to Mary, but her friend didn't even turn around. Instead the other children imitated her, calling out 'Marewee, Mareweee' in shrill voices like parrots, bursting into giggles. They used Mary's Kikuyu name, calling Edith '*mzungu*' – foreigner – and '*kirigu*' – 'uncircumcised girl'.

She felt like a white ghost, an underworld shade, watching them walk by, her stomach churning with a mixture of longing and resentment.

LAUREN

A COUPLE WERE LYING on a double mattress, in the boarded-up doorway of an old bank. You could just see the tops of their sleeping heads sticking out under piles of dirty blankets. They looked like they'd been magically beamed from their bedroom onto the pavement without even waking up.

As I walked round them, this mop of grey, matted curls popped up out of its sleeping bag like one of them puppets off kid's TV, only not so cute. A toothless mouth gave a big yawn, a pair of bloodshot eyes stared round. Of course she spotted me. Homeless people and beggars always zero in on me. It's like I've got 'Try me, I'm a soft touch' tattooed on my forehead.

'Got any change, love?'

She stuck out a filthy hand, the cracked palm lined with dirt. It'd take some manicure to get that clean.

I gave her a pound. I knew she'd only spend it on cans of white cider, or crack or whatever, but if I was homeless I'd want to get out of it too.

I'd never admitted this to anyone, but I had this secret fear that one day the homeless person would turn out to be my dad. My dad was very proud. I'd looked up to him as a kid, thought he was amazing, but that was eight years ago – anything could've happened to him since then. It might explain why he'd never got in touch with any of us for all these years. He'd be too ashamed.

I'd never been to wherever it was he lived. A couple of times, when he'd asked me what I wanted to do, I'd said, 'I want to go to your house.' But he'd just laughed and told me it was a bachelor's pad, that I'd be bored there. Looking back, it seemed a bit weird. I'd asked Mum about it and she'd just shrugged and said he lived in a bedsit. It was easier for him to come to ours where all my toys and stuff were. I suppose that made sense. Maybe it was Mum who vetoed me going to his – she could be very controlling. And, you know, considering the way he disappeared, maybe she was right to be.

The handles of my plastic shopping bag were cutting into my fingers. I shouldn't've bought the bananas – I'd forgotten how heavy they are. I'd only gone into the supermarket for milk, then I'd seen the fresh apple tart made with sultanas and cinnamon in an all-butter shortcrust case, glazed with caramel. I knew how happy Edith would be if I brought that out for afters.

Then of course I had to buy cream to go with the tart. Never go into a food store when you're hungry – should've remembered that.

'It's good for your biceps,' I told myself as I shifted the bag over to my right hand.

When I tried to open the front door, my key stuck. For a paranoid moment I thought Edith might've changed the locks. I jiggled the key slowly, twisting it backwards and forwards, telling myself not to panic. Why would Edith get the locks changed? I hadn't done anything to make her do that.

'Come on, House, let me in,' I whispered. 'You know I've got a right to be here.'

At last the key slipped round, the bolt turned and the door opened. I let out a big sigh of relief, making sure I thanked the house before kicking off my shoes and dumping my bag on the floor.

Normally the hall was lovely and cool. It was always a relief to feel the cold stone tiles under my swollen feet, but today even the tiles felt warm. As I straightened up, my head swam. I had to hold onto the radiator. My period was very heavy – maybe it was loss of blood giving me a head rush. It'd been busy at work too and then there were delays on the Victoria line and the tube was jammed. I hadn't sat down since lunchtime.

I rested on the bottom of the stairs for a minute, listening to the quiet, steady ticking of the grandmother clock. Edith said that being under six feet it was too short to be a grandfather clock. '*Tempus fugit*' was written on its face. She told me that's Latin for 'Time flies', meaning, like, nothing lasts forever so grab it while you can. I always stop in the hall and look at it as a reminder.

Suddenly it struck six, making me jump. I didn't normally hear the clock because Edith always had the radio on full blast. Why was the house so quiet? Edith never went out on her own. Where could she be?

I shouted up the stairs, but there was no answer. Maybe she'd forgotten to turn her hearing aid on. My skin prickled with alarm. Calling her name, I ran into the living room, heart racing.

Edith was sitting bolt upright in her chair with her eyes closed and her coat on. I forced myself to touch her cheek. It was warm. I could feel the pulse beating on her neck. I nearly cried with relief, and not just because it would've been bad timing. I liked living with Edith – weirdly, I was even getting kind of fond of her. She looked small and frail, wrapped up in her trench-coat. Like a sweet, innocent old grandma out of a cartoon, with her white hair puffed up behind her head and her face all smoothed out in sleep.

I reminded myself that she wasn't innocent. She wasn't even a grandma. And the way she bitched about her daughter, I don't think she was very maternal neither. Unless Joanna literally was the daughter from hell. Sometimes when Edith came out with something really bad, I wanted to tell her everything just to see her expression. But I was scared she might drop dead of the shock.

I had to give her a shake to wake her up. Just a gentle one. She nearly leapt out of her chair, looked at me like I was a vampire. Called out for someone named Mary.

'It's Lauren, and it's dinner time. Shall we get that coat off? Why'd you put your coat on anyway? Were you waiting for me? Did you want to go out somewhere?'

She let me help her out of her coat, but didn't speak.

Edith perked up over dinner, seemed embarrassed I'd found her napping.

'This afternoon tired me out completely,' she said, as she finished off a second big slice of apple tart.

For someone so skinny she can put her food away. Poured half a jug of cream over her dessert. Edith loves cream, ice cream – anything like that. I'm trying to stay off it, keep my weight down, but it was satisfying to see her eat. Satisfying and then sickening.

After all those years breaking her back nursing others, my nan died on her own on the freezing cold floor of a kitchen with not enough food in it to feed a mouse and here I was pouring cream down Edith's throat. Was this the right way to go about making amends? I didn't really know any more. Sometimes everything got confused in my head and I didn't know who I should blame for what.

If I hadn't been so obsessed with my own life I might've been with Nan when she died – might've realised how bad things had got. Instead I'd been wasting my time with a shitty boyfriend who couldn't keep his dick in his pants.

I couldn't remember if I'd told Nan, the last time I spoke to her on the phone, how much I loved her. I would've said, 'lots of love, Nan, see you soon.' I always said that instead of 'goodbye'. Don't like goodbyes – too final. But 'lots of love' isn't the same really, not like coming out with 'I love you' so a person knows you mean it. I might've said, 'love you, see you soon', but casually, not so she'd know how important she was to me. How unique.

I thought of all the times she'd been waiting at the school gates for me, her massive handbag tucked under one arm. She'd let me rummage around in it for ages before conjuring up a bag of sweets or a chocolate bar for me to eat as we walked home together. Every school fair, she was there behind the cake stall. Every school play or concert she'd be sitting in the audience, spine straight, shoulders back, looking so proud.

She was stricter in some ways than my mum, but I knew she'd do anything for me. She was a genuine Christian – lived by her principles. Not like people who act all holy but are mean as shit. I don't believe she ever did a bad thing in her life – never hurt another soul – and look where it got her. If there was ever an advert for screwing others over or getting screwed yourself that was my nan. She got screwed every which way and she still turned the other cheek.

'The pastry was nice and crisp, but the raisins didn't really add anything.'

Edith dabbed at her mouth with her napkin, leaving a blob of cream on her chin. That was going to annoy me, but I knew it would annoy her more if I mentioned it.

'All that legal business exhausted me.' Edith dropped her napkin into her bowl. 'We took a taxi there and back, but even so, the traffic was dreadful.'

'What legal business? Where?'

'I went to see my solicitor, with Paul.'

Edith looked at me like I ought to know what the hell she was talking about. I pulled a face and she sighed.

'Since I'm growing so forgetful I need to make sure my finances are looked after. I've given Paul power of attorney. My solicitor agreed it was the right procedure to take.'

'Power of attorney?'

'It just means Paul can oversee my financial affairs. Nothing for you to worry about, dear. Paul's going to make sure my money's safe.'

'What on earth are you doing?'

'Taking a photo, for Instagram.' I turned the tray round so the pink roses hung down behind the teapot. 'People love this shit.'

'Language!' Edith leant forward and pulled a plate off the tray, nearly knocking the milk jug over and spoiling my arrangement. 'Hardboiled eggs and toast are hardly *haute cuisine*. If you want to develop your photographic skills you should get yourself a proper camera. I can't imagine a mobile phone takes good-quality pictures.'

Like I could afford a decent camera.

It was so hot we'd agreed to have breakfast in the garden. Edith had been going on about the sort of picnics they used to take on safari in *Keenya*. The 'boys' would carry hampers filled with fresh bread, cold chicken, ham, fruit salads and champagne. I'd done my best with what we'd got.

She'd nabbed the only seat in the shade, leaving me screwing up my eyes against the sun. She was wearing sunglasses and a battered old straw hat. Don't know how she was going to get her Vitamin D quota all wrapped up like that. The hat looked like a man's – maybe it'd been Graham's. I suppose he used to sit out here with her, enjoying the sun.

The butter was turning liquid. It dripped off the butter-knife as I smeared it over the toast. Even the jam had to have a special spoon in Edith's house. She went mental if you got crumbs in it.

She picked an egg up out of the cute little blue-and-white Chinese bowl I'd put them in and immediately dropped it.

'Good God, that's boiling! Did you pour cold water on them?'

I nodded, stopping myself from commenting on her language. Never take the Lord's name in vain, Nan used to say.

'It is extraordinary how they retain their heat. Let's eat the oranges first, leave the eggs to cool down a bit.'

I'd offered to juice the oranges, but Edith likes to eat them in segments, with salt. She says it brings out the sweetness. I told her salt's bad for her, but she claims you need it in the heat. Not that she does much sweating.

A wasp kept buzzing round the orange skins, so I dumped them onto the compost heap at the end of the garden. It was peak – smelt rank and was full of worms wriggling about. I thought Edith'd be pleased though. She loved that compost pile, for real. She even tried to get me to dig it over. I told her Paul could do that. It would make me ill. I don't mind housework, but I draw the line at gardening.

Her eyes had closed. Her hat had slipped off her head and lay on the grass beside her chair. Her hair was so thin you could see her scalp. I thought it was only men who went bald. I balanced the hat back on her head. I was going to peel an egg for her, but it was still so hot I had to drop it from hand to hand, as the shell burnt my fingers.

Edith was snoring softly, her head tilted back. For a crazy second I was tempted to push one of the unpeeled eggs into her open mouth. Let her suck on that and see how she liked it.

Her eyelids fluttered. She raised a bony hand to brush something away from her face. I was shocked at myself – how could I be so fucked up? Edith was just a fragile old lady.

'Are we going to eat those eggs then?' Edith tapped an egg on the side of the table and half the shell came away cleanly in her hand. 'That's the way to do it,' she said with satisfaction.

The wasp had come back. He hovered around the egg as she bit into it. She swallowed half in one go, uncovering a pale-yellow yolk with grey all round it. Made me feel a bit sick.

She waved the wasp away. 'I've never understood the point of wasps – it's not as if they pollinate anything, they're just pests.'

She rolled up the newspaper that was lying across her lap and whacked at the wasp pointlessly. It landed on the melting butter.

'Better get this in the fridge,' I said, stacking up the tray.

I watched Edith from the kitchen window. She'd unrolled the newspaper and was doing the crossword. The garden was full of flowers. It looked amazing. My nan would've loved a garden like that. She only had plants in pots on her balcony. I used to sit out there in the summer, trying to get a tan, my feet propped up on the railings.

'Watch yourself! Don't fall.' Nan was always worrying about me. Wished I'd never caused her any anxiety now, but I guess it was in her nature to worry.

If Nan hadn't died I'd probably be living with her now, instead of with Edith. Even when I was in secondary I'd go round hers a couple of times a week. I liked hanging out with Nan. She always made my favourite food and let me watch what I wanted on TV. Not like at home where it was either kid's TV or sport. Of if Mum got her way, some depressing documentary about hospitals or people on the dole. Me and Nan actually liked the same comedies. I even got her into *Friends*.

Also, it was easier to do my homework at Nan's – without Leo and Amber making noise. I'd spread my books out over the table while she sat next to me reading her church newsletter or preparing something for her bible class. She used to joke that we were study buddies. That was before I started going out with Joel.

It was stupid really, but I just thought she'd go on forever. I keep seeing the way she'd smile at me, her eyes soft with love. Now I feel like I didn't deserve it. I know you can't go back in time and put things right and I know she wouldn't like the methods I'm using, but I don't feel like I've got a choice. Now I'm here I have to stick to the plan. And Nan always said that so long as I was safe and happy, so long as I was financially secure, that's all that mattered.

KENYA, 1956

'THE SHOPS ARE CLOSING. I must go or I won't make it back to school in time.' Charity pushed herself away from Githii, but he kept his hands clasped tightly around her waist.

'They always pack up early. There's plenty of time before your bus.'

He pulled her towards him so that their bodies were pressed together and she couldn't think of anything except her longing to feel his skin against hers. He planted little kisses along her neck, making her giggle.

A van beeped as it drove past them, a small boy hanging from the door. 'Better get going,' he shouted. 'Curfew's coming.'

'Come on.' Githii took Charity's hand. 'I'll walk you to the bus stop.'

'You go on home,' she urged Githii. 'My stop's the wrong direction for you.'

'You sure you don't want me to wait with you?' His forehead

furrowed in the anxious expression she'd grown to recognise.

The consequences would be worse for him than for her if he was caught out after curfew. 'Of course, you need to get home.' As she spoke she noticed how dark it had got. All the shops were closed and the street was empty.

'See you next Saturday.'

Githii gave her one of his cheeky grins, his mouth lifting slightly higher on the right side in a way that always made her smile back in response. She watched for a second as he ran off down the road, his long legs carrying him effortlessly away, then she picked up her own speed, marching determinedly towards the bus stop.

This was the first time she'd met Githii on her own; they'd hung out together in a group with other girls from her school before. She felt a little nervous now about making the journey back to school by herself. She'd told her friends not to worry, to go on ahead without her, but she hadn't meant to stay out so late. Now she regretted sneaking out without the well-known Sacred Heart uniform which they were supposed to wear at all times. She would have felt safer inside the respected blazer, proclaiming her convent-school status.

Githii hadn't even been impressed by her dress. He'd laughed and called her a tai-tai. Would he rather see her in a cow-skin skirt? And the dress was such a pretty sky-blue colour. She loved the way it hugged her waist before flaring out in soft pleats. It had belonged to one of the daughters of her mother's employer. Mama said the girl had never even worn it before Mrs Johnson gave it to her. She had a whole wardrobe full of dresses, more than she could ever wear. Charity's friend Victoria, who kept up with all the fashions, said it fitted Charity perfectly. That she looked like a movie star in it. But Githii obviously didn't approve of European clothing.

Githii's parents had been detained. Charity was shocked when he told her he didn't know where they were or when they might be released. Now he survived by working odd jobs around the city for whoever would give him work. He said his younger brothers and sisters had been sent to a reserve somewhere in the countryside, but he was proud of being a city boy. He wasn't going to be locked up in a camp and forced to dig roads for the Europeans. So he'd managed to escape and come back to Nairobi.

He was working for a tea vendor when she met him. He'd seated her and her friends on stools, bowing elaborately and treating them like queens. He made them all laugh with his constant patter. 'You're crazy' they told him, but were delighted with all this attention from such a good-looking boy. When he started singing to her, Charity had blushed and looked away, but secretly she was flattered to have been singled out. Her friends, excited by the romance of an illicit affair (they were studying *Romeo and Juliet* at school), encouraged her to go out walking with Githii on their next Saturday outing to Nairobi.

This was the third time she'd met him and their time together had just disappeared. Despite their very different lives they'd never run out of things to talk about. Beneath the jokey charm, Githii was thoughtful and his responses to her chatter showed how seriously he'd been listening to her.

She told him about her older brother, Joseph, who was studying in London. How lucky he was to get to go to university abroad. She wished she could go someplace else, but the Women's Group at Church would never raise the money for her to travel like they'd done for Joseph. Her father, who was a teacher, was worried Joseph wasn't taking his studies seriously enough. In his last letter, Joseph said he'd been to a rally in Trafalgar Square where people were protesting against England's invasion of

Egypt. Her parents wanted him to get away from protests, not get involved in more.

Githii had nodded seriously. 'He must come back with an education, like Kenyatta, to show the British we can rule ourselves without them.'

But when she asked Githii if he would like to be at school, he just shrugged. 'You know me, I always get by,' he grinned.

Her parents wouldn't approve of course. They'd question what Githii's parents had done to get arrested, even though they knew innocent people were rounded up all the time. They'd worry about her getting involved with someone with no future. Baba would give her a lecture about the need to focus on her schoolwork and the danger of offending the nuns. Of course she was grateful for the sacrifices her family had made in sending her to school and knew it was a great honour to win a scholarship to Sacred Heart. It was just…sometimes she wished she didn't have to be good all the time, that she didn't have to worry constantly about God, or the Home Guard or soldiers or the Mau Mau.

As she turned the corner, Charity saw her bus pulling away from the stop. Dismay swept over her. It was probably the last bus to Limuru, it would take her hours to walk back to school. She'd never make it in before the doors were locked and then she'd be seen not wearing her uniform. What would Mother Winifride say? Would she be expelled? Her parents would be so ashamed of her.

She looked about, but there was no one else at the bus stop to ask about later buses. She started walking as fast as she could, keeping her head down. Perhaps she could catch the bus up at the next stop. She put her fingers to her neck to check for the little bag she kept her passbook in. She couldn't feel the ribbons that secured it. She groped under her collar, the ribbons must have come undone. She reached up under her dress. It had to be there, she'd have noticed if it had fallen out. But there was nothing. The bag was gone. She jumped up and down, praying to dislodge it from beneath her dress, to see it fluttering down from under the airy rayon folds of her skirts. But still, nothing. The ribbon must have come undone when Githii kissed her neck. They'd been too absorbed in each other to notice.

'Oh Jesus, St. Anthony, please let me get back to school without being stopped,' she prayed as she walked. The bus conductor wouldn't let her on without her pass. If only she had the money for a taxi. Perhaps she should go to the cathedral and ask for help. Maybe a priest could drive her back to school.

She kept on at a semi-run, the breath burning in her lungs. Maybe the bus driver would be sympathetic and let her on. If she could get a bus. She'd been to Mass at The Holy Family Minor Basilica before and was sure it was nearby, but all the streets were starting to look the same. She was tempted to veer off down a road on the right, but, having no idea where it led, was afraid of getting lost and ending up in a forbidden neighbourhood. Now she wished she'd let Githii wait with her; he'd know what to do. Maybe she should go back and look for him. She swallowed, trying not to give in to her rising panic.

'Are you Kikuyu, Embu, or Meru?'

A weight descended on her shoulder. She was spun round to find a man in a Home Guard uniform staring down at her, his hand gripping her shoulder. For a moment she was tempted to pretend she belonged to a different tribe, but was afraid of getting into worse trouble if she was caught lying. Most of the men from her village had to join the Home Guards if they didn't want to be seen as terrorists. She hated it when her brother and father helped them patrol the village at night, because she knew they'd be the first targets of the Mau Mau. She would lie awake, waiting anxiously for their return. It was another reason her parents had been keen for Joseph to study abroad, to send him somewhere safer. Githii said the Home Guards in Nairobi were thugs. The ones from Pumwani district were the worst, he said. If you didn't pay their bribes they'd arrest you. All she had was her bus fare back to school.

'I'm Kikuyu, but my family are Christians. We support the British Government.' She tried to smile calmly at the man.

He just snorted. 'What are you doing out during curfew?'

'I didn't realise what time it was and I missed the bus.' She avoided meeting his eyes. Another Home Guard stood just behind the first, she could see his fingers tapping on the gun in his belt.

'Missed the bus?' The man sneered. 'It's your duty to be inside before curfew. Show me your passbook.'

Charity squeezed her hands together. 'I've lost it,' she whispered. 'I always carry it round my neck but my bag must have come undone. I just don't understand where it's gone.'

'So, you're a prostitute. We know about Nairobi women.' The men laughed. 'You're all prostitutes, or the daughters of prostitutes.'

'I'm not from Nairobi, I'm from Kiambu. I go to the Sacred Heart Convent School. I just need to get back there.' Her bladder suddenly felt full to bursting and she was afraid of wetting herself.

'If you go to Sacred Heart why aren't you wearing the school uniform?' The Home Guard pushed his fat fingers between the buttons on the front of her dress, rubbing the silky fabric between his thumb and index finger. 'Where did you get a dress like that? From your lover?'

Charity shook her head. 'The *memsahib* my mother works for, she gave it to me. If you call the school they'll tell you who I am.'

'You answering back?' He turned to his companion. 'You can

tell she's a prostitute. They're all full of talk.'

The men laughed again. Charity felt her knees giving way beneath her. An armoured truck drew up beside them. The back was full of frightened-looking people, caged in under the wire roof like chickens in a coop. The Home Guards gestured to the driver, a young European solider who looked at them nervously.

'We've picked up a Mau Mau spy,' the Home Guard told the soldier.

Charity shook her head vociferously as the Home Guard forced her hands behind her back. 'It's not true,' she cried.

The Home Guard yanked her arms until they felt like they'd be pulled out of their sockets. Another soldier jumped out of the vehicle and opened the back of the truck.

'Please,' Charity tried appealing to the soldier. 'I haven't done anything wrong. I just need to get back to my school.'

The soldier ignored her and Charity found herself being lifted up and thrown into the truck, landing painfully on her knees. A woman beside her pulled her up to standing before the truck started up. Charity clung to her as they were jolted against the wire.

They were driven into a compound, fenced in with barbed wire. As they stumbled off the truck, soldiers separated the men from the women. Charity, feeling giddy and nauseous, followed the line of women into a dark room. The heat and the smell of fear-induced sweat and urine were overwhelming. It was so crowded there was hardly room to sit. Charity heard a key clanging against a metal lock.

'I need the toilet,' Charity, in desperation, told the woman next to her.

The woman shouted for a guard, but her calls were ignored. As the night wore on women moved to a corner of the room to relieve themselves and Charity was forced to do the same, despite the terrible smell. Her empty belly made her feel light-headed, but at least the stink stopped her from wanting to eat.

Women around her called to each other, announcing their names and where they were from. 'If you get out before me tell my husband, my mother, my brother, where I am', was a refrain passed on from one person to another. One of the women had a baby who wailed for most of the night, despite various attempts to console it.

As the hours passed Charity sank onto the dirty floor. She sat squashed in, with someone's knees and feet pressed against her back, no longer caring if her skirts were dirtied. Every time she started to nod off she was jerked awake by the pain in her neck as her head fell forward.

At last the glimmerings of daylight crept in under the tin roof. There was the blast of a trumpet and the doors were pulled open. The women stumbled out into the yard, shaking their cramped limbs. They were pushed into a line by the Home Guards, their bodies roughly handled under the pretext of a search. Charity was even made to open her mouth. A Home Guard stared into it, pulling her lip out and checking her cheeks like a belligerent dentist looking for ulcers. She longed for some comforting sweet porridge, but no breakfast was forthcoming, not even a drink of water. Her mouth was horribly dry and now it was sore as well.

They waited in the sun for what felt like hours, until finally the gates opened and a car drove in. A white man got out, accompanied by two Askari. The Home Guards stood to attention, saluting as the European and the policemen disappeared into a tent.

'That's good,' the woman standing behind Charity said in Gikuyu. 'A white man will treat us more kindly than these traitors.' She nodded at the Home Guards.

Charity said nothing. The woman would probably consider

her family traitors too. Still, she was also relieved to see a white official. The English were famous for their sense of fair play after all. She rehearsed in her mind what she would say to the officer, grateful to her school for her excellent English. She had never once had to wear the shameful badge declaring 'I am an idiot. I have been speaking in my mother tongue'. She and her friends all spoke in English, even at home where no one else could understand them.

Soon all this mess would be cleared up and she would be driven back to school. She didn't care any more if she was punished, just so long as she got back there. She would beg the Sisters for mercy and promise not to leave the building until she graduated. And if she was sent home she'd throw herself into her mother's arms and feel herself cocooned in the safety of that strong embrace. Her mother would be so happy to see her she'd forgive her for being out after curfew and for losing her passbook.

At last it was her turn to enter the tent. A Home Guard stood behind her, pushing her forward with his rifle butt. The white officer sat behind a desk, flanked by the Askari.

'Please sir,' Charity began in English. Immediately she felt a whack to the back of her head.

'Do not speak until spoken to,' the Home Guard shouted in Kiswahili.

The white officer didn't look surprised by this violence or say anything to the Home Guard. He just shuffled through the papers on the desk in front of him, sighing wearily as though it was all rather tedious.

'She's Kikuyu, suspected Mau Mau collaborator,' the Home Guard told one of the Askari who then translated what he'd said into English for the benefit of the officer.

Charity vehemently shook her aching head.

'Where's her passbook?' the officer asked in English.

'Doesn't have one. She was out after curfew, probably a prostitute. The Mau Mau use them as scouts.' The message was relayed from Home Guard to policeman to officer.

'I'm not. I'm a schoolgirl, from Sacred Heart Convent School.' Charity didn't care if she was hit again, she had to convince this Englishman to let her go.

He finally looked at her directly. 'What were you doing in Nairobi then?'

'We're allowed into the city on Saturdays, sir.'

'After curfew?' His face was shiny with sweat. He seemed irritated rather than impressed by her command of English.

'I missed my bus,' she said quietly. It was stuffy in the tent and she was so thirsty she couldn't think straight. She couldn't admit to seeing a boy. Mother Winifride would definitely expel her for that. Her family would be so ashamed of her.

'Age?' The officer had returned to his forms, his pen hovered above a dotted line.

'Sixteen.'

He stared up at her again, eyebrows raised. 'Very well developed for a sixteen-year-old.' His tone was scathing.

She didn't know how to respond to this. Her friends were envious of her curves. But the nuns had taught her never to look at her own body and to guard against vanity at all times. Her carefully prepared speech dissolved in the cloud of humiliation and pain filling her head.

The white officer turned back to the Home Guard. 'Phone this school she claims to attend and see if her story tallies. If it doesn't, send her for further screening.'

The policeman translated swiftly, but Charity wasn't listening to him, she was so relieved. Soon she would be out of this nightmare and back to her normal life, struggling over algebra and learning poems about the English countryside. She'd never complain about her schoolwork ever again.

She stepped out of the tent expecting to be taken to an office, somewhere with a telephone, but instead the Home Guard, his hand curled tightly round her arm, marched her over to a waiting truck.

She twisted round to look up at him. 'Are you taking me back to school?'

'Yes, yes,' he said, pushing her onto the back of the vehicle.

It was already full, but they kept adding more women; one by one as they left the tent they were shoved onto the truck, like cans on a conveyor belt. Were they going to drop all these women off one by one?

'Are they taking you home?' she asked the woman squashed in next to her.

The woman smiled pityingly at her. 'I don't know where they're taking us, darling, but it won't be home.'

Charity tried to call out to the Home Guards to ask about the phone call to her school, but if they heard her, they pretended not to understand.

By the time the truck finally began to move, the women on board were so hot and dehydrated they swayed together in silence, not questioning where they were going, just glad to have a little breeze on their faces.

Charity castigated herself bitterly for not managing to convince the officer to release her. She had learnt Wordsworth's 'Composed Upon Westminster Bridge' off by heart at school, what if she had ignored the blows of the guard and recited it to him? That would surely have persuaded him of her innocence. The only city she had ever seen was Nairobi and she'd never been able to picture the 'Ships, towers, domes, theatres, and temples' all crammed together in Wordsworth's London, but the officer must have seen them. Perhaps he even came from London. She could imagine it now; filled with pity and admiration by her rendition of his nation's poetry, he would drive her back to school himself and explain to Mother Winifride how there had been a terrible mistake.

A guard post on wooden stilts, towering ominously over rows of grey tents, came into view. They stopped for an armed sentry to open up the gates. Above them a sign in Gikuyu declared in capital letters, '*MWITHEITHIA NIATEITHAGIO*' –'He who helps himself is helped.' They passed through the first set of gates, driving over a narrow wooden bridge. Staring down through the wire mesh that covered the truck, Charity could see, instead of water, lines of wooden stakes, like rows of giant sharpened pencils, pointing upwards from the bottom of a deep ditch. They stopped at a second gate for a second African sentry to let them in, before finally passing into another compound enclosed with more rolls of barbed wire.

Two African female warders stood by to escort the women into one of several long huts. Here, to Charity's horror, they were told to take off their clothes. Charity tried to speak to one of the warders to explain that she shouldn't be here, she was supposed to go back to school, but the woman slapped her legs with a cane, screaming at her to strip. Charity unbuttoned her dress with trembling fingers, dropped it into a wire basket and ran with the other women to be hosed down with cold water.

Shivering and wet she was handed back the dress she had come to loathe, before being moved on to have her fingers pressed onto an inkpad and again onto a sheet of white paper. She was glad when her photograph was taken; thinking this at least would be a means for her parents to identify her and prove her innocence.

The women were being split up into groups of about fifteen.

Charity was too frightened by this time to attempt to speak to the warders. She just hoped that soon she would be given the chance to explain herself. That the promised phone call to her headmistress would be made and she would be released from this horror story.

Armed guards stood in the next hut, waiting for them. They were ordered to lie on the ground with their legs apart. Charity's heart was beating so fast she could hardly breathe. Were they about to be examined? Was this to see if she was a virgin? Would they be satisfied then that she wasn't a prostitute? Despite not having had anything to drink since the previous afternoon, she felt like she might pee and prayed that she wouldn't wet herself when the nurse or doctor came to inspect her.

The guards stood over them laughing and commenting on their private parts. Charity stared up at the iron roof. A big fat fly kept buzzing pointlessly against the metal as though it could force its way out to the sky beyond.

Instead of a doctor, a group of women in calico dresses came in. They were giggling and whispering in Gikuyu. Not nurses then, but not prisoners either – they were too bold and too cheerful. She could see that one of them was carrying a basket of eggs. The woman put them on the ground by Charity's legs. Suddenly she grabbed Charity's wrists. Another woman seized her ankles and they pulled until Charity was spread out like a starfish. When she struggled, the one holding her arms slapped her around the head, and when she tried to fight back with her freed hand, the woman rubbed her face into the dirt floor, so that her mouth and nose filled with dust and she thought she'd choke.

She could hear the guards, laughing and taunting her. She felt something burning being rammed up inside her. Heavy hands forced her legs together. A ball of fire was cracking right inside her, burning into her womb. She could hear an agonised groaning, like an animal whose throat has been slit and she didn't even know if the sound was coming from her or someone else.

She thought she was going to die.

A woman's voice, speaking Gikuyu with an English accent, rang out. 'Admit to taking the oath and this will stop. Your choice.'

Charity licked at the salt tears running down her face, her throat too dry for her to speak. How could she admit to something she hadn't done? Something she didn't even have any knowledge of? A heavy weight collided with her hip. She hadn't even realised she'd been squeezing her eyes closed until she opened them and saw a tanned white face with livid red cheeks staring down at her.

'You,' the woman kicked her again. 'Admit it, you've drunk blood, taken the Mau Mau oath.'

Charity rolled her head from side to side. 'I'm a Christian,' she said, as if this was all the proof required. Something warm and sticky landed on her cheek. The woman had spat on her. But the pain in her vagina was so bad she hardly cared. The boots moved. She could hear the same question being put to the other women still lying on the floor. No one admitted to taking the oath.

Eventually Charity's limbs were released. She and the other prisoners stumbled up, hopping from foot to foot, trying to get rid of the bits of egg and cracked shell from their scalding vaginas, not caring how the guards mocked them.

'You'll soon be dancing to another tune,' the white woman told them. 'The sooner you confess, the sooner you can be rehabilitated.'

Charity didn't know what being rehabilitated meant. If no one would listen to her how could she explain herself? This woman was obviously one of those settlers who hated the Kikuyu. She just needed to a chance to speak to another English officer, someone honourable and kindly, like Father Timothy who taught maths at school. Someone who would pluck her out of this terrible ordeal and see her safely home again.

EDITH

I'D BEEN CALLING LAUREN from the bottom of the stairs until my voice was hoarse, but still she didn't respond. She was either deaf or asleep. I'd have to go up and talk to her. I needed to see the chiropodist about my corns and I couldn't remember whether Lauren had made me an appointment, and if she had, for what day.

I hadn't been into that room since she moved in. I just assumed she kept it as clean and tidy as the rest of the house. She was always nicely presented. It certainly couldn't be any worse than when Joanna lived at home, but Lauren was nothing like my daughter, thank goodness.

She was lying on the bed plugged into her phone with those ear pods, her eyes closed. I paused in the doorway, holding onto the frame. Climbing all those stairs had taken it out of me. I'd used the banisters to haul myself up, but my legs ached and my hands were shaking again. I could feel my joints seizing up.

Piles of clothes dotted the floor like molehills. Dirty glasses, mugs and make-up accessories littered the shelves. I leant against the chest of drawers. Cheap jewellery was scattered across the top; hoop ear-rings and bangles. One of the bracelets caught my eye. There were two in fact, one on top of the other, made of thin grey metal. I picked the top one up. A number was etched onto the side. I had seen these bracelets before.

'Where did you get these?'

Lauren looked up at me, startled. She pulled the plugs out of her ears.

'Sorry Edith, did you need me?'

I made my way unsteadily across the room and held the band up in front of her.

'Where did this come from?'

'I don't know.'

'What do you mean you don't know?'

She just shrugged. I turned the band round and round in my hand. It was unmistakable, the detention number neatly inscribed on the metal. Two bands for grey prisoners, not the worst, but not the most innocent either.

'Do you know what they are?'

It took her a long time to answer me; too long.

'Just bracelets,' she mumbled.

'And what do you think the number signifies?'

'I don't know.' She sounded like a surly schoolchild.

'You must at least know where you got them.'

Lauren jumped up off the bed.

'I don't know anything more about them than you do.' She was shouting at me.

She had never raised her voice at me before. I felt dizzy. I reached out for the bedside cabinet to steady myself, but my hand knocked over a mug. Lauren grabbed a box of tissues and began to mop up the brown liquid that was pouring onto the carpet. I moved out of her way and sank down onto the bed.

As I leant back on one arm, my hand slid under the pillow. I could feel something hard and smooth concealed beneath it. What was she hiding under there? I pulled out a folded silver photograph frame. Lauren still had her back to me. I opened out the frame. On one side was a picture of a young woman with long auburn hair, holding a toddler on her knee. The other side contained a picture of an elderly black woman and a little girl. They were hugging each other as they looked at the camera. The child nestled into the arms of the woman. Their faces pressed together. The same broad smile. The same large, oval eyes that crinkled at the edges. The woman wore a bright blue head wrap. The little girl was unmistakably Lauren.

'It's all right, Edith. It's nothing to worry about.'

Lauren's voice was as brisk as a nurse's. I didn't know if she was referring to the spilt tea, my physical decline or her own secretiveness. She tossed a ball of soggy tissues carelessly into the wastepaper basket.

'Who is this?' I held up the picture.

Lauren spun round. Her face grew pale when she saw what I was holding.

'That's mine.'

She held out her hand, but I grasped the frame as tightly as my trembling fingers would allow.

'Who's the woman?'

'My mum.'

'Not her, the black woman.'

'That's my nan.' Lauren's voice caught on the name.

How had I been so blind? I could see it in her now, the curly hair, the wide nose and plump lips. I had been deceived by her pale skin and hazel eyes.

'Where was your grandmother from?'

'Edmonton,' she said, and looked down at me with a coldness, a hostility in her eyes that I had not encountered there before.

'Originally.'

'Africa.'

'Were they hers?' I nodded at the bracelets in my lap.

'Why should they be my nan's?'

'Where in Africa was she from?

'I'm not sure.' Lauren's voice brightened. 'To be honest I never really thought about where she'd come from. She never talked about her life before she came to Britain. She was just my nan.' Lauren smiled her wide innocent smile, but I wasn't falling for that now.

'You have encouraged me to talk about Kenya and yet deliberately withheld the fact your own grandmother was African. Kenyan even, if these detention bracelets belonged to her.'

'I don't know where those bracelets came from, Edith. There was loads of stuff still in this room when I moved in. Maybe they're your daughter's.'

'Why on earth would Joanna have them?'

But as I spoke I realised that this was quite possible. The only reason I knew what the bracelets were was because Graham had kept some. Exhibits from his days as an overseer at the prison camp. It was Graham who had explained to me how the system worked. The grading of the prisoners, those with one bracelet were the most militant, Mau Mau hard-core who needed to be kept apart; women with three bracelets were accomplices, usually young girls and the easiest to rehabilitate. Those with two were the greys and might go either way.

Graham had kept all his memorabilia in a case in his study, but Joanna might have picked these up, thinking they were bangles. Or perhaps Graham had given them to her. He might have hoped they would serve some educational purpose.

Mementos he called them. I thought it a little ghoulish, but he liked his souvenirs. Most people wanted to forget, but of course Graham couldn't afford to forget; he applied the lessons learnt in Kenya to other places – Northern Ireland for example.

'There's someone at the door.'

It took me a moment to process what Lauren way saying. I hadn't heard anything.

'They're ringing the bell again. I'd better answer it.'

Lauren sped out of the room leaving me sitting in the midst of her detritus. I wondered whether she was fabricating the bell ringing in order to escape an awkward situation.

I stared at the photograph. At the little girl cuddling her granny. The delight on both their faces. The love. Envy bubbled in my chest like heartburn. Sorrow pushed it down. I had trusted Lauren and I thought she trusted me. I thought we had become close. But why conceal her background?

I became aware of a stinging pain in my hand. I had clenched my fist around one of the bracelets, pressing the metal into my palm so hard it left a circular indentation there. I shoved it into my cardigan pocket and surveyed the room. I wasn't sure how I was going to get myself off the bed and back downstairs. There was nothing to hold onto.

KENYA, 1953

IT WAS FATHER WHO beckoned Edith over. He was standing on the lawn in front of the house conferring with two soldiers. They were nodding in an affable, but business-like manner, as though they were discussing the price of tobacco or coffee.

'Edith can tell you where Mary's hiding. You were always sneaking about, the two of you. Where'd you go to?'

Edith looked at the men uneasily. Although they were no longer friends, she had spoken to Mary only a few days before. Mary was walking home from the station, dressed in her boarding-school uniform. As they stopped to chat, Mary pulled on the lapel of her blazer, drawing Edith's attention to her prefect's badge.

'You should get your parents to send you to school. White girls don't have to pass exams for their schools so you'll get in no problem. You must get so bored stuck here with only a governess. We have a different teacher for every subject; they are all specialists.'

Edith tried to ignore Mary's jibes, but it was true, Miss Chandler, her governess, was as much a companion for her mother as a teacher for Edith, and her educational background was dubious to say the least.

Edith looked down at Mary's sandals. She'd never seen any of the squatter children wearing shoes before. Not even the adolescents. These were scuffed and dusty from the dirt road. Edith wondered if Mary had got them new or if they'd been passed on to her.

'Our headmistress went to Oxford University. She could have been a professor, but she got a calling to come to Africa and set up a girls' school.'

Mary had laughed and Edith couldn't tell whether she was mocking her or her headmistress's vocation. But there'd been no hostility in her eyes; only the usual mischievous spark. And when she smiled dimples still appeared in Mary's smooth, round cheeks.

Now, the older of the two soldiers turned to her. 'The girl's brother has joined the Mau Mau. We know she's been taking messages and food to the forest gangs. She must know where he is.'

'Which brother?' Edith couldn't help asking. It couldn't be Kamau, surely, or George, who was at Kagumo teacher training college. They wouldn't succumb to Mau Mau witchcraft.

The soldier just shrugged. She could tell from the badges on their caps they weren't Kenya Regiment and it was obvious from their pale skin they weren't settlers. The younger one, a ginger-haired youth, didn't look much older than she was. He was probably doing his National Service. His neck was red and blistered where the collar of his khaki jacket rubbed against it. His face was covered in acne; angry red spots inflamed by the sweat that bubbled on his forehead. His bloodshot eyes stared at her wildly, the watery blue irises darting from Edith to the land around them. She couldn't tell if it was fear or excitement that made them bulge so. He kept licking his chapped lips and she wondered if she ought to send Mathenge for some tea or lemonade.

Father dropped his cigarette, grinding it into the grass with his heel. 'The girl's helping those murdering bastards – what does it matter which of her brothers is involved? The whole family must be complicit.'

The soldiers looked at Edith expectantly. She glanced around to see if any of the workers were nearby. That was how bad things had got. The raiding of settler farms had them all on the edge of their nerves. Thank God no one they knew had been murdered, but the slaughter of the Ruck family, especially that poor little boy, was never far from their minds. Edith was haunted by the photograph in the newspaper of his blood-stained nursery. And to think the Rucks' own servants had been involved. Edith had grown up with their houseboys and trusted them completely, but her parents said the Mau Mau targeted loyal workers.

Edith and her mother now slept with pistols under their pillows, while her father spent his nights on a chair facing the front door, a loaded rifle on his knee. The trouble was, he said, the colonial administration was too soft – let the blacks get away with murder, quite literally. All this fuss about legal rights and trials – they should let the settlers deal with the bastards. They'd soon put them down.

When she couldn't sleep her mother told her to keep her chin up and think of those incredible women in Nyeri, two of whom managed to fend off a Mau Mau attack single-handed. Shot three men dead. Not bad for a pair of old ladies. It was just so sad about their pet dog, a boxer who got caught in the crossfire.

Mother even looked into getting a boxer puppy. She and Edith were going to deliver it to them as a token of their admiration, but, as usual with her mother, the idea came to nothing.

'Don't just stand there gawping, Edith. These men don't have all day.' Father slung his rifle over his shoulder.

Edith thought of all the times she'd called to Mary and her former friend had pretended not to hear. How the other children had mocked her, and Mary had said nothing. A light rain was starting to fall, beading the hairs on her arms with drops of water. They should get going before the path became too slippery.

Edith could hear the men scrabbling up the rocks behind her. It was exciting to take the lead, to think of herself as Boadicea and the men as her foot soldiers. For once she was getting to be the warrior princess of her childhood games instead of the lowly follower. Now Mary would see who was superior.

She stopped at the bottom of the waterfall. There, to the right, just a few feet away, was the stone shelf that led into their secret hideaway. She hadn't been here in years; perhaps Mary hadn't either. Colobus monkeys shrieked from the trees above them. She could hear animals rustling in the undergrowth. Her mouth had turned dry and her heart pounded. If she didn't tell them, they would never guess there was a cave behind the screen of water. They would never find the playhouse, swept clean with a brush made of sticks. Edith thought of the stones they'd pretended to cook over, the imaginary babies they'd nursed, the shop selling everything from food to jewels. It was the perfect place to hide supplies.

The sergeant was staring uneasily up at the sky. The clouds were getting thicker and the rain heavier.

'Well?' said Father. 'Is this it?'

This was Edith's chance at last, to impress him with her usefulness. She pointed, whispering, 'There's a cave behind there.'

'Call for Mary,' he urged.

The men waited in silence.

'Mary,' Edith shouted, hesitantly at first and then louder.

While telling herself Mary wouldn't be there, part of Edith longed to catch her red-handed. To triumphantly march her back to the village between two soldiers. To see her shamed and brought low, to make her see that for all her scholarships and ambitions, she couldn't outwit Edith. Edith was the smarter one.

'Mary!' Edith yelled above the cascading water. 'Mary come out, I need you.'

Mary emerged slowly, a flash of white and brown behind the water materialising into human form, sidling along the narrow ledge, trying not to get her clothes wet. She stopped when she saw who Edith's companions were, her eyes wide in her face, her mouth open in shock.

Edith held her breath, it was as if she had conjured an imaginary being into life. She was astonished by her own power, thrilled and horrified in equal measure.

Later, as Edith turned the moment over and over in her mind, she told herself that if Mary had only stayed still and put up her hands, if she had just obeyed the instructions the soldiers shouted, everything would have been different. But as soon as she had cleared the ledge Mary turned towards the forest, running as fast as she could, her head jutting forward, a look of grim concentration on her face.

There was a sudden movement to the right of Edith. One of the soldiers was lifting his rifle. Shots rang out, ricocheting off the rocks. They must be firing into the waterfall, she thought. There might be men hiding in there. But then, as if in slow motion, she watched Mary fall to her knees. Mary's back juddered, a red stain blossomed out across the white cotton of her school shirt.

She slumped forward, face down on the ground, hands spread out before her.

Edith heard Father cursing. She wanted to go to Mary, to lift her up out of the earth and wrap her arms so tightly around her friend she would stop the blood leaving her body. But her feet would not move, the breath stopped in her lungs and she could not even cry out.

'We'll check the cave. You wait here.' The sergeant raised his hand.

The soldiers left Mary where she lay, the rain soaking her clothes, turning the ground around her to mud. They shuffled across the stone ridge, gripping their rifles. Parting the curtain of water with their bayonets, they disappeared into the cave.

Edith listened for an exchange of gunfire, shouts, but could hear only the hollow roar of the water and the shrieking of the monkeys.

The soldiers quickly reappeared. 'No weapons,' the sergeant shouted. 'But we found supplies of food, a bag of maize, some bananas. She was working for the Mau Mau all right.'

Mary's body hadn't moved, but Edith was sure she could still be saved; they just needed to get her to a hospital in time.

'Wait there, behind those trees.' Father pushed her towards a grove of eucalyptus trees.

The trees screened Mary and the soldiers from view, but Edith crept forward to watch them from between the trunks. After that day, she always hated the smell of eucalyptus.

The ginger-haired soldier was rolling Mary onto her back. Her head lolled to one side, her eyes open, her cheeks coated in dust.

She heard the soldier ask his sergeant, 'Shall I take a hand?'

Edith thought he meant to make a gesture of comfort, to hold Mary's hand while they got help, called for an air ambulance.

She shuffled further forwards, clutching onto roots and clumps of grass to keep her balance, her fear of snakes forgotten.

'Don't know if they'll accept a girl's hand. Could be a boy's I suppose.' The sergeant looked over at Father. 'It's evidence,' he explained. 'So we get our five pounds.'

The boy had pulled a knife out of his belt, he was jerking it in a sawing motion across Mary's wrist.

Edith's legs gave way beneath her. Vomit rose up into her mouth. She felt her shoulders being grasped. Father had come up behind her. He spun her round towards him so she could no longer see the soldiers or Mary. She pressed her head into his chest, one of his jacket buttons cold and hard against her eye. She hoped it would blind her.

'Don't waste your tears.' His voice was muffled. 'She was working for the Mau Mau, had taken their vile oaths. Once they've submitted to that wickedness they're lost anyway.'

They said you could see it in a person's face, when they had taken the Mau Mau oath. Witchcraft was involved; animal sacrifice, human blood and body parts, even babies. No European had seen an oath-taking – they were carried out in secret – but afterwards the oath-takers' faces changed. Their mouths twisted in a perpetual sneer and their eyes were filled with hatred and savagery. Some even turned yellow, like a leopard's eyes.

Why would Mary, the only girl for miles to get into secondary school, who was so proud of her prefect's badge, why would she take the Mau Mau oath?

Father was holding Edith up by the elbow. 'Let's get you home.'

'What about Mary?'

'Leave her body for the hyenas, or let her brother come and get it.'

Edith tried to remember whether Mary had been wearing

her sandals. She thought her feet were bare, she remembered the upturned soles coated in red dust. But why hadn't Mary changed out of her school blouse? Had she been in such a hurry? Someone must tell her mother. But who would tell Wacheera that her only surviving child, the girl destined for university, was now a body lying by the river where she used to fetch water?

Edith lay awake most of the night, listening to the rain drumming on the roof, as if the sky itself was weeping for Mary. She could hear the distant cries of women and children. Perhaps the village had discovered Mary's body. They were holding a funeral for her. Everyone was crying. Edith didn't think she would ever cry again – not at anything.

Waking to sunshine late the next morning, it took a moment before the horror of the previous day broke upon her consciousness. She lay like a stranded fish, gulping air until she felt calm enough to get out of bed. In the dining room her mother was bewailing the loss of Mathenge, the houseboy in charge of laundry. Who was going to wash the dress she needed for dinner at the Smythes?

'Where's Mathenge gone?' Edith asked, hoping he hadn't left in disgust over the shooting. He was a cousin of Mary's.

'He's been relocated with the rest of the Kikuyus. They were all moved in the early hours to a resettlement camp, God knows where. I'm surprised you didn't wake up. The army came, loaded them onto trucks and drove them away. Insisted on taking Mathenge though I told them he's a loyalist.'

Edith left her mother wondering where she was supposed to find a trustworthy replacement, and ran all the way to the squatters' village.

Apart from the goats bleating to be fed, the village was silent. There were no children playing in the dirt outside their huts, no women singing as they made the morning porridge. Smashed pots and overturned stools were scattered on the ground. Chickens pecked over spilt millet. She stepped into an empty hut. Everything was still there, blankets and clothes, a pot of burnt food on the embers of a fire.

She moved through the deserted village to where Mary's homestead had been, but there was nothing left, just heaps of blackened mud and charred sticks. Wisps of straw stuck to the claggy piles, fluttering in the breeze.

A figure came striding towards her making her jump, but it was only Father.

'Mary's home,' she waved at the smouldering rubble. 'It's been burnt down.'

Father nodded. 'To send out a signal to anyone else planning to help the Mau Mau. Mary's family are all right, they've been relocated with the rest of them,' he added, as if guessing Edith's horrible suspicion that the family had been set alight with their home.

Edith remembered the night she had spent curled up next to Mary, listening to her mother's storytelling. How Wacheera had been able to conjure ogres and demons up out of the smoky air. How she had given voices to animals and got them all cheering for the little bird whose chicks were crushed by the heedless elephant. How terrible the mother bird's vengeance had been as it flew up right inside the elephant's fundament and pecked away at the elephant's entrails until it sank to its knees and died. 'The careless elephant must still be punished,' the elephant's children were told.

What stories would Wacheera tell now? Had she been able to take Mary's blazer, with its prefect's badge? Had she packed up the sandals? She might hang them up in her new hut, waiting for Mary to reclaim them. Had she been told, before she was moved? Did she know? She might think Mary had run off into the forest or eloped with a boyfriend. She would wait for a letter, for news, and wonder why it never came.

Vultures perched on the branches of a nearby tree. Edith thought she saw a dog running off with a hand in its mouth, but couldn't get close enough to tell. She must have imagined it, Father told her; she must put such images out of her mind.

Edith's mother finally agreed to Father's demands to send Edith to boarding school in England. Edith hadn't been herself since 'the incident'. She spent all her time in bed, refusing to get up for her lessons with Miss Chandler. She wouldn't take a bath and smelt dreadful.

'Do you think they've put some sort of Mau Mau curse on her?' Edith overheard Mother ask Father.

'Don't be ridiculous, Irene. She just needs to be at school with girls her age. Discipline and distraction will stop all this moping.'

Edith didn't really care whether she went or stayed. She just felt so tired. All she wanted to do was sleep. The crossing was good for that; she spent most of the journey to England in her cabin pleading seasickness, while Mother socialised. Mother had decided to accompany her, using the trip to visit relatives in England. Apart from forcing her out on deck twice a day to take the sea air and into the dining room to pick at her food, Mother left her to her own devices.

The sombre, grey school building looked like a suitable place of punishment. Mother insisted on accompanying her all the way there, as though afraid she might abscond. Edith, however, was too lethargic to run away and too numb to be embarrassed by her mother's tearful, public farewell.

Despite her general apathy, Edith struggled with the rules and the lack of freedom. She wasn't used to spending so much time indoors or being constantly surrounded by other girls, all with their own strict social codes. She found them rather silly and insipid, screaming over harmless English spiders and mooning over boys. At least all they wanted to know about Africa was whether she'd seen lions or ridden on an elephant. The English girls had never heard of the Mau Mau and didn't give two hoots about Kenyan independence.

It was strange, but the shooting of Mary and what came after it was all a bit of a blur. She could no longer remember exactly what had happened, and didn't want to either. As Mother said, better to put it all behind her, focus on the here and now.

After her governess's lackadaisical teaching, Edith needed every ounce of concentration trying to catch up with the school curriculum. Even then she only just scraped a couple of O-Levels. But they allowed her into the sixth form, which was a relief. She spent most of her time on cookery lessons and dance classes, and then there were the plays they put on once a term. It was here Edith discovered her love of acting and that she was good at it, or so her drama teacher told her. It came naturally to her, to turn herself into someone else. So many dramatic characters to inhabit and none, no matter how steeped in blood, so awful as the one she'd left behind.

She never spoke of Mary again, except once, when she tried to tell Graham what had happened.

'All soldiers take trophies,' he said. 'A few units competed for the highest number of kills and that might have encouraged some carelessness. But you saw what we were up against, the bestiality of the Mau Mau. The bastards had to be wiped out. Can't blame a man for not taking any chances.'

It wasn't the answer she'd been hoping for, but then no answer could have been. She thought she wanted Graham to tell her that she'd done the right thing, that Mary must have been guilty.

But equally she wanted him to know how brilliant and beautiful Mary was; how much she had wanted to be her best friend and how hurt she'd been by Mary's disdain. How she'd never meant for Mary to get killed and that for the rest of her life, even though she refused to think of Mary, she would feel a sharp little beak ripping at her insides.

LAUREN

'YOU MUST BE LAUREN.'

This skinny white woman was standing on the doorstep grinning at me.

'And you are?' I didn't mean to be rude but I was a bit freaked out, what with everything that'd just happened with Edith and then this stranger knowing my name.

'Didn't Mum tell you? I'm Jo, Edith's daughter. I've come to stay.'

I just stood there staring at her, completely gobsmacked. The thing I'd been dreading had finally happened, only Joanna seemed really friendly and a bit apologetic. I should've guessed who she was – she had that hippyish vibe about her. She was carrying this massive cloth bag made up of all different patterns and colours, her beach blonde hair was long and messy. Only she looked too healthy to be an ex-junkie. Maybe Edith had exaggerated that part.

She was holding out her hand so I gave it a shake. She wiped it on her jeans and I remembered my hand was wet from mopping up the tea Edith spilt.

'Edith had an accident,' I explained. The look of disgust on Jo's face was something else. 'Not like that,' I said quickly. 'She just knocked over a cup of tea.'

'Oh,' she said. 'That's a relief.'

'You'd better come upstairs.' I figured Edith was gonna throw me out anyway, so what did it matter that Jo had turned up now?

'Is Mum OK?' She sounded alarmed.

'Yeah, well, she's just…acting a bit strange.'

Edith was still sitting on the bed, her hands resting palms up in her lap.

'Has Mum moved into my bedroom?' Jo looked a bit baffled.

I glanced round the room, taking in all the clothes I'd left on the floor. Really? Like Edith shopped at New Look?

'Joanna, when did you arrive?' Edith looked at Jo with surprise.

'We agreed I'd come for a visit, remember?' Jo sat down on the bed next to her mum.

Edith put her hand up to her forehead, rubbing the loose skin up and down with the tips of her fingers. 'I thought you were coming next week. My memory's like a sieve these days.'

God forgive me but I was thankful to hear her say that.

'I decided to come a few days early.' Jo gave a fake-sounding laugh. 'I've been staying at Ottie's – remember my old friend from school? She's got two children now, can you believe it?' She picked up Edith's hand and held it in her lap. 'There's a lot of tension between Ottie and Tom – you know, her husband, the architect? Thought I'd better give them some space.'

'She isn't what I thought she was,' Edith was mumbling and I wasn't sure if she was talking about me or Jo.

'None of my friends seem to get much pleasure out of parenting; it's all stress and exhaustion.' Jo shook her head. 'Makes me grateful I'm footloose and fancy free.'

Edith just snorted. 'So you're still a hippy?'

'I was never a hippy, Mum. I was running a guest house and retreat. It was actually a successful business.'

'Why have you given it up then?'

Jo sighed loudly. 'Remember, I told you Mum. I'm training to be a yoga teacher. I've enrolled in a very highly regarded school here in London.' She dragged her fingers through her tangled hair. 'It was time for me and Stefano to pursue different paths.'

'He's left you, has he? Doesn't surprise me.' Edith pushed herself forwards. 'Help me downstairs, Joanna. I need to lie down.'

Jo spent ages in Edith's bedroom. 'Looks like it might be *adios* from me then, House. Think we might be parting ways, yeah?' I started shovelling my clothes up off the floor and stuffing them into my suitcase. Didn't even check if they were clean or dirty, never mind folding them. I was in such a panic, thinking were they calling the police on me. What would they arrest me for though? I hadn't done anything illegal. Not really.

I heard Jo calling my name softly from the landing. I followed her into the sitting room and she hopped up onto the sofa and crossed her legs. She made me think of a frog, though I think she fancied herself as a bit of a guru, or Buddha or something. I don't know what her beauty routine was, but she was a good advert for yoga. She was very well-toned – skinny, but muscular enough not to look scrawny. Tanned skin, but not leathery looking – always a danger for older white women.

'I would love it if you'd tell me what's going on.'

I was feeling a bit sick, my stomach was all clenched up. But then she asked if her mum had dementia. I let out a big sigh of relief, maybe I hadn't fucked up everything then.

'I couldn't say exactly. I mean, I'm not a doctor. But she does get confused.'

Jo nodded, lifting her head up and down in big, slow movements.

'Like, she never told me you were coming over. Last I heard, you was in Italy.'

'Does she talk about me much?'

I didn't know what to say then, thinking about all the times Edith had bad-mouthed her daughter.

'She mentioned you'd had a bit of a falling out.'

Jo raised her eyebrows. 'Is that how she put it?'

'Something like that.'

Jo nodded again – she looked like she was doing neck exercises. Maybe she was.

'We've always had an explosive relationship. You've been living with Mum, you know what she's like.'

Jo looked like she needed me to agree, so I smiled and shrugged. She had the same bright blue eyes as Edith. Hers stood out especially against her bronzed cheek bones. She wasn't wearing much make-up, just a lot of eyeliner. Bit dated, but it suited her.

'I've sought a lot of guidance on this and it feels like now is the time for me to return. Me living here will be really sweet for Mum. That's precious at her stage in life. We need to re-build some bridges.'

My heart curled up like a fist. 'Do you want me to move out then?'

'Oh God, no.' Jo's eyes looked like they were gonna pop out of her head. 'I wouldn't dream of pushing you out. Mum told me on the phone what an amazing job you've been doing, looking after her.'

Yeah, I thought, but that was before she'd seen not only the detention bracelets, but a photo of my nan as well. Like I just had to leave every bit of incriminating evidence I had out on display. What was wrong with me? I wanted to slap myself for being so fucking careless.

Jo stretched her long legs out in front of her and then crossed them again. 'There's loads of room here for all of us. I can sleep in the spare room. I don't suppose it's being used for anything, is it?'

'I haven't been in there. It's full of boxes. I mean, I've looked in, put my head round the door.' I was so stressed I didn't know what I was saying.

'Must be Dad's stuff. I'll have to sort through it all at some stage.' She sighed. 'Need to gather my strength for that.' She jumped up, suddenly looking all cheerful and energetic. 'I'd love you to share some tea with me, my friend.'

She rummaged about in her shoulder bag, finally pulling out a packet of what looked like weed. She held it up like she expected me to applaud.

'Revitalising, balances the elements.'

The tea tasted like the seaweed face masks we used at college. We stood in the kitchen drinking it. It felt a bit weird, Jo being so at home. I felt like her guest. I didn't know if she was playing me with all this 'friend' business. She told me all about growing up there, where she'd gone to school, how she used to hang out in the park. She even got as far as her first boyfriend. I didn't know what to say to all that personal information, but Jo didn't seem to mind if I said anything or not, she just carried on talking. She took after her mum that way.

'Sweetie, one thing that occurs to me is, once we've cleared the spare room it would make so much more sense for you to move in there. That way you're on the same floor as Mum, if she needs you in the night or anything like that.'

'Oh, she never needs me in the night,' I said. 'She always takes a sleeping tablet and sleeps right through to seven.'

'Hmm, not sure that's very good for her. What if she gets up in the night half-drugged and has a fall? Sleeping pills are highly addictive. They shouldn't be taken regularly.'

'That was her routine before I moved in.' I said quickly, in case she thought I was drugging Edith or something.

'I don't doubt it. Mum never does anything unless she wants to. I wouldn't try prising her away from her routines.'

Jo laughed and stretched her arms up over her head. Her sleeves slipped back to show some serious tats. She had a lotus flower on her left arm and a massive one of that Indian elephant god, with some Asian writing underneath, on her right bicep. My friend Riya used to have a poster of Ganesh on her wall, but her family was actually Hindu. I wondered if Jo even knew what the writing meant. I guessed she'd been one of those 'gap yah' white girls who thought she'd discovered India. I kind of hoped the writing said 'I'm a twat' or something like that.

She did a couple of side-bends. 'The other issue is, I need somewhere for my yoga practice and there isn't the floor or wall space in the spare room. It's vital that I practise every day.' Jo put her hands together like she was praying and looked at me imploringly. 'It would be so helpful if I could move back into my old room. Meditation would be impossible for me across the landing from my mother. The sort of negative energy she gives off – I couldn't shut it out at that distance.'

'Though, if you're in the top room, your floor will be her ceiling, so in that sense you'll be even nearer.' I had to point it out.

Jo looked really pained then. She closed her eyes and did her slow nodding thing. She suddenly reminded me of that dog off the Churchill ads and I had to stop myself from giggling.

'I hear what you are saying, my friend, but the space is crucial.' She opened her eyes. 'The spare room is lovely and light. I'd happily go in there if I had a studio or somewhere else I could practise. If the weather wasn't so unreliable here I'd just practise in the garden.'

'It's fine, Jo, I don't mind moving. It's your bedroom anyway.' I didn't even know if Edith was going to let me stay.

'Well, if you're sure.' Jo was smiling again.

'It's no trouble to me.'

'Great, let's get started on shifting those boxes.' And Jo was off, bounding up the stairs. That tea had given her a bigger hit than it had given me. That was for sure.

EDITH

I COULDN'T THINK STRAIGHT with Joanna hovering over me, doing her mumbo jumbo. She spent so long sitting on my bed I had to ask her to leave. It was Paul I wanted to speak to. Joanna talks such a lot of nonsense, she'd probably accuse me of being a racialist. Paul is very level-headed and as a man of the world I knew he'd understand my dilemma. We often chat as we work on the garden. I say 'we', but I'm just the overseer now. Paul has become my arms and legs. When he first suggested I got a girl in to help me round the house I wanted to say, 'but I have you, Paul, what do I need with anyone else?' But of course, he can't be there all the time and if I were to have an accident in the house he wouldn't necessarily know. We don't see each other every day.

I was so upset I rang him from my bedroom. I didn't feel well enough to go down to the basement. Lying on the bed I watched the curtains swelling and subsiding against the open window, sucked in and blown out by the wind. I wished my lungs could fill so effortlessly. Old age prevents one from taking anything for granted.

Paul listened quietly, without interrupting, as I explained what had happened. Graham would never have been so patient.

It took me a while to convince him of what the detention bracelets were and he was certain Lauren couldn't have any connection to them. I thought she might be hiding her grandmother's involvement in terrorism, but he made me realise I was jumping to some awfully large conclusions. I didn't even know which country in Africa the woman came from. It could have been anywhere. I wasn't even sure Lauren knew. Joanna turning up out of the blue had distracted me.

Paul was very interested to hear about Joanna's arrival and said he'd like to meet her. I wasn't sure how I felt about that. I hoped she wouldn't embarrass me.

My sinuses were throbbing. Joanna had left the window open – rather thoughtless of her. The bracelets probably were Graham's. It would be too much of a coincidence for Lauren to own a pair as well. And, as Paul pointed out, she was a good girl. He'd been keeping an eye on her for me and hadn't detected anything untoward. A lot of English people had mixed heritage, himself included, and there was no reason why it would have occurred to Lauren to tell me about her grandmother. But he promised he'd have a word with her. By the end of the call I felt a little foolish. I really had made a big fuss over nothing. Times had changed and I needed to change with them.

I could almost feel the warmth of Paul's laughter down the phone line as he told me I wasn't foolish at all. I had every right to be concerned and he was very glad I'd spoken to him about it. He was always there for me; I could come to him with any worry, no matter how trivial.

Sometimes I can't help wondering what it would have been

like to be married to a man as considerate and kind as Paul. Father and Graham were cut from the same cloth – men's men, with little time for women's concerns. They were honourable, dedicated, fearless, and I admired them both hugely. But sometimes I had longed for a little more…sensitivity…I suppose one would call it. Women today are lucky – men seem to fall over backwards to keep them happy. Joanna has had a string of men, all desperate to please her, and yet she seems unable to settle down. If I had a man like Paul I'd never let him go.

LAUREN

SHE HAD LOVELY FEET, Jo. I didn't even need to use separators on her toes, she just held them spread out while I painted her nails. She said she'd show me some exercises to stretch out my feet. She was all into me doing yoga with her, but I said it wasn't really my thing. I go down the gym, when I can find the time. I tried yoga once, but I couldn't get the hang of it. All that putting your left foot under your right thigh and balancing on one hand – I got into such a tangle. I never was any good at telling my left from my right. Jo asked if I had tried Ashtanga yoga, but I like to work out to music – keeps me going. It was nice though, sitting in the garden with her.

'I used to do my mum's nails, before she threw me out.' She'd told me so much about her life, I thought I might as well say something about mine.

'What did she throw you out for?' Jo closed her eyes and raised her face up to the sun.

'Well, it was more my stepdad really. They went away for the weekend, said I could have, like, a gathering. I only asked a few friends, but then my boyfriend, Joel, invited a load of his mates. I never even knew half of them. They were older than me. It got a bit out of hand. The neighbours called the police. I cleaned the house after, but there were a few things I missed.'

Jo laughed. 'Like what?'

'The vodka bottles in the recycling for starters. I mean, they literally went through the bins. You'd think they'd be pleased I was recycling. And this old whisky of Mike's got drunk. It was, like, a collector's item or something.'

'Is that all?'

'Promise you won't tell Edith?' God knows why I was confiding in Jo, but she put her hand on her heart and nodded like she meant it. 'Someone left a used condom in my mum and stepdad's bed. And, you know, basically left the bed in a bit of a state. They'd pulled the covers over so I never noticed when I was cleaning up. Mum and Mike only found it when they were getting into bed.'

Jo grinned. 'That could so have been me as a teenager, only I never dared throw a party at home. My folks did hire a barn for my eighteenth, out in the country. That was OK – people could just vomit in the bushes or whatever.'

'Mike, my stepdad, he was just looking for an excuse to get me out anyway. He's a total control freak, know what I mean? Can't handle teenagers. I'm just waiting to see what happens when Leo and Amber hit their teens – see how he likes that.'

'What about your mum?' Jo stuck her nose into the bunch of flowers she'd picked. She'd snapped off just about every flower in the garden, left the borders bare. Edith would go mad.

'She goes along with whatever Mike says. She never sticks up for me.'

'Sounds like my mother.' Jo nodded. 'Though I only really appreciated my father after he'd died. I'd no idea what an amazing career he'd had until I read the obituaries. I mean, obviously I'm not a great fan of the military machine per se. You know, peace and love and all that. But all the humanitarian work he did for the UN – I'd just never thought about that.'

My hand swerved and a blob of orange polish landed on Jo's skin.

'What kind of work?'

I wiped off the smudged polish, trying to sound casual. But she turned the conversation back to me, asking about my dad.

'Can't remember much about him. He split up with my mum when I was little.' A pale blue butterfly landed for a second on the bottle of nail polish, before realising its mistake and flying off to look for a flower. 'Used to take me out, bring me presents. But then he just stopped coming. I think he might've gone abroad. Even my nan didn't know where he'd gone. He never even phoned.'

'Better off without him.' Jo stretched her arms out behind her and arched her back. 'Matriarchal systems – much better for raising children. Who needs men anyway? They're only good for one thing.' She winked. 'Still with your boyfriend?'

'He cheated on me so I dumped him.' I suddenly felt like I might cry.

'Let me give you some advice, sweetie. Don't get caught up in the whole monogamy, nuclear family thing. It's not a happy way to live, believe me.'

'You girls seem to be getting on well.' Edith was groping her way slowly down the garden steps, leaning onto the handrail.

I jumped up. 'Can I give you a hand?'

'I can manage, thank you. But some tea would be nice. I shall sit at the table, I'm too old for picnic rugs.'

'I'll do your topcoat after,' I said to Jo and hurried up the steps to the kitchen.

Edith still hadn't said nothing about that scene and her finding the detention rings. It was so weird. I didn't know if she'd forgotten, but she just went along with Jo's suggestions.

I'd moved all my stuff out of Jo's room and given it a good clean. Jo had helped me clear some space in the spare room. We'd stacked the boxes along one wall and put a throw over them, so I could use them as shelves. It looked all right and I could get into the wardrobe now. Colonel Forbes' old suits were still hanging up in there. Jo didn't say anything to her mum, she just bagged them all up, said she'd take them down the Oxfam shop. I told her she could make some money selling them online. They were good-quality suits. She thought about it for a minute, then shook her head.

'Better karma this way. Dad did a lot of work for charities – he'd want them to go to a good cause.'

I needed an extra teapot for Jo's herb tea – she didn't take black tea or coffee because of the caffeine, and Edith would never let me get away with tea bags. In the end I had to use a jug. I'd already sold the silver tea-set.

Turned out it was only silver-plated. A bit disappointing really – thought I'd get a lot more for it than I did. The fuss Edith made over it you'd think it was sterling at least. As far as she was concerned it was back in the attic where it'd spent the last forty years. Neither of them would ever notice it'd gone. And what you don't know can't hurt you – that's what Edith believes anyway. The things I sold, they belonged to me as much as to anyone else. I reckon I'm 'a good cause'.

If the worst came to the worst I'd earn enough to make a new start. Enough for a deposit to rent a flat somewhere far away from here. I only wanted enough to get myself somewhere to live. That's all.

When I came back outside I nearly dropped the tray. Paul was sitting next to Jo on the rug. She was flirting like crazy, tossing her honey blonde locks over her shoulder and laughing. He was relaxed as usual, leaning in close to her, his right arm resting on one knee, nodding and smiling at Edith and Jo.

I put the tray down on the wrought-iron table.

'Could you fetch an extra cup, Lauren? Paul is joining us for tea. Have we got any biscuits?' Edith asked.

'Don't worry about me,' Paul said.

'S'all right, we've got some chocolate digestives.' I trudged back up the stairs.

Well, Paul knew about Jo now and he didn't seem all that bothered. It was only a matter of time before Edith told him about me though and finding Nan's photo and bracelets. I was really scared he might tell me to piss off and not come back. I'd been so lax – I wouldn't blame him if he was angry with me. When it came down to it, I didn't really know him all that well. Not so I could predict how he'd react.

KENYA, 1956

CHARITY LAY ON HER CAMP BED, too exhausted to join the other women who were sitting under the shade of the only tree in the yard, sewing coloured thread onto old Christmas cards. She ached all over and her hands were bleeding. She touched her scalp cautiously with the tips of her fingers. She was afraid her skull would be permanently dented, she might even get brain damage.

All day, every day, for the past two weeks she had been carrying murram from the quarry in a tin basin on her head. She had no idea what the earth was for, only that she had to run with the heavy load, dump it out and then run back for another and that if she didn't run fast enough the warders would beat her.

She was too tired even to cry. When were her parents going to find her? Why hadn't they got her out yet? Her brother was in London – he could petition Queen Elizabeth. The Queen had visited Kenya, surely she'd be horrified if she knew what was going on in her name?

Maybe her family didn't know she'd been arrested. They might think she'd been kidnapped by a Mau Mau gang on her way home. What if Victoria and Eunice told Mother Winifride that she'd been seeing a boy? Would they try to find Githii or would they think she'd run off with him? No, her friends knew her too well to think she'd do anything so stupid. If they went into Nairobi they'd see Githii was still there and he'd tell them how she'd gone to catch the bus.

'*Jambo.*' Wairimu, all jutting bones, greeted Charity as she plonked herself down on the bed beside her.

Charity hugged her arms in, trying to avoid Wairimu's sharp elbows. Why couldn't Wairimu sit on her own camp bed, it was only two down from Charity's. The girl was like a fly; no matter how often Charity batted her away, she kept on buzzing back with the same unshakable good humour.

'Don't stay in here moping, it'll only get you in trouble.' Wairimu got up, but remained beside the bed, looking down at Charity.

Charity turned away. Wairimu openly supported the Mau Mau and she didn't want anything to do with her.

'Here, this is what you need to do.' Wairimu pulled Charity's tin basin from under her bed, placed it upside down and jumped up and down on it with her cracked, bare feet.

'What the hell are you doing? You're the one who'll get me in trouble.' Charity was roused from her weariness by a sudden surge of anger.

Wairimu just laughed. 'You make a dent in the bottom, see, then it can't hold so much murram.' She shoved the basin at Charity. 'Looks full but it's lighter.'

'What if the guards notice?'

Wairimu just shrugged. 'They'll always find a reason to beat you so what difference does it make?'

Charity had to concede she had a point.

Wairimu dropped the basin back under the bed. 'Come outside. If you want to get out of here you have to show willing. I don't know why you don't just tell them you've taken the oath, that's what they want to hear.'

'Because it isn't true.' Charity clenched her teeth together. 'And it's a sin to lie.'

The second time she was screened it was in the commandant's office. He had placed a photograph on the desk in front of her. It was a picture of a dead black man, his body hacked to pieces. His guts spilled out onto the ground, half his head was missing and what looked like his brains were oozing out of his smashed skull. Charity looked at it in horror, wondering if this was something the Mau Mau had done, if the commandant thought she had been involved in the atrocity.

'What do you see?' he demanded.

But when Charity described what she saw, he shook his head sadly and tapped a finger on the corner of the photograph. 'What's that?'

Charity squinted at the black-and-white picture. There was something tiny, balanced on a leaf. 'A butterfly?'

'Hmmm.' The commandant stared at her with cold, fishy eyes, before turning to the warder next to him. 'This is a psychological test of my own devising. If she had noticed the butterfly, I might have classified her as white. Generally, those who see only the violence are classified black.' He paused. 'She is young in age group; there's hope for her yet. We'll classify her grey and see how it goes.'

Even the warder looked perplexed.

It was only later that Charity understood these classifications referred not to skin colour, but to innocence and guilt. The

Blacks were the hardcore, unrepentant Mau Mau. To become White you had to be considered rehabilitated.

'I thought your god was supposed to be so forgiving.' Wairimu sat back down on the edge of the bed. 'It's not evil witchcraft like they say, you know. The first oath I took, all I had to do was walk through a sugarcane arch in my underwear. Then I did have to drink some disgusting goat blood mixture. But we don't eat babies or make human sacrifices or anything like that.' She picked at a scab on her knee. 'Don't you want Kenya to be free from the whites?

'I want us to be equal. Not all whites are bad.' Charity thought of Sister Kathleen, her favourite teacher at school, who was always kind and full of praise for Charity's schoolwork.

'D'you really think they'll ever let us have equality? Look at South Africa. We have to fight for our land and maybe when we've won they'll show us some respect.'

'What are you girls up to?' Mrs Eastfield, the rehabilitation officer poked her head into the tent.

'We're coming; Charity has a headache, that's all.' Wairimu grabbed Charity's hand and pulled her up off the bed, their detention bracelets clanging together.

'You need some fresh air. Lounging about in bed isn't going to do you any good.'

Mrs Eastfield never looked the detainees straight in the face; her gaze always hovered somewhere over Charity's shoulder. Now she marched ahead, expecting to be followed. Charity was forced to accept Wairimu's arm as she limped over to join the other women.

'Tomorrow evening,' Mrs Eastfield clasped her hands together enthusiastically. 'If you behave, I will be giving a cookery lesson. I'll show you how to make a perfect Victoria sponge.'

Charity's mouth watered. All she'd had to eat since arriving at the camp was unsweetened maize porridge and there was never enough even of that. What she really longed for was a bowl of her mother's spicy bean stew served with chapatis and arrowroot, but English cake with jam would be better than nothing.

'Do we each make our own cake?' she asked in English. She imagined it would be like the cookery classes at school.

Mrs Eastfield's pink face went even pinker. 'Of course not, it will be a demonstration.' She stared off, somewhere past the barbed-wire compound, her chin pulled into her neck like an indignant pigeon. 'Where do you think you are? Finishing school?' She barked out a short laugh.

The other women watched her warily. Few of them spoke English and were unaware of the treat being bestowed on them, or what exactly it was that Mrs Eastfield wanted from them.

Mrs Eastfield gathered up the leftover bits of brightly coloured wool and old Christmas cards so kindly donated by the British Red Cross towards their re-education, putting them all in her basket. 'Right, well, I'll see you tomorrow.' She nodded at one of the warders to escort her out.

Despite the rebuff, Charity hobbled after her.

'Please Mrs Eastfield, may I speak with you?'

Mrs Eastfield stopped. The warder waiting by her side looked ready to lash out at the slightest provocation. Charity swallowed.

'Did you call my school or contact my parents?'

'Do you know how many thousands of prisoners are being held here? Do you think we have time to make personal phone calls for each one? The commandant assures me you have been given every opportunity to confess, but that you still refuse to do so. When you are ready to be returned to society you will be, but not before.' Having addressed her speech to the lowering sun, Mrs Eastfield turned on her heel.

Charity watched the woman in her flowery dress and white gloves being escorted out of the compound and was filled with despair. If confessing got you out, why was Wairimu still here? If she agreed that she was guilty they would keep her here even longer, inflicting further punishments on her for being Mau Mau. It was a trap and she could see no way out.

LAUREN

'YOU ALL RIGHT LOR? You seem a bit quiet, not your usual bubbly self.' Ash looked at me with concern.

'Just a bit tired that's all.'

I moved the make-up brushes around so they were all lined up neatly, smallest to biggest. What if I told Ash? Just spilled it all out to him. He was the only person I could think of who might not hate me for it.

'Who's been keeping you from your sleep then? I hope he's worth it.'

'I wish.' I forced my mouth into a smile. Tell Ash? I must be losing it. Ash couldn't keep anything to himself. 'No, it's just been a bit tricky, with Edith's daughter back and everything.'

'The bitch, has she been giving you a hard time? I'll come round and give it her.'

'No, nothing like that. It's just, the dynamic's changed. I think she might be seeing Paul, the guy who lives downstairs.

She's totally wrong for him. And Edith wouldn't like it.'

I checked the lipstick testers weren't looking too worn down. Some girls – early teens – had just been swarming over the counter like a bunch of locusts. I was surprised everything was still there. Ash put an arm around my shoulders.

'And does someone else have a bit of a soft spot for this Paul? Someone standing next to me maybe?' He gave me a squeeze.

'God no!' I accidently sliced the top of a lipstick off with my nail, leaving a sticky crimson smear over my fingers.

'Well that got a strong reaction.' Ash grabbed a wipe from under the counter and started to clean my hand. 'What's so wrong with Paul? Go on, give Uncle Ash the gossip.'

'There's nothing wrong with him. I just wouldn't think of him that way.'

Ash raised his eyebrows like he didn't believe a word.

'He's in his thirties, Christ's sake.'

'Bit hung up on age aren't we? Trust me, an experienced older man is just what you need, after that little arsewipe did the dirty on you.' Ash lowered his voice. 'He'll be a lot more attentive to your needs, if you know what I mean.' Ash stuck out his tongue and flapped it from side to side.

I gave him a shove, but I couldn't help laughing. 'Don't be disgusting!'

'If you think that's disgusting you really are missing out. Have you slept with anyone apart from your ex?'

'I am not discussing my personal life here.'

I glanced around the store, but the lunchtime rush was over and there was hardly anyone about. Stacey still hadn't come back from her lunch break – she'd been gone over an hour. Lucky for her our manager was at the dentist.

'I'd take you out for a drink tonight, but Fabian's working late and I've got to get home and walk Mitzi. D'you want to come back with me? I'll cook you dinner.'

An evening with Ash was just what I needed. He'd pour me a big glass of wine and I'd curl up on the sofa with Mitzi while he cooked something tasty. I could forget all about Gainsford Square.

'Won't Fabian mind?'

'Course not, he adores you. Anyway, he won't be back till after ten. Come on, you can walk Mitzi with me. It'll do you good. You look like you could do with some fresh air.'

'Thanks, bro.' I glanced in the mirror. My face was a bit pasty.

I was so tempted, but Jo was going to be out, so I'd need to be in for Edith. I hadn't been on my own with Edith since she'd found the bracelets. I felt a bit nervous about it, but I'd have to get over that. Also, with Jo out I might get the chance to talk to Paul in private.

❁

'You were supposed to leave the bracelets by her bed.' Paul muted the TV, leaving a football match playing in the background.

'I was going to do it that day. I was just waiting for her to go downstairs.'

'What were you thinking, leaving photos around?'

'They were under my pillow and I never expected her to start poking round in my bedroom.'

'You can't take those kinds of chances, Lauren. You've got to be smarter than that.'

Paul massaged his chin. He needed a shave. I hoped he wasn't growing a beard like every other man in London.

'Why can't we just pretend Edith imagined the whole thing? I could sneak into her room tonight and get them back. I've been in there enough times. She never wakes up.'

'Because she's shown the bracelets to Jo, hasn't she?'

'Shit.' I got up and stood in front of the window, looking up at the pavement above. 'What did Jo say?'

'Hadn't seen them before. Thinks they must have ended up in her room by accident.'

I picked at my nails. The gel polish was coming off. I needed to get them redone or I'd get in trouble at work.

'What's the story with you and Jo, anyway?'

'Got to keep her sweet, haven't I?'

'Yeah, but, how sweet?'

I could see Paul's reflection in the window, watching me. 'You jealous?'

'Jealous?' I snorted. 'Why would I be jealous?'

In one smooth movement he was out of his chair and standing behind me. He put one hand on my shoulder.

'I'm only yanking your chain, Lauri – chill.'

His face was so close to mine I could feel the warmth of his breath on my cheek, smell the familiar, citrusy fragrance of his aftershave. I still hadn't found out what make it was. I kept meaning to take a sneaky peak in his bathroom so I could get him some for his birthday. He gave my shoulder a squeeze.

'She likes you. Thinks you're doing a great job with her mum.'

'Good, but what do we do now? What's the plan?'

'Just keep going as we are. We can win Jo over.'

'And then what?' I drew a flower into the dust on the window. 'Share the house with her? I guess that would be fair.'

Paul laughed and shook his head. 'Oh, Lauri, what's fairness got to do with anything? Fairness is for kids. What we're about is justice.'

EDITH

'WELL IT'S NICE TO HAVE an evening in with you at last, Joanna.'

She had cooked some sort of vegetable curry; the smell had travelled all the way up to my bedroom. I peered into the saucepan bubbling on the stove. It was certainly very colourful. I gave it a stir. The bottom was sticking; it would burn if she wasn't careful.

'Do sit down, Mum.'

Joanna wrapped her hair her around her hand, tying it into a loose knot at the back of her head. She was getting too old for long hair. Graham always said women over forty should cut their hair short. It was pitiful, seeing a middle-aged woman dressing like a girl. Not that Joanna looked middle-aged; forty was the new thirty, isn't that what they said now? She could probably still have children. That would be the making of her.

'And what's this?' I pointed at the bowl she had just placed on the table.

'Quinoa, full of protein, very good for you.' She ladled a huge pile onto my plate.

'You *are* taking care of me. I wish I'd been able to look after my mother at the end of her life, but of course I had you and your father to consider. I couldn't just take off for Africa and leave you both behind.'

I tried a mouthful of the quinoa. It was like eating something you'd find at the bottom of a hamster's cage.

'You could have taken me with you.'

'And disrupted your education? That would have been utterly irresponsible. You had exams. Besides, at that age you were refusing to visit South Africa because of apartheid.'

Joanna put the saucepan directly onto the table. I pushed a placemat towards her. I suppose she didn't think it was worth using serving dishes for just the two of us, but there was no need to burn a ring on the table. They probably thought that sort of thing rustic, on her Italian farm.

'It's such a shame Granny and Grandpa didn't stay in Kenya. Imagine having a place there now – all that amazing wildlife.'

'Very few whites stayed on after independence. The government gave them a decent price for the farm and, well, their generation couldn't contemplate being ruled by blacks.'

'So they took the money and ran? Why didn't they come back to England?'

'And work some middle-sized farm in the rain, or retire to the suburbs? That wasn't your grandmother's style.'

Joanna chuckled. 'Now that I can understand. But if you had wanted to go out there, Dad and I could have looked after ourselves.'

'Your father relied on me entirely when it came to his domestic life. A single man can't host a dinner party, and we often had important guests to entertain.' At least the curry was edible –

not too spicy. 'A man needs his wife by his side.'

'And what about the wife? What does she need?' Joanna gave me a sharp look. She and her father had never seen eye to eye. They both had strong temperaments; it was inevitable they would clash.

I looked around the kitchen I had spent so many hours of my life in. It was a bright room, south-facing, with fine views of the garden. I still got a sense of satisfaction from the glass-fronted cabinets with their concealed lighting – they really were rather elegant. The cupboards underneath were crammed with cooking paraphernalia; a fish kettle and various jelly moulds were buried in there somewhere. Not to mention all the different accessories for the Magimix which still stood proudly on the worktop. It must be almost as old as Joanna. So many dishes I'd used it for: soups, pastries, mayonnaise, chocolate mousse. The kitchen was my workspace, my 'territory' as Graham used to say. I liked to linger over breakfast now, watching the birds pecking at the feeder that hung from the walnut tree, knowing there was no need to rush, no chicks for me to feed.

'I used to have quite a reputation as a cook. Do you remember the Deacons? Bob worked with your father. He was very fond of my cooking – always had seconds. I don't think Heather fed him properly. She was always on some faddish diet and trying to impose it on poor old Bob too.'

'Oh God, I remember those awkward evenings hanging out with their sons. While you grown-ups drank Campari and played kinky games with fondues and forfeits for dropping your food into the molten cheese.'

'What on earth are you talking about? The only game I recall playing with the Deacons was bridge.'

'The oldest son was good-looking though.' A dreamy look came over Joanna's face. Really, she was incorrigible, turning a little innocent fun into something dirty.

'I enjoyed being a wife and mother. It may not be fashionable to say so, but I found it an enormously fulfilling role.'

'Even when he hit you?' Joanna was pushing the food around her plate, just like she used to do as a child.

'That only happened once and it was because of the medication he was on at the time. We've been through this before. Isn't it about time you left the past behind?'

'The past has to be acknowledged before it can be laid to rest. Beating your children is illegal now you know.'

'How you love to exaggerate; always the drama queen. You received the occasional smack, which, quite frankly, is far more effective than all this endless explaining parents go in for now. Far more confusing for the poor child.'

I was getting indigestion, the quinoa didn't agree with me. I didn't want to upset her further by saying anything, but I preferred the simple English dishes that Lauren prepared; shepherd's pie, fish and chips – that sort of thing – even if they were frozen. My days of dabbling in *haute cuisine* were long gone. Not that Joanna's cooking could be placed in that category. I wouldn't have minded if she'd made pasta. Lauren did a very nice penne with pesto. It was all this New Age food I couldn't cope with.

Joanna let out a big, adolescent sort of sigh, lifting and dropping her shoulders emphatically. 'Aren't you going to finish your supper? You're looking awfully thin, Mum.'

'Goodness, we seem to have come full circle. I recall saying the same thing to you, many's the time.' Our first evening alone together and it wasn't going at all how I had hoped. 'What's for dessert?' I needed something sweet.

'Sorry, Mum, didn't occur to me you'd want a pudding. Never eat them myself.'

'Lauren always provides a dessert. She says they're good for one, at my age. She learnt that in her food technology classes,' I added, as I could see Joanna looking sceptical. 'I expect she's left some choc ices in the freezer.'

'I'll get you some fruit.' Joanna whisked up the plates and clattered them into the dishwasher. 'Shall I cut up an apple for you?'

'If you must, though I find them rather hard on my dentures.'

'That's why I'll cut it up for you.'

I was evidently not going to be allowed a choc ice.

'Sounds like it's been working out pretty well with Lauren.'

Joanna stood at the counter, hacking an apple to pieces with a carving knife. How on earth had she run a guest house? I wondered whether they'd had many complaints. Perhaps that was why she'd left.

'I'm still not sure my trust in her wasn't misplaced. And since you've come home I don't see that she's required any more.'

Joanna put down the knife and turned to face me.

'Maybe not, but I do have to lay down some boundaries here. I cannot become your full-time carer; that would not be good for either of us. The yoga training is a big commitment. I need to be able to give myself to it fully.'

'I'm not senile yet! I hardly need full-time care.'

'That's not what I'm saying, but you do need someone to prepare your meals, do your shopping – that sort of thing.'

She resumed her seat at the table, putting the plate of chopped apple between us and absent-mindedly popping a chunk into her mouth.

'We don't need live-in help for that.'

'But are you prepared to pay for someone professional to come in? That's very expensive you know.'

I looked down at the bits of apple. She hadn't even removed the core properly. 'Are you worried about your inheritance? Well

I suppose you should be – with these low interest rates I can't be making anything on my savings.'

She swallowed another piece of apple. 'You're sitting on a pretty big investment in this house.'

'It will be yours when I die.'

Joanna leant forward, placing one hand over mine. Her palm was warm and soft. She gazed at me earnestly, just like she did as a child when she wanted a skateboard, or riding lessons, or a puppy. The puppy was the only thing I refused her; she hardly used the skateboard and after several expensive riding holidays, quickly grew out of her horse mania. The amount of money I wasted on her fads. She tucked a strand of hair behind her ear.

'Mum, a sensible solution would be for you to sell the house. Think of the upkeep old properties like this require. When did you last have the central heating serviced or the roof tiles checked? It's only a matter of time before things start to go wrong. I can feel damp in my bedroom and have you ever had the chimneys cleaned?'

I was surprised by her practicality. Perhaps she had learnt something running that Italian guesthouse after all. Not that I ever used the fireplaces.

'And let's face it, this house is way too big for two people.'

'Three. Four including Paul.'

'Well you've become more liberal in your old age, including someone racially different in your family group.' She pulled a silly face.

'What on earth are you talking about?'

'Paul, who you've got so fond of – he's black.' She raised her eyebrows. 'What would Dad say?'

I knew she was only trying to provoke me.

'Paul isn't black. He might be a half-caste, but I've never thought of him that way. He went to St. Edmunds you know.

He's very well-spoken. He said his father was from Cornwall, or Devon. Both his parents were accountants, or perhaps his father was an engineer. I think he said his mother is Nigerian; hardworking, ambitious, she wanted Paul to be a lawyer. Besides, you seem to be forgetting I grew up in Kenya, surrounded by Africans.'

I thought suddenly of the time Graham and I had taken my parents to The Stanley Hotel for dinner to celebrate our engagement. There was an awful commotion in the lobby. An African had come in, tried to buy a drink. When he was refused, as of course he knew he would be, he sat down on the carpet, legs and arms crossed. The doormen had to pick him up and throw him out. Then a group of them outside started shouting slogans through a megaphone, demanding an end to the colour-bar. They were socialists, radicals, probably linked to the Mau Mau. It was dreadful, ruined my engagement dinner. I was furious. Now it occurred to me that Paul would not have been admitted to the Stanley. It was an odd thought, because I really had forgotten that he wasn't white.

Joanna gave me a patronising smile. 'I don't care where people originate from – we're all children of the universe.'

Where did she learn to spout such rubbish?

'The other thing is, leaving me the house means I'll be crippled by inheritance tax.' She squeezed my hand. 'You know how Dad hated losing anything more in tax than he had to. I'm sure it's what he would do, if he was here.'

'And where am I supposed to go?'

Joanna pulled some magazines out of the monstrous, multicoloured shoulder bag she carried everywhere. Once I'd located my glasses I saw they were brochures, for something called 'Retirement Villages'. She had clearly been planning this.

'Isn't this one beautiful?' She opened one of the brochures

at a page she had folded over. 'A ground-floor apartment in an eighteenth-century manor house with a walled garden and an ornamental lake. Twenty-four-hour security and nursing staff on call should you need them. There's even a restaurant on site.'

I squinted at the tiny map beneath the picture. 'Easy access to the M11,' it boasted.

'It's in Essex!'

'You were saying only yesterday how much you hate London now. You rarely go beyond the square. Why not live somewhere peaceful, with clean air and the sound of birdsong instead of constant traffic?'

I turned the page over to a photograph of a 'delightful cottage' in the grounds of the 'Manor House'. It looked more like a bungalow stuck onto a prison. Jazzy writing at the bottom of the page advertised a 'Downsizing Event', promising it would 'uplift and motivate' me about my future.

I stared into Joanna's eyes, attempting the laser-like penetration Graham had been so good at. At least she had the decency to drop her gaze.

'How can you be so heartless? I bought this house with your father. You grew up here.'

'I thought you believed in leaving the past behind.'

'Certain things are worth preserving.'

We sat in silence for a few moments. Are all children so ungrateful, or is it just my daughter who is stuck being a perpetual adolescent?

Joanna smiled at me in a conciliatory way. 'This is a gloomy old house and you can hardly manage the stairs as it is. Here's an opportunity for a new beginning, a cosy place of your own with a society of like-minded people.' She grasped both my hands now. 'I'd love it if you would just think about it, Mum. Wouldn't it be nice to choose something for yourself for once?'

'Indeed it would. And what about you? Where are you planning to live?'

'Wherever it is I'll make sure it's close to you, less than an hour by train. I'll be a regular guest. We're free to live wherever we want – isn't that wonderful? We can pick somewhere together.'

I took the brochures up to bed with me. Told her I'd read through them. Being stuck with a bunch of doddery old fools, dropping like flies – I couldn't think of anything worse. It was all very well her talking about taxes, but Graham never trusted Joanna financially. He certainly wouldn't let her sell the house from underneath him. I'd discuss it with Paul. He'd know what to do.

KENYA, 1956

A VOICE ON THE loudspeaker called out Wairimu's number, ordering her to the commandant's office. All sound in the tent hushed. Everyone dreaded the summons; it meant more screening, which meant more mind games and more beatings.

Wairimu just grinned. 'Aren't I the popular one?' She wiggled her narrow hips as she strutted out of the tent.

Charity watched her with a mixture of admiration and anxiety. Wairimu was the bravest person she knew; nothing seemed to crush her resilient spirit. Where other women returned from the screenings in tears, Wairimu came back singing. Even after days of solitary confinement spent in one of the tiny huts, denied food or water, her eyes never lost their fire. Other detainees returned like ghosts from purgatory, but after a little rest and a mug of water, Wairimu would be back to cracking jokes.

Charity had stopped avoiding Wairimu and learnt to appreciate her strength and good humour. Her jokes were terrible, but there was nothing else in the camp to laugh about. Wairimu, having grown up in the slums of Nairobi, was sharp and cunning. She knew which of the warders could be bribed, who was sympathetic and who to avoid. She was able to relay all the latest news – not only what was in the newspapers but what was happening elsewhere in the camp, having channels of communication with other older, hardcore women held in different compounds.

When Wairimu asked Charity to translate a letter into English, Charity had at first been wary. She'd read through the letter carefully. She wasn't going to be involved in anything violent. But the letter was very reasonable; it listed the brutal treatment the women had to endure, as well as the lack of proper food and the suffering of the babies and children in the camp. She was impressed to see that it was addressed to Queen Elizabeth the second; the colonial secretary, Sir Evelyn Baring; the Commissioner of Prisons and all members of the House of Commons.

Wairimu knew a warder who would smuggle the letter out, get it posted. It would never be traced back to the writers, or the translator, Wairimu assured her. There was a lady politician in England who'd been agitating on their behalf. Questions had been asked in Parliament.

For the next few weeks life ground on as usual. Every day the women hoped for some change, but none came. Then, one afternoon, two women from the Kenyan branch of the British Red Cross appeared at the camp with blankets and clothes for the prisoners. Mrs Eastfield showed them around the yard and a few of the tents. It was clear from the women's expressions that they were shocked by what they saw. 'You wouldn't keep animals like this.' Charity overheard one of them say. Later she watched them in the yard, deep in conversation with Mrs Eastfield and the commandant.

'Is this because of the letter?' she asked Wairimu.

'I hope the letter will get us more than an extra layer of clothing.' Wairimu said. 'If it doesn't get us freed, it might at least mean a proper inspection and a change of conditions.'

Charity fixed all her hopes on the women from the Red Cross. Her school had collected money for the Red Cross; it was an important, international organisation. The women had seen just a little of the camp and were disgusted. They would surely deliver her from this hell. If only she'd tried to speak to them, to tell them she was innocent, but it was impossible with Mrs Eastfield constantly hovering over them.

At least they'd given her a new dress. The sky-blue frock she had once been so proud of was filthy and ragged, the white polka dots no longer distinguishable on the uniformly brown material. The extra blanket, too, meant she didn't spend the night shivering, muscles clenched against the cold. Instead, every night, she begged God to get her released.

When she had first gone away to school she'd missed her mother terribly. She missed working with her on their farm. She missed the goats she used to herd, especially her pet black and white kid-goat, Ngoto. He was very sweet and affectionate but always up to mischief and had to be watched carefully to make sure he didn't escape. But she also enjoyed learning and quickly made friends. All the girls at school were aware of how lucky they were to be there and were determined to do well. School was their ticket to a better life.

What an alien world that seemed now. How could she have been homesick when she was so well cared for? Even the harshest nun, Sister Agatha, was kind compared to the warders in the camp.

She had failed her parents and everything they'd sacrificed

to send her to school. When her uncles asked why they were bothering to educate a daughter, her parents had always insisted she was worth the investment. That she might one day become a teacher and pass on her learning. If only she'd obeyed the rules. She wished she'd never gone into Nairobi. She should have stayed in school and read, or gone to the chapel to pray.

Her parents must be sick with worry not knowing what had become of her. She kept seeing her mother's face smiling at her, the way she'd done the last time they said goodbye. She knew it was hard for her mother not having her help on the farm, but she never complained. Her smile was always full of reassurance and encouragement. Sometimes she was afraid she'd never see her again.

When the Red Cross women returned with another group of Europeans, Charity thought her prayers had been answered. Once again the delegation was shown around a selection of the tents, avoiding the isolation huts and the medical tent where the dying prisoners were kept. The detainees were ordered to stand beside their beds. A man Charity assumed to be a doctor took out a stethoscope and listened to their chests. They were told to stick out their tongues and he looked inside their mouths. Another man took notes.

'You can see the women are well-clothed and kept warm.' Mrs Eastfield gestured towards the folded blankets placed at the ends of their beds.

The visitors nodded. The women looked at them expectantly, waiting for further questions. 'What about the beatings, the torture?' Charity wanted to scream. The white people put away their notebooks and left the tent.

After the inspection their food rations got better. The prisoners were given vitamin pills and some of the women were taken to hospital. The sores in their mouths and the crusty, burning patches on their skin started to heal. Charity no longer had to run to the open latrines to relieve herself as what little she had to eat poured out of her. The work was just as brutal, but she didn't feel as if she was about to collapse and die.

She was still there though. They were all still there. The outside world had abandoned them.

The loudspeaker clanged again. All the women were to go out into the yard. They were made to sit in rows out in the hot sun. Wairimu was brought out between two warders. She was already limping. To Charity's surprise Mrs Eastfield was there too. She stood to one side, gazing out over their heads as if she were studying the clouds for portents.

The camp commandant strode out in front of the squatting women. 'Make no mistake, while you are here you have no other parent, no other husband, no other master, no other god. You have only me and you will obey and respect me in all things. There will be no more tale-telling in this camp.'

Unlike Mrs Eastfield he stared right at them, his blue eyes boring into their faces as if he could see right into their minds. 'We don't stop anyone from writing letters home if they wish to, but as you know, all correspondence must go through the proper channels. If you have a letter to write you can dictate it to Mrs Eastfield here and she will pass it on to me.'

Charity knew what that meant. She'd written several letters home, supposedly posted by Mrs Eastfield. If they'd reached her parents they'd have got her out by now, she was sure of it.

'I know some of you have been smuggling illegal letters out of the camp. Letters packed with slander. Number 6743 here has admitted to just such a crime and lest any of you are in any doubt about the consequences, you can witness the punishment for yourselves.'

Usually the beatings were left to the African warders, while the white officers stood by, watching, but this time the commandant took out a black truncheon. Something glinted on it and it took Charity a moment to make out the nails sticking out of its sides.

Afterwards, they were all amazed that Wairimu survived. Any other woman would have died after a beating so ferocious. She was taken away to a solitary cell. On the second evening two women managed to sneak her some porridge, but they said her mouth was too swollen to eat.

Charity was seized with fear that Wairimu would give away her involvement in the letter-writing. It was well-known that after a session with the commandant a woman would say anything – tell him her own mother was in the Mau Mau, if that's what he wanted to hear. She could trust Wairimu, she told herself. She was the one person strong enough not to break.

She lay awake all night, listening to the coughs and snores of the other women. Someone was sobbing in the corner; probably the new arrival – a girl even younger than she was. She was about to get up and go to her when she heard one of the other detainees singing softly. She looked over to where the girl lay and saw her being cradled in Sarah's arms. Sarah had had a baby in the camp, but it had died, strapped to her back as she worked in the quarry. Now she hummed a lullaby as she rocked the new girl to sleep.

Sleep while you can, Charity thought. You won't get much rest here.

LAUREN

'OH DEAR, WHAT A DISASTER!'

'What's that, Edith?'

'Her cake – it's collapsed.' Edith pointed at the TV. 'She should have beaten the egg whites separately.'

I squinted at the screen. I'd been sleeping really badly and my eyes were so tired the whole world seemed grey and pixelated.

'That young man's surprisingly good, but I suppose men do make better chefs – they're more daring. Women are better everyday cooks.'

'Maybe women don't get the chance to show off in the kitchen.'

Edith shook her head. She gets impatient with what she calls my 'women's lib' attitude. If she goes on one more time about how great her husband was, I might just blow the lid on it all.

I didn't trust Jo neither. She liked to think she was really open-minded, going on about how she didn't believe in the patriarchy or any of that stuff, but I'd noticed how she liked to get her own way. She might spout off about community, the universe, us all being one, but when it came down to it she always put herself first. She'd gone out again tonight. I wouldn't mind if she'd just let me know in advance. Edith was always fretting about her – where she was, when she'd be back. You'd think Jo was the teenager in the house.

Edith had to watch the ten o'clock news every night. It was like some anti-bedtime story. I kept telling her it would only keep us both awake and what good did seeing all that misery do anyway? Those desperate people crammed into dinghies, trying to get somewhere safe and drowning instead, or being stuck in shitty camps. The women with hollowed-out faces, the kids screaming in terror – or worse, not crying at all – as if they'd already given up and nothing could touch them any more.

'We can't have them coming here,' Edith would say. 'We're over-stretched as it is. We're just a small island. We don't have the resources.'

So I looked it up online and it turns out we hadn't even fulfilled our quota – the measly number of refugees we'd promised to take – and that was nothing compared to countries like Jordan, Lebanon and Turkey.

'Kenya's in the top ten countries for taking refugees,' I told Edith.

'Yes, well they've got plenty of space.' She put her glasses away. 'You're young and therefore naïve – you can't help it, but you have to be practical. We don't know who these people are, whether they've really had to flee from their own countries or if they're just looking for somewhere nicer. Why do they want to come to England? Because we have a welfare state – that's why. Most of them are young men intent on making money to send back home.' She paused, before adding triumphantly. 'They're economic migrants, not genuine refugees.'

She'd got that off *Question Time*. Another programme she made me watch every week.

I swallowed. The blood was rushing in my ears, I couldn't just sit there and say nothing, not any more. 'So, your family were economic immigrants too. They didn't have to go to Africa, they weren't fleeing war or famine or persecution. They just wanted to live in a nicer place and make some money.'

Of course white people are never called immigrants, unless they come from Poland, that is. Edith looked outraged, she pulled herself up straighter in her chair.

'And they had to work jolly hard to do it. My father built our farm up from scratch. There was nothing there before. He created jobs, wealth, security.'

'There wasn't 'nothing' there. There was people, living differently to how English people lived, but it was still their land – land the English colonists stole off them. I mean, imagine if I suddenly told you this was my house now, that you're just a squatter and if you want to stay you've got to work for me, obey my orders.'

I thought I'd gone too far, but instead of making her angry, what I'd said seemed to excite Edith. She was looking at me weirdly, kind of like she was in awe of me.

'Have you been talking to Mary?'

'Who?'

'Where did you get those ideas from?'

Why couldn't Edith ever credit me with any intelligence? She was always talking down to me. Just because I worked in the beauty industry didn't make me stupid.

I shrugged. 'I did social studies and geography at school, didn't I? I still read blogs, look at the news.' I nodded at the telly. I was tempted to tell her to talk to Paul about it – he'd set her straight. I was a bit sick of having to do all the dirty work while he was the golden boy.

Edith gave a little bark of a laugh. 'So that's the sort of left-wing clap-trap they teach you. No wonder this county's going to the dogs.' She grabbed her frame from beside her chair with shaking hands and hauled herself upright. 'You can't possibly compare the state of Africa in the 1940s to modern Western countries. I don't object to people with skills coming here – scientists, doctors, people we actually need. It's all the others, burdening the NHS with their infectious diseases, so that decent taxpayers have to wait months for treatment. Your generation have been cosseted – you don't know what tuberculosis, or what smallpox looks like – but let me tell you, you would not want to see an outbreak in London.'

She was really riled – her cheeks had gone red and she was swaying over her walking-frame, but I was too pissed off at this stage to go easy on her.

I stood up too. 'Immigrants pay more in taxes than British people do. My nan was a nurse. She paid her taxes and she put her health on the line, so don't tell me about the NHS and infectious diseases.' I realised I was shaking a finger at her, I stuffed my hands in my pockets. I needed to calm down.

Edith just shook her head. 'Time for bed.'

She thumped out of the room, leaning on her extra set of metal legs. I hurried out after her. I didn't want her going up the stairs on her own, especially not in the mood she was in.

It was nearly eleven by the time I finally saw Edith to bed. I went straight down the stairs to Paul's before I could change my mind. I didn't care how late it was. Anyway, I knew he was still up – I'd heard music coming though the floorboards.

The door to the basement flat hadn't been closed properly. It opened as I raised my hand to the knocker. Trance music was booming out of the sitting room. Not Paul's usual taste. Was he having a party? He was standing in the doorway to the sitting room with his back to me. The place stank of patchouli and the sort of incense they burn in those head shops in Camden Town. The only light came from the coloured candles glowing on the shelves.

'Hey,' I said, but he couldn't hear me over the bass.

I tapped him on the shoulder and he spun round with a startled expression on his face. Behind him, in the centre of the room, Jo was waving her arms in the air and shaking her flat little booty for all she was worth. It took my mind a minute to catch up with what my eyes were seeing. Jo was stark-bollock-naked.

'What the fuck?' I turned to Paul.

I'd never seen him look panicked before. Jo just laughed and grabbed his hand. She spun herself along Paul's arm until she was pressed up against his chest. Draping her arms over his shoulders she nestled into his neck.

'Jo, that's enough.' Paul lifted up her arms and tried to steer her away, but she was all over him like an octopus. 'She's totally wasted,' he said to me.

'And what were you doing while she was getting her kit off – standing back and watching?'

'I've only just got in. She was already like this.'

Fair enough – he was wearing a tracksuit and clutching his gym bag in one hand.

Jo swung Paul's arm up and down. 'Make a baby with me while I still have a few eggs left. We'd make beautiful babies together.'

'Oh my days! You don't know how twisted that is,' I couldn't help shouting at her – not that it made any impact.

'Lauren, now is not the time.' Paul's voice was severe, but he was still wrestling with Jo, whose body glistened with oil. She kept slithering out of his grip and finding a new part of his anatomy to stick herself to.

They ended up doing a freaky kind of slow dance round the room. Jo rubbing herself against Paul in what she clearly thought were some sexy moves while he tried to push her away.

'Jo, you've got to stop. This is totally inappropriate.' He sounded like a desperate supply teacher.

Jo's eyebrows shot up and her mouth formed a big O as she looked at me for the first time.

'Lauren, sweetie, would you mind giving us a bit of privacy?' She actually winked at me. I thought I might throw up.

Since Paul was unable to detach himself from vampire squid lady, I grabbed a towel from the bathroom and threw it over her. Paul managed to pull it tightly round her shoulders, pinning her arms to her sides, and together we pushed her into a sitting position on the sofa.

'Shut your legs for God's sake.' I shoved her knees together.

Jo just kept nodding her head to the music, her eyes half-closed. Paul found the remote and hit the mute button. The silence seemed to bring her round. She stopped swaying and looked up at us. Her pupils were still like black holes, but her eyes were starting to focus.

'We need to get her upstairs without Edith seeing her,' I said.

'Why is everyone round here so uptight? You both need to chillax.' Jo made a scissoring movement with her arms and the towel fell down around her waist. Paul turned to look away.

'You should lighten up – you might actually enjoy yourself.' Jo giggled. 'I'm not bad in bed you know.'

'I'm really not interested.'

I have to admit I was relieved to hear Paul say that.

'Are you gay?' Jo raised her eyebrows in surprise.

'No I'm not gay, I'm just not into you.' Paul was starting to sound pissed off.

Jo slumped backwards. 'Do I disgust you?'

She suddenly looked so sad and dejected I sat down beside her, wrapping the towel back round her like she was a little kid just out of the swimming-pool. She rested her head on my shoulder.

'You're a lovely girl, Lauren. Mum doesn't deserve you.'

I looked over at Paul. He was staring down at his trainers like they were going to solve all his problems. This whole situation had got so fucked-up I just didn't know what to say. Paul started picking Jo's clothes up off the floor.

'Maybe you can help her get these back on.' He handed the pile to me.

Once she was dressed Jo was all on for going out clubbing. We managed to persuade her it would be more fun to lie on the sofa and listen to some Latin jazz. She settled back, closing her eyes and smiling blissfully. I hoped for her sake the previous hour had been wiped from her memory. Paul and me lay side by side on the rug, our heads resting on bean bags.

'These are nice.' I nestled my head into the stuffing.

'Yeah,' he gave an awkward laugh. 'Jo bought them.'

'Did she think she'd be moving in down here?' I whispered.

'Hope not.'

Weird though this sounds, it was really relaxing – the three of us lying there, listening to music. I felt safe and snug beside Paul. My eyes began to close and for the first time in over a week I fell into a deep sleep.

EDITH

A COLD BREEZE WAS BLOWING across the right side of my body, bristling the hairs on my arms. My nightdress had ridden up, hitching round my hips, exposing my legs and buttocks. The duvet twitched as though someone was tugging at it, I grabbed a corner before it was pulled right off me. As I leant over I saw a hand, small and dark, resting on its finger tips on the far side of the bed.

It moved slowly towards me, feeling its way over the ridges of the bedclothes, then stopped suddenly, halfway. I lay still, holding my breath, too afraid to cry out. The forefinger lifted slowly upwards to point at my face. There was no arm, no body, just a severed wrist, caked in dried black blood.

Warm liquid seeped out between my thighs, soaking into the sheet beneath me. Tears collected in the corners of my eyes, sweat ran down my spine. I didn't care, I hoped I would melt completely, that my brain would dissolve before the hand could reach me.

The forefinger quivered like an antenna sensing what was around it. I shut my eyes, expecting it to pounce, to claw at my face. What was it waiting for? When I opened my eyes it was still there. The pink fingernails clipped short and even, like a row of tiny seashells. The clock on my dressing-table ticked steadily on. In the distance a motorbike roared. Downstairs the grandmother clock chimed three times. The forefinger lowered, joining the other fingers in drumming slowly on the bed, beside the resting thumb. The knuckles rolled, the tendons rose and fell beneath the smooth brown skin. I would not allow it to lure me into movement. It would give up before I did.

'Oops, did you have an accident?'

The reassuringly familiar pattern of Royal Copenhagen blue and white china formed itself into a cup, placed at eye level on my bedside table. I rolled over and felt the still damp, now cold, patch of sheet beneath me. Lauren's head bobbed up as she gathered the fallen duvet off the floor and threw it clumsily over the end of the bed.

'I was ill in the night, must have had a fever. The sweat has soaked right through.'

Lauren put the palm of her hand against my forehead. I flinched involuntarily.

'You don't feel hot. Have you got a thermometer? My mum always keeps a thermometer in the house, because of the kids.'

'I don't recall, I don't think I have one.'

I pushed myself upright and surveyed the room, half-expecting to see the hand, curled up in a fist under the wardrobe, or tapping its fingers in the shadowy corner behind the open door.

'I had such terrible visions.'

'Hallucinations – happens with a temperature. Hope you

don't have the flu. Do you feel achy?' Lauren frowned.

'I'm always achy – comes with age.'

I managed a sip of tea, such a comfort. My mouth was parched.

'My nan always swore by Vick's VapoRub.'

'Ugh no, I can't abide the smell of eucalyptus. Something about the smell, makes me feel sick.'

'Just as well we're going to the doctor's tomorrow.'

Lauren pulled the curtains open and sunlight flooded the room, restoring normality, making the disembodied hand seem like nothing more than the stuff of dreams. A bright blue sky glowed behind the lace curtains.

'Looks like another scorcher,' I said, with as much enthusiasm as I could muster.

She held one of the lace curtains aside and stood looking out onto the square. I could hear the dustbin men dragging the wheelie bins out to their truck. I was about to ask her if she'd remembered to put the recycling out when she started speaking, her voice uncharacteristically sombre.

'I had the worst nightmare ever a few days ago. It was so real I seriously didn't know if I was dreaming or there was someone there, in the room with me.'

My skin turned icy cold.

'Do you often have nightmares?'

I hoped she'd say she'd been having them regularly before moving in with me.

'Not since I was little and never as bad as that one.' She remained by the window, talking with her back to me. 'It was like something out of a horror film. Like a ghost whispering in my ear, wanting to know why these bad things had been done to her.'

'What bad things?' A dizzying sense of dread descended on

me. 'What did she look like?'

'I couldn't see, couldn't get my eyes open. It was a girlish voice, African. She was angry. She said the evil would be punished.'

I felt sick. There was a rushing noise in my ears.

'How?'

Lauren swung round to face me. 'That's what I've been trying to work out.'

I didn't like the way she was staring at me – as though I were responsible in some way, as though I ought to have the answers.

'Did she tell you her name?'

Lauren thought for a moment then shook her head. 'Why?'

She moved over to my dressing table and started re-arranging the bottles and jars, fiddling unnecessarily. I could see myself faintly reflected in the mirror, as grey as any ghost. Perhaps nightmares were infectious, we were both becoming hysterical. It was ridiculous to think that Mary might have popped up sixty-three years after her death, seeking revenge. I needed to assert myself, to act the wise elder even if I didn't feel it.

I swallowed another mouthful of tea, trying to hold the cup steady, and said, as casually as I could: 'I just thought, knowing who the girl was might help you to understand your dream.'

'What are your nightmares about?' Lauren perched on the edge of the bed, which reminded me of the unfortunate damp patch.

I drew myself up in an attempt to look dignified. 'I read an article about dreams once, written by a doctor. He said there is no meaning, no significance to them. It's just the mind clearing out the day's debris.'

Lauren nodded. 'Yeah, that makes sense.' She stood up, brushing down her skirt. 'Why don't I help you into the shower? You'll feel a lot better after a wash. Then I can get this bed stripped and changed.'

I wished I could do it myself, but I hadn't the strength. What if bedwetting became a regular occurrence? The shame of it, I couldn't bear it.

'Is Joanna up?' I glanced over at the open door.

'She's at her yoga training.'

'Don't tell her, about the bed. She wants to pack me off to a care home. This will just encourage her.'

Lauren squatted down beside me, her forehead furrowed with concern.

'What's she want to do that for? There's been some terrible stuff in the news about what goes on in nursing homes – you don't want to end up in one of them.'

'Exactly, and then you'd be out of a home too.'

She straightened up.

'Well, yeah, but you're my main concern. You're much better off here than being drugged up to the eyeballs and left to rot in some care home. No offence, but I'm surprised at Jo. Me and Paul, we've been looking after you just fine, haven't we?'

It was reassuring to know that I had allies against Joanna. I should put aside my misgivings about Lauren for the time-being at least; she was a great help around the house. Joanna liked her and once she'd got this notion about selling the house out of her head I could always look for another girl. I'd insist on a medical student next time though; someone from a more compatible background – not so political.

I swung my legs slowly over the edge of the bed, planting my feet on the floor. Looking down at my calloused, wrinkled toes made me shudder as I recalled the disembodied hand. I pushed it firmly out of my mind. I was not going to dwell on the macabre; it was just a dream, some arbitrary nonsense. There was nothing to fear.

❂

'You don't have to do anything you don't want to, Edith.' Paul put his coffee cup down and took my hand between his palms. 'No one has the right to pressurise you into selling your home.'

I curled my fingers around his large, soft palm, feeling the hairs on the back of his hand brush my fingertips. Such security in masculine hands. What would it feel like to press my fingers against his cheek, to feel the stubble prickle against my skin, to smell his aftershave on my fingers?

He squeezed my hand and then pulled away. I carefully pressed my fork down into the creamy beige layers of walnut cake.

'Joanna will get it when I die anyway. I don't know why she's being so impatient.'

Paul leant his elbows on the wrought-iron table, gazing at me earnestly. The only other person I'd known to meet one's eyes so directly was Graham, but with Graham it was like having a searchlight beamed into one's brain, illuminating all the hidden thoughts and buried emotions, all the embarrassing moments. Paul's gaze was kinder, as though he sought to understand rather than expose. Graham was quick to ridicule, Paul to sympathy.

Building work was going on a few gardens away, the usual peace of a weekday morning was broken by drilling, clanking and the shouts of workmen – obscenities no doubt.

'Can you see what they're doing? It's not another ghastly extension is it?'

Paul stood up, sliding his hands into his trouser pockets and surveying the horizon.

'Can't tell from here – might just be re-pointing the brickwork.'

He sauntered to the end of the garden. Catching hold of an overhanging branch, he leapt lightly up onto the wall, where he balanced on the balls of his feet, peering through the trellis. His trousers stretched taut over his behind, the belt accentuating his narrow waist. He had the grace of a ballet dancer, as well as the muscular physique of a soldier. Had it been anyone else I'd be afraid they'd damage the latticework, but he had the poise of a cat.

'Watch yourself on that climbing rose; the thorns are vicious.'

He jumped nimbly back onto the lawn. 'Don't you worry about me, Edith.' He smiled playfully at me. 'Couldn't see through the leaves, but planning must be strict round here, they'd have to let you know if they were building anything major.'

'I'd hope so. Mr Nicholls, at number forty-two, is a retired architect so I'm sure he'd have something to say about it. I've been to his house; very restrained decor, lots of glass – walls and so forth. Rather exposing, I'd have thought. All right if you don't mind being on display.' I found myself chuckling as I looked at Paul. 'Perhaps he's an exhibitionist. He shares the house with a man, his partner, and I don't mean that in the business sense.'

I tried to remember the partner's name. It was something foreign. Russian perhaps, or was I getting distracted by the Russian vine growing over the wall? We'd only been there once. I'd invited them over for Christmas drinks several years in a row, but they were always away, or busy. I feared Graham might have said something to offend them. I hardly knew any of the neighbours now. Not that I'd ever known many of them well. One doesn't, in London.

I suddenly realised Paul was speaking.

'Going to St. Edmund's I had a lot of wealthy friends. It was tough at the time, as you know I was a scholarship boy, so I couldn't afford all the holidays, the ski trips, the new trainers etc. But now I'm so thankful I didn't have their kind of money. It's been the making of me, and I've seen first-hand the damage that money does.'

He poured himself more coffee, gesturing to my cup with the cafetière. I shook my head. Too much coffee makes me jittery.

'Take one of my best friends, Giles. He spent his entire adult life waiting for his inheritance. He was the most talented, intelligent person I knew, but he had no incentive to make anything of himself. It was a tragedy, I'm telling you, Edith.' Paul shook his head. 'Giles ended up addicted to drugs and alcohol. We tried to get him into rehab, but he refused. He died of a fatal overdose three years ago. We'll never know if it was intentional or not.'

'What an appalling story.' I pushed the last bit of walnut cake to the edge of my plate.

'It is appalling, and I wouldn't burden you with it if I didn't think it was important.'

Perhaps it was Paul's brown eyes that made his gaze softer, warmer, than Graham's steely-blue.

'You mentioned Joanna's impatience and I wonder if she has similar tendencies. Giles was always flitting from one project to another, never able to form lasting attachments. He believed the money from his parents' house would enable him to settle, to start his life proper, when in fact it was doing the opposite. It was the very thing preventing him.'

A sparrow landed on the birdfeeder. It pecked rapidly at the nuts, releasing a shower of seeds onto the ground below. That would be another lot of weeds taking root in the lawn. Sometimes I wondered why I put those things up.

'I was reading this article the other day, about very wealthy people who've made the decision not to support their children financially – Bill Gates, Warren Buffet, Andrew Lloyd Webber, Nigella Lawson – not leaving their kids a penny, giving it all to charity instead. Nigella Lawson said financial security ruins people's lives. She wants her kids to earn their own way.'

'She should know I suppose. Wasn't her father chancellor of the exchequer?' I'd no idea who the first two were though. 'Graham wouldn't invest in Joanna's Italian project, didn't trust her financially. Trouble was she had her grandmother's money to fall back on. Perhaps that spoilt her.'

We sat looking out on the garden, while the construction work hammered away around us.

'I could leave some of my money to charity; there's the wildlife trust Graham set up.'

'That's one option.'

'And of course I'd want to leave something to human development, worthy as animals are, I've always thought people must come first. It's just knowing which charity. There are so many and I don't want my money being wasted on a lot of bureaucrats.'

'You're quite right, Edith. These big charities are all competing with each other for business. You should see the salaries some of the people working for them earn.'

'Yes, I read something in the *Mail* about that. People don't realise that the money they donate all goes to over-paid pen-pushers.'

'Exactly. I'm glad to say, being a smaller charity, we avoid that trap. We don't have the overhead costs, you see. Every penny we raise goes straight to the people who deserve support: ex-service men and women. The trouble is when people read about the big, overly bureaucratic charities, we end up losing vital donations too. We all get tarred with the same brush, even though we're completely different.'

Paul folded his napkin into a neat square and placed it under his cup. He stared up at the sky for a moment. It was starting to cloud over. Thunder was forecast later.

'You've created such a beautiful garden, Edith, you must be very proud of it. It's so important for children to have outdoor space to play in, isn't it?'

I smiled. 'Oh yes, Joanna even had her own little flowerbed, over there on the right. Graham thought she ought to take full responsibility for it, but she forgot to water it and the seeds she planted failed. She was so upset, I bought some annuals and planted them out while she was asleep. Her little face in the morning when I showed her the flowers that had miraculously appeared was a picture.'

Such a happy memory – Joanna's sense of wonder as she gazed open-mouthed at the pink and mauve Busy Lizzies. She had danced round and round the garden in delight. She must have been about six. Graham was very cross with me, said she'd never learn from her mistakes if I kept interfering. I suppose he was right, considering the way she turned out.

'They were Busy Lizzies, proper name *Impatiens* – very apt flowers for Joanna.' I surveyed the garden. There was an empty patch where the peonies had finished flowering. 'We ought to plant some more.'

'She's always been impatient then?' Paul hesitated. 'What do you think about this yoga training? Can you see Jo as a teacher?'

'Well, I certainly wouldn't let her loose on children,' I said automatically, and then felt a twinge of guilt. 'Of course, it would be different if she had her own. Motherhood would make her settle down. My father used to say breeding mares calms them. Though it only seemed to last while they were in foal.'

'I know you'd have liked grandchildren.' Paul looked at me sadly.

'I'm still not ruling it out entirely.' I sighed. Who was I deceiving? Joanna didn't have the remotest desire to reproduce and, without a husband to encourage her, why would she? 'But time is running out. Joanna's always been unconventional.'

This was why I'd longed for a large family; then at least I was sure to get some sensible, well-balanced children, with careers in medicine or law, with husbands in banking. Children who'd take me out for Sunday lunch, children with big houses in Richmond or Buckinghamshire, big enough to build an annexe for their mother to live in. Children who would never dream of putting me in any home other than their own. Children who were financially secure.

'She was a very difficult teenager.' I might as well tell Paul everything; he of all people would understand, given his work. 'The school suggested counselling once, but Graham didn't believe in that sort of thing.' I stirred my spoon around my empty cup. 'We had to pick her up from police stations on a couple of occasions.' I looked up at Paul. 'She'd been taking drugs. I'll never forget those phone calls.' The horror of it still made me shudder, all these years later.

'I'm so sorry you had to go through all that. It must have been terrible for you.'

I nodded, remembering the set look on Graham's face when he locked Joanna in her room, the muscle in his jaw twitching. Her screams and cries, lapsing into tears and pleas. Her promises to behave, to be good.

I unknotted my scarf. The silk material slipped through my fingers and onto the ground. Paul retrieved it for me.

'What kind of drugs was she on?'

'Various things. She smoked marijuana, but when she was arrested she'd taken LSD.' Even in the shade the heat was oppressive. It was the humidity; we needed a storm to clear the air. 'She grew out of all that nonsense a long time ago.'

Paul sighed heavily, twisting uncomfortably in his chair. 'I didn't want to have to burden you with this; I'd been hoping it was a one-off.' He broke off abruptly, getting up and walking round the lawn.

'What? What is it?' A horrible feeling of inevitability was rising through my bones.

'I would never have said anything.' He clasped his face in his hands. 'This is very embarrassing, but now I know the history, I feel duty-bound to tell you.' He resumed his seat beside me. His eyes were filled with sorrow as he said, very gently, 'Joanna's still taking drugs.'

My heart almost stopped. I could feel the blood congealing in my veins, paralysing my limbs.

'Are you sure?'

After hearing the whole sordid story of Joanna's inebriated Salomé impersonation, I felt quite nauseous.

'I am concerned that Joanna would make herself so vulnerable.' Paul looked grave.

'But as you said, it could be a one-off, a moment's aberration.'

'Drug addiction doesn't work that way, unfortunately. Whoever supplied Jo with those drugs will make sure she keeps on taking more.'

'What's wrong with her?'

My voice sounded more quavery, more desperate, than I'd intended, but I just couldn't understand it. She'd had the most stable, cosseted upbringing anyone could wish for. Perhaps there was some mental deficiency. I remembered my mother's slurred speech, her incoherent words, the bottle of gin at the back of her wardrobe. They say inherited traits often skip a generation.

'Disgraceful, idiotic behaviour, I'm so sorry you had to witness it.'

She was lucky Paul was such a gentleman. I twisted my napkin so hard it came apart, bits of shredded paper fell onto my plate like snow. Looking down at the ragged tissue clutched between my fists I was shocked at how old my hands seemed; mottled with brown liver spots, the loose dry skin so criss-crossed with lines it resembled alligator leather. It took me a moment to recognise them as my own.

'You have nothing to apologise for.' Paul was smiling gently at me. 'She's an adult who makes her own decisions; she's not your responsibility any more. It's your wellbeing we have to think about. I would never have said anything, only her wanting you to sell the house rings alarm bells.'

If only she'd married Stefano and stayed in Italy, it was obviously a better place for her. It wasn't fair, to inflict her problems on me, an elderly widow.

'What can we do?'

'There are treatment programmes, 'rehab' you might have heard of. Some people send their children abroad to break the drug habit, but they're usually teenagers.'

Joanna needed to grow up. 'Can we make her go?'

'Not at this stage, but it might be worth raising the subject with Dr. Morahan. You've got an appointment with her tomorrow haven't you?'

'Did Lauren tell you about that? She said she'd accompany me.'

Paul's brow furrowed. 'We agreed that I would take you, don't you remember? I've told them at work I'll have to leave early.'

I felt terrible then. I had no recollection of making any arrangement with Paul. I'd discussed my appointment with Lauren only yesterday, I was sure of it.

'Well of course I'd rather go with you,' I told him.

'Great. We can explain your fears about Joanna to the doctor. Tell her that Joanna's back on the drugs and behaving erratically. The doctor can't do anything directly, but at least she can offer you some support and advice. I'll go through it all with you beforehand. There's nothing to worry about.'

'Oh Paul,' I squeezed his arm. 'Sometimes I think Graham's spirit directed you to me, to look after me in his absence.'

Paul just smiled and nodded thoughtfully.

KENYA, 1956

IT WAS EVENING WHEN Charity was summoned to the commandant's office. That was unusual in itself; more unusual still was that the female warder did not enter the hut with her. She had never been left alone with Captain Forbes before.

He was sitting on the corner of his desk, a cigarette in one hand. He smiled at her and told her to sit down, gesturing to a wooden chair. After knocking back the contents of the glass he was holding, he refilled it with an amber-coloured liquid, then offered her a drink from the same bottle. She shook her head nervously.

'Go on – it'll do you good.' He lifted the tin mug tied around her waist and poured some of the brown liquid into it before handing it back to her.

Charity had no choice but to take a sip. She coughed as the earthy smelling drink burnt its way down her throat. Was he poisoning her? Was this some kind of truth drug? Captain

Forbes looked amused.

'So, you have a good level of English?'

'Quite good, *Effendi*.' She had learnt in the camp to address all white people with this title.

Forbes leant forward, placing one hand on her knee. 'Go on, finish your drink.'

Charity thought she would throw up. At least when she'd finished, he didn't pour any more of the disgusting liquid into her mug. His hand remained on her knee though. He had pushed her dress up and his damp palm pressed heavily against her skin. She wanted to move away, to stand up, but feared the repercussions if she dared to shift a muscle without his permission.

'English good enough for writing letters to VIPs, I believe.'

The commandant's bloodshot eyes were locked on hers. She could smell the alcohol on his breath, feel its heat against her face. She shrank back in her chair.

'I've only written letters to my family and my headmistress,' she whispered.

There was a sharp stinging sensation on the back of her hand and a smell of burning. The pain made her cry out. He'd stubbed his cigarette out on her skin.

'Let's start again, shall we?' He settled himself back on the desk. 'You've been working for the Mau Mau, doing their dirty work.'

'No, *Effendi*, no. My family are loyal to the British Crown. I believe in Her Majesty the Queen. I am thankful for all the improvements the British have brought to Kenya.' It was a litany she'd learnt to recite as well as she'd previously known the Hail Mary or the Our Father.

Forbes grabbed her head. Holding it between his hands he thrust his face into hers. She could feel the wetness of his saliva spraying out between his words. 'You've been translating propaganda for those Mau Mau bitches.' His hands slid down to her breasts. He pinched her nipples, twisting them as he pulled her towards him. 'I'll show you what happens to bad girls.'

It was a clear night with a full moon so Charity was easily seen when she was finally returned to her tent. Sarah and another woman called Wanjiku helped her to lie down. They cleaned her as best they could, then tore strips of material from the side of the tent, tying them carefully between her bloody thighs. Sarah lay down beside her. Embracing Charity's shaking body, she stroked her hair and told her that one day she would be free from this hell and would forget everything that had happened here.

They lay enfolded together until the sun rose and the loudspeakers summoned them to work. Charity walked slowly, wincing as the warders' whips slashed against her calves, but incapable of moving any faster.

She wondered if the commandant had raped Wairimu too – if that was how he'd got her to rat on Charity. She couldn't ask Wairimu because she'd been moved to another camp. One for hardcore Mau Mau detainees categorised black. So Wairimu couldn't pollute the greys any more, Mrs Eastfield told them.

Charity was taken off the murram shift and put on toilet duty. This was a privilege. Even though what they were carrying stank, it wasn't as heavy as the clods of murram, under which some of the women's bodies were bent permanently out of shape. Commandant Forbes didn't want Charity crippled; at least, not physically.

After Forbes raped her the second time, Charity stopped speaking. It was as if all the words in her head had disappeared. Her thoughts were inexpressible, even in Gikuyu. The other detainees cared for her as though she were a little child again, feeding her when she refused to eat, telling her stories to strengthen her, singing her to sleep.

Mrs Eastfield was not so sympathetic, however. 'This attitude is very disappointing,' she scolded. 'How do you expect to go home when instead of improving, you've become sullen and unresponsive?' She shook her head in frustration, turning to the visiting missionary who stood nervously by her side. 'Number 6743 should have been moved earlier; she was a bad influence on this girl. It wouldn't surprise me if she's done some sort of Mau Mau voodoo on her.'

The missionary, a young English woman, stared at Charity as though she were a wild beast about to strike. Charity wished she were as dangerous and powerful as the woman seemed to think.

'You see a bad woman is extremely difficult to rehabilitate and the better ones get contaminated by the hardcore,' Mrs Eastfield continued. 'The idea is to keep them separate, but there are so many of them it's not always easy to do.'

'Shall I read to them now?' The missionary held up the bible she'd been gripping tightly in both hands.

'Give it a go, why not?' Before leaving her terrified charge, Mrs Eastfield glanced over the top of Charity's head. 'If you don't start speaking again soon we'll have to send you to the clinic,' she warned.

The English girl smiled nervously at the waiting women. 'Do make yourselves comfortable.'

They looked round the sun-baked yard, the rolls of barbed wire fencing glinting in the sun, before sitting on the dusty ground.

'Romans 13:2. Therefore, whoever resists the authorities resists what God has appointed, and those who resist will incur judgment. For rulers are not a terror to good conduct, but to bad. Would you have no fear of the one who is in authority? Then do what is good, and you will receive his approval, for he is God's servant for your good. But if you do wrong, be afraid, for he does not bear the sword in vain.'

The missionary read too fast and kept tripping up over names and words familiar to Charity from school and church. Some of the women closed their eyes and began to doze, grateful for a respite from enforced labour.

Charity thought of Githii; his crooked smile and inquisitive eyes, the fizzing low down in her belly whenever he touched her, the excitement she felt when they kissed. How could she have enjoyed a man's hands on her flesh, even a young man's? Now the idea made her skin crawl. God was punishing her for her disgusting, lustful impulses. No wonder the commandant had singled her out; she must have reeked of sin.

If only she was plain and flat-chested like Eunice, he might have left her alone. If only she'd obeyed her parents and teachers and been sensible like her friends. She should never have gone off alone with Githii. He was the devil in the shape of a boy and she'd been too lecherous and stupid to realise. How could she have gone against everything the nuns had taught about chastity and piety? Now she knew they were only trying to protect her.

Someone was tapping her knee.

'Don't let them send you to the clinic, Charity,' Sarah whispered. 'They fry your brain there. You'll never get out if they label you insane.'

Charity felt as though her brain was being fried anyway. At least the clinic would get her away from Forbes.

LAUREN

'COUCH POTATOES!'

'What's that, Edith? You still hungry?' I put down the TV remote.

'You may be stuck in with me on a Saturday evening, but that doesn't mean we have to sit watching endless drivel on television. Why don't you make us both a martini?'

'All right,' I said. 'But you'll have to show me how.'

She had a real silver cocktail shaker in the drinks cabinet. I poured in the gin and vermouth, then Edith followed me into the kitchen to get olives and ice.

'Shaken, not stirred,' I said, holding up the shaker. It was a cheesy line, but it made Edith laugh. It was nice to see her in a cheerful mood for a change.

We ended up staying in the kitchen, sipping our drinks out of big triangular cocktail glasses at the wooden table, looking out of the open windows at the garden. I liked it better in the kitchen – it was more relaxed than the cold, stuffy living room. 'No offence, House,' I thought, then realised I hadn't talked to the house since Jo arrived.

Edith put the radio on. Some jazz was playing. Jazz wasn't really my thing, but the mellow sounds went well with the martini. Felt very sophisticated, like we were in a film.

'We ought to be dancing.' Edith started swaying in time to the music. 'I loved to dance when I was young.'

She leant towards me like she was about to grab my arms. I was scared she'd try to make me slow-dance round the kitchen with her, but she steadied herself and sat back in her chair.

'Do you know any African stories?' she asked.

'No,' I said, nervous we were getting onto dangerous ground.

'Just thought your grandmother might have told you some.'

I frowned and shook my head. Since I told Edith I'd had a nightmare too, we'd been getting on better, like it created a bond between us. She seemed to of got over me not telling her about Nan. I think she finally believed the detention bracelets weren't mine, but I was careful not to say anything about Africa, especially Kenya, in case I said the wrong thing and raised her suspicions.

But Edith just smiled at me. She looked kind of dreamy. 'When I was a girl I loved to listen to my friend's mother telling stories. She was well-known locally for her tales, used to command quite an audience.'

'What kind of stories?' I couldn't help being curious.

'Make me another one and I'll tell you.' Edith lifted her glass.

She had problems trying to remember a whole story. She started one about an ogre luring girls into the forest but couldn't remember if it was the girls who got eaten by the ogre or the ogre who got eaten by other ogres when the girls escaped, or maybe the girls got swallowed whole and then cut out of the ogre's belly by their brothers. We were onto our third martini by the time she finally remembered a full story.

'Once upon a time…'

'Do African stories start like that as well?'

'Don't interrupt, I'll lose the thread again. A hyena and a squirrel lived together quite happily, working their bit of land, growing enough vegetables to eat, looking after their goats.'

I was about to ask how a squirrel could keep goats, but Edith gave me one of her looks, so I just got on with refilling our glasses.

'The squirrel was a hard worker, but as everyone knows, the hyena is a greedy beast. And very soon he hatched a plan to eat the squirrel and keep all the land and the animals for himself. The trouble was, the hyena talked in his sleep and the squirrel overheard his plans. So the cunning squirrel came up with a plan of his own.

'While the hyena was out in the fields the squirrel stoked up the fire, getting it as hot as possible. On this fire he cooked the hyena's favourite dish, a delicious piece of roasted meat. Under the meat he heated a stone until it was red hot.

'Very soon he heard the hyena return. The hyena demanded his dinner, shouting about how empty his belly was and threatening to eat the squirrel if he didn't feed him quickly. The squirrel carefully rolled the hot stone up in the tender strip of meat. "Open your mouth, friend Hyena, and taste this special meat," he said. "Swallow it at once and I'll get you a larger piece." The squirrel threw the meat wrapped stone into the hyena's open mouth and the hyena swallowed it whole. Immediately the hyena began to howl in pain. The red-hot stone burnt right through his stomach and killed him dead. So the squirrel took possession of all the land and the animals and lived happily ever after.'

'Wowzers, that's dark. Not exactly Disney, is it?'

Edith just looked pleased she'd finally managed to tell a whole story.

Maybe it was the martinis, or the fox screeching in the garden, but I lay awake most of the rest of that night. Nan had only ever told me bible stories to teach some lesson, and I kept thinking how weird it was that the one story Edith properly remembered was about a big greedy animal getting killed by the smaller one it was exploiting. It was probably just the alcohol and the lack of sleep making me paranoid, but I started wondering if she saw us that way. Then, was she the hyena and I the squirrel? Or, you could see it as Kenya being the squirrel and the hyena being the British.

I rolled over, trying to get comfortable. I was overthinking it. Edith was just telling a story she'd heard as a kid. She didn't have a clue what it might mean. There was probably loads of stories with hyenas in them. It was funny though, how she'd got so into it. She'd sat very still when she told that story, her eyes glazed over, totally there, with the hyena and the squirrel in their shamba, looking after the goats and the chickens.

Tired and hungover, I rang Paul next morning, said I really needed to speak to him. He told me to meet him in the Lebanese cafe round the corner from his gym. It was a dimly lit place with tinted windows, not very popular – perfect for a private chat, especially with a hangover.

I told him I couldn't take the posing no more. It was all right for him – he didn't have to live in the house with Edith, eating his meals and spending his evenings with her, all the time acting like he didn't know about Forbes, like there was no connection.

'You've got to get some distance. Think of yourself as a

professional carer on a contract. It isn't going to last for ever.'
He mopped up the sauce on his plate with a piece of pitta bread.

'She loves you so much she'd probably forgive you anything.'
I took a sip of orange juice. It went down like acid on my
stomach.

Paul just sighed and shook his head. 'You know why Edith
accepts me? Because she's whitewashed me. I tell her what she
wants to hear, act how she expects me to act, and she sees the
man she wants to see in the empty space she's created. As soon as
I tell her who I really am, as soon as I become real to her, she'll
change her mind about me.'

I pushed a chicken kebab off its skewer. The pale cube of meat
lay on my plate – it was a bit pink in the middle where the hole
was. Made me think of the stone the squirrel fed to the hyena.

'I dunno, maybe you're underestimating her. I don't think
she's so racist as all that. She was best friends with a black kid
growing up.'

Paul snorted. 'Have you forgotten how she reacted when she
found out you had a black granny? If I hadn't convinced her to
let you stay, she'd have thrown you out.'

'She seems to of accepted it now though.'

Paul gave me one of his full-on stares. 'You've been brought
up white, Lauren. You think everything's just going to come to
you, doors will open, people will welcome you, because that's
the way it's always been. No one's ever seen you as a threat, so
they've never been hostile.'

I got what Paul was saying – I knew I'd been protected by the
pale colour of my skin. Like an invisible forcefield my whiteness
shielded me from the sort of abusive crap most black people –
people like Dad and Nan – faced every day. It wasn't like I could
help it though.

'I didn't get any choice over how my genes got played out.' I pushed my finger through the granules of salt scattered on the tablecloth.

'None of us did, but you do get a choice over how you live your life.' He rubbed his cheek wearily. 'The thing is, Lauren, as a black man, I know no one in this country is ever going to take me seriously. Our lives have no value. No policeman has ever been sent down for killing a black person. Where are the inquiries, where are the consequences? And if they can get away with it over here, do you think there's ever going to be any soul-searching about what they did in Kenya? The concentration camps? The cover-ups? No, we have to take matters into our own hands, seek justice in our own way.'

The waiter came over to see if we wanted any desserts. We both shook our heads and he gave us a sad smile before taking our plates away. I brushed the spilt salt into my hand, but then I didn't have anywhere to put it so I ended up pouring it back onto the table in a little pile.

The waiter came back with a plate of baklava. You can't grow up near Green Lanes without having your fill of them.

'On the house,' he said, putting the plate down with a wave of his hand.

I took a piece just to cheer him up. It was a bit stale but the honey syrup helped lift my hangover.

Paul was gesturing out the window. 'All this nostalgia about the good old days, when Britain ruled the waves and everything was soft-focus, cricket and teatime, African elephants and Indian tigers. When black and brown people knew their place was to give up their lives for the white man so he could get rich. They don't want to admit that all their wealth, everything they've acquired and built is tainted with blood.' He turned to look at me. 'Why would anyone open up that can of worms if they didn't have to? No, in this society if you don't help yourself there's no one going to hold out a hand – not if you're black.' He pushed the plate of pastries to one side, leaning towards me over the table. 'You can drop out if you want. It'll make it a lot more difficult for me, but I'm going to see this through to the end.'

Paul wasn't bitter or angry – he was just practical. He knew the score. He'd told me about the bullying he went through at the private school his mum sent him to, all the racist slurs the rich boys landed on him. Maybe he knew Edith's kind of people better than I did. And it was true, Edith was a Tory through and through, very attached to the system, her property – all that. She even called Nelson Mandela a terrorist. Maybe he was right – it was too much to expect her to see things from our perspective.

I looked up at Paul, at his handsome, open face that reminded me so much of my dad. At his rich, multi-toned brown skin, whose shade I could never quite pin down. It seemed to get lighter or darker depending on the time of year, the light, and even the company.

'Course I'm not going to drop out,' I said. 'I'm with you all the way.'

EDITH

I WOKE TO THE SMELL of burning. A thick, cloying smoke filled the room. I pushed myself out of my chair and onto my walking frame. Where were Lauren and Jo? Why had no one come to get me?

'Fire!' I shouted, but my voice was so feeble it would be a miracle if anyone heard it.

Then I saw Joanna. She was standing with her back to me waving a bunch of leaves in the air and chanting some gobbledygook. On the side table a newspaper was blazing.

'Joanna!' I screamed.

She looked round with a start, noticed the conflagration, threw her burning bundle into the fireplace and tipped a large vase of lilies over the flames. Water dripped over the table and onto the carpet.

'What the hell are you doing now?'

'Sorry, Mum, that was an accident. I'll clean up the mess.'

The sickly smell rising up from the leaves was making me feel quite dizzy. 'This is the last straw. Your drug addiction has nearly caused a major catastrophe.'

Joanna looked surprised and then she actually began to laugh. I suppose she was high as a kite.

'For God's sake Mum – they're smudge sticks.' She picked the bunch of leaves up and thrust them towards me. 'North American sage, as used for cleansing. I'm detoxing this house.'

She obviously took me for a fool. 'Smells like marijuana to me.'

'Have you ever smelt it? Might actually do you good, help you to relax a bit. Some cannabis oil would work wonders on your arthritis.'

'I don't want your drugs.' I made my way back to my chair, thumping the frame down in front of me. 'What are you trying to do? Kill me off? I know what you're after. You can't pull the wool over my eyes – not any more.'

'This is ridiculous. You're over-reacting. There's a lot of negative energy in this house. I'm using an ancient technique to flush it out; that's all.' She waved her leaves in big sweeping movements round the room.

It was heart-breaking how she could lie so brazenly. Paul was right: the sooner I got her into treatment the better. She was a danger to herself and others.

LAUREN

I HAD TO FIGHT MY WAY onto the tube – the carriage was packed with tourists. They were so unaware how they were annoying the other passengers, leaning over them to study the tube map, pointing at random stops, chattering away in different languages.

I wished I was on holiday somewhere, instead of spending my summer working, working, and then working some more. Sometimes I thought, is this how it's going to be for the rest of my life – just a couple of weeks off a year and the rest of the time slogging my guts out for other people? Some of my friends were going to Zante to celebrate finishing their AS-levels. They'd asked me if I wanted to come, but I was halfway through my diploma and couldn't've afforded it anyway. We didn't seem to have so much in common any more. When they moaned about school, I just thought they had it easy. I wasn't much of a party girl these days. Must be living with Edith – it was ageing me.

When I got up onto street level I saw I'd got a text from Jo.

Can you meet me in The Albion after work? I'll be there from 6.30 xx. Followed by an emoji of praying hands.

I was tired, hot and sweaty, my feet hurt. All I wanted was pizza and Netflix. But the Albion was only a short walk from Highbury Corner and I guessed Jo wanted to talk to me in private about what'd happened last Saturday. I felt a bit sorry for her to be honest. I'd hardly seen her all week. She must've been dying of embarrassment – I would be.

Paul would tell me to get on it straightaway. He said we needed to persuade her to leave – to go back to Italy, or better still some yoga commune in Thailand or India where she'd be out of contact. He had an idea about how to get Edith to pay for it.

Be with you in 5, I texted back with a smiley face.

The Albion was covered in that same plant Edith has round the back of hers – like ivy only with purple flowers that look a bit like bunches of grapes. It grew all over a frame over the patio at the back, shading the tables. Reminded me of this island scene painted on the wall of the pizza restaurant in Palmers Green. So when you sat down to have a pizza you felt like you was sitting on a veranda, looking out over a blue sea – like you could reach out and pick a grape if you wanted. At least that was the idea, I guess.

The place was packed. I spotted Jo sitting at the sunny end of a long wooden table with a space saved beside her. Hadn't bothered getting me a drink in though. I waved to her and pointed inside, miming raising a glass to my lips. She nodded enthusiastically, lifting her half empty glass and mouthing, 'White, Pinot Grigio, large.'

She'd finished her drink by the time I got outside again.

'Thank you, sweet friend,' she said, like she was surprised, as I put a new one down in front of her.

She was smoking a rollie – not very health-conscious. I was tempted to ask her for one but reminded myself that I'd given up and didn't want to get a taste for them again. I squeezed onto the end of the bench, beside a group of women, early forties, wearing statement jewellery and neutral linens in taupe and slate. They were discussing their holiday plans.

'You've got to have a villa with a pool. What will you do with the kids otherwise?'

I seriously considered asking that woman to adopt me, or maybe she needed an au pair?

Jo exhaled smoke carefully over her shoulder, not noticing that the breeze brought it straight back over my way. One of the linen ladies gave her a dirty look.

'So, I thought it would be really lovely to meet outside the house for once. Just the two of us.'

She gave me a big smile. She was wearing a floaty pink kaftan style top over a white vest. Showed off her tan nicely, and her biceps. I had to give it to her – all that yoga was paying off – she was well fit. It was only the lines round her mouth and eyes gave her age away. She could get some dermal filler on those – smooth them out.

'Sure,' I said, tearing into a packet of peanuts. I was starving.

'Here we are, fellow students, both on journeys to help others realise their best possible selves.' She was doing her nodding thing again. 'You may only be working on the outside, but that's precious too.' She waved her rollie in the air and her silver bangles slid down her arm, clanking together at her elbow. 'How's your course going?'

'All right. I was working on the counter today though.' I swallowed a mouthful of vodka and lime. It was tangy and refreshing, cooling my throat as it went down. 'Didn't reach my target again this week so I got a bollocking from my manager.

I only needed to make two more sales – if I could just have persuaded that woman to buy the Midnight Mocha lipstick.' I sighed. 'She must've tried every colour we have. Didn't take any of them.'

'A really beautiful thing to do, when you feel like the universe is against you, is to offer up a prayer of gratitude. So you repeat this mantra, focusing on your manager, for example.' Jo closed her eyes and held the palm of her right hand flat against her left tit. "'I'm Sorry. Please Forgive Me. Thank You. I Love You.' It might feel hard to do at first, and it can open up some really deep emotions so you have to be careful, but it is deliciously healing.' She looked at me expectantly.

I put both my hands up, surrender-style. 'I'm sorry, please forgive me, but the woman's a bitch, the sales targets are impossible to reach – everyone says so – and she has some personal vendetta against me. Don't know why, but she's always picking on me.'

Jo just smiled at me in this really condescending way.

'I hear you my friend, believe me. I know how hard it is to let go of that negative energy, but the release when you do is so sweet.'

She threw her head back, stretching her arms out behind her, like someone off an ad for vitamin tablets or a low-fat spread. I was tempted to ask her if she'd offered that prayer to her mum, but chickened out and asked her how the yoga course was going.

'The teacher's amazing, really, very disciplined, but literally enlightened – an inspiration. She's actually German, but very chilled – spent a long time in India studying under some incredible teachers.'

She dropped her fag butt on the patchy yellow grass and ground it out under her sandal. This was my chance to suggest the whole India thing, but I was too slow off the mark, she got in there first.

'So, there's a strange thing I wanted to ask you about.' She leant forward, tucking her hair behind her ears like she meant business. 'I was using Mum's iPad to check out TripAdvisor. I wanted to see how Casale Alfredo's been doing without me. Its ratings are better than I expected.' She gave a little snort. 'Anyway, eBay came up on the browser.'

She twisted one of her rings round and round on her finger. I held my breath, waiting for what she was going to say next.

'It went straight to a silver cigarette case, exactly the same as one Dad used to have. It even had his old regiment's badge on it. Whoever's selling it is asking for £80.'

My heart was thumping so loudly I thought she'd hear it.

'I showed it to Mum, but she didn't know anything about it. She said she hadn't seen the case in years. Dad gave up smoking in his sixties, but I remember him keeping it on his desk.'

I smiled and nodded like Jo does, opening my eyes as wide as I could in what I hoped was a look of pure innocence. Felt like my eyeballs might burst out of their sockets.

'Oh that, yeah, Edith told me about it the other day. She was trying to remember what it looked like so I Googled it for her.' I felt like such a shit.

'Why was she talking about Dad's cigarette case?'

'We were talking about smoking. I said how I used to smoke a bit. She was surprised anyone my age smokes, with what we know about the health effects now. She's a bit worried about you smoking, to be honest. But she did say she smoked, back in the day, her and Forb – your dad.'

That was all true – we had had that conversation. 'She said how it seemed very glamorous back then. That's when she started talking about the cigarette case.' That last bit wasn't true. 'I was thinking I could get one as a present for her, because she said she'd lost his old one, but then I saw the price...' What the fuck was I saying?

'Mum's very anti-smoking now, the last thing she'd want is a cigarette case that looked like Dad's.' Jo stared at me for a while, like she was weighing up what I'd said.

I forced out a laugh. 'Dunno what I was thinking.'

That was true. How could I've been so stupid? Jo seemed so airy-fairy I never thought she'd go on the iPad. My phone had run out and I'd needed to check the bids. Paul could easily have seen it too. I had to be more careful.

'I wanted to get her something for her birthday – she was saying how she was dreading it, another year closer to death and all that. Then she started saying how she just wanted to die anyway, her life was over, what was the point.' I picked at my nails. Edith did keep saying things like that. 'I wanted to cheer her up with something special.'

'God, I'd forgotten her birthday's coming up. What's the date?' Jo checked her phone. 'It was a nice thought, Lauren – sweet of you – but, yeah, not really the right gift for Mum.'

She carried on looking at her phone and I couldn't tell if she believed me for real or was just pretending, to see what I'd say next. I took another gulp of my drink. The ice had melted and it tasted kind of watery now.

'The way she keeps going on about wishing she was dead, I just thought, she might as well take up smoking again.' I was really scraping the barrel.

'Hmmm.' Jo gave me a funny look. 'I was a bit concerned that she might have asked you to help her sell stuff, like family heirlooms and things – which would be a dreadful mistake.' She lowered her voice. 'Has Mum ever mentioned anything to you about her finances? Savings, shares, that sort of thing?'

I suddenly needed to wee, very badly. Should I tell Jo that

Edith had given Paul power of attorney? She was going to find out sooner or later – it wasn't like Edith kept it secret. I tried to think like Paul, to work out what he'd say, but it wasn't easy to know what was going on in Paul's mind.

'She doesn't really talk to me about stuff like that. Paul's the one to ask,' I added lamely.

'That makes sense.' Jo drummed her fingers on the table. 'If she ever does though, I'd really love it if you could tell me, as quickly as possible.'

'Of course.' I nodded. And there was me thinking she wanted to talk about her and Paul. Fuck, but I'd got that wrong.

'Have you been to Corsica?' The woman next to me leant across the table, topping up her friends' glasses from a fresh bottle of wine. The liquid glowed a golden rosy-pink in the evening light.

'D'you want another drink?' I asked Jo.

'Since you're offering.' She handed me her empty glass.

Yeah, I thought, I could die of thirst before you got a round in.

I went to the toilet first. I needed a moment to think. I was playing this all wrong. Why'd I go and tell her to ask Paul about the finances? What if she told him about the cigarette case on eBay? Whatever happened I mustn't forget to erase the browsing history off the iPad as soon as I got home.

Jo was on her phone when I got back outside. I wondered who she was talking to. For a paranoid moment I thought it might be Paul, or the police – to come and arrest me for stealing. I nearly walked straight out of the pub garden. I could go to Sam's – no one had her address. I could run away to Zante with her. But Jo was smiling over at me in a friendly way and rolling her eyes at her phone like it was someone annoying.

She mouthed 'thank you' as I set the drinks down. I'd gone

for a glass of rosé this time – it looked so pretty. By the time she finally finished with her phone call I'd drunk half of it. From what I could make out it was just someone off her yoga course.

She turned to me looking serious. 'When I first arrived you told me about Mum's confused mental state, and I've seen it for myself now – her forgetfulness, muddle etc. We have to face the fact that her condition is only going to get worse. As much as we'd love her to stay at home, that's not going to be the best place for her. Eventually she will need residential care.'

'That's a long way off though. She isn't that bad yet.'

I was relieved we'd got off the topic of selling stuff. And Jo focusing on Edith's fuzzy mind was just what we wanted, but still I couldn't help feeling guilty. Trouble was, me and Paul were in a bind. We couldn't have Edith moving out, but we didn't want nurses coming in either. It was bad enough with Jo poking her nose into everything.

'There's been a lot of stuff in the news lately about what goes on in nursing homes. It's not nice,' I said. But I don't think Jo heard me.

The linen ladies' laughter was getting more raucous. It was distracting. I needed to focus.

Jo coiled her hair into a rope and wound it round her hand. 'Mum could go downhill very rapidly. You're wonderful with her, but you're not a professional nurse. I don't want to leave it too late. It would be really sad if she didn't get to choose where she goes.'

I thought of Edith sitting in her wet bed, clutching my hands and begging me not to tell Jo. Made me want to cry to see how scared she was of her own daughter.

'Edith definitely wouldn't choose to go into a home.'

Jo sighed and put her hand on mine. 'I know you care about Mum, it really would be in her best interests if you can encourage her to change her mind. I've shown her some beautiful places she could move to. Maybe you'd like to take a look at them with her. You know – be really positive about them.'

'OK,' I said slowly.

Jo had a way of asking questions that made them feel more like orders. What did she want to get rid of her mum for anyway? There was plenty of room there for the two of them. I might have my differences with my mum, but I'd never treat her like that.

Jo rapped her rings on the table. 'She needs to think about selling the house. It's time.'

Startled, I looked straight into her blue eyes and it hit me for the first time that for all I knew they might be more like Forbes' than Edith's.

'Where will you go if Edith sells the house?'

Jo looked surprised. 'Me? Well, I'd get a place of my own – a flat or something. Long-term I want to move back to Italy.'

She stared around the pub garden. When she turned back to me, her expression had changed. She looked like she'd found dog shit on her yoga mat. Her lip curled.

'I can't stand this country.'

EDITH

THE DOORBELL WOKE ME from a nap – gave me quite a start.

'Who is it?' I called from the hall.

I don't like answering the door to strangers when I'm alone in the house.

'It's Bob, Edith,' he shouted through the letterbox.

'Goodness,' I said, opening the door. 'I wasn't expecting you. Was I?'

'No, no.' He smiled. 'I came up to town to meet my son for lunch at St. John's, Clerkenwell. It's only up the road and I thought, why not pop in on Edith, see how she's doing?' He pressed a bunch of yellow tulips into my hand.

I stood aside to let him in. Squeezing into the hallway, he kissed me on the cheek. Beneath the bristles of his moustache his lips were wet. His breath smelt of alcohol and onions.

'If you'd given me some advance warning I'd have got a cake, or scones, or something.'

Bob patted his football of a stomach. 'Just had a tremendous meal. Lamb's tongue, followed by tripe, and then a slab of bread pudding. Took me back to my childhood.'

'Goodness, rather you than me. I assume you didn't drink red wine as a boy.'

Bob's lips were stained claret red and his cheeks were flushed. He chuckled.

'You've got me there. We were celebrating. Richard's just set up his own financial consultancy.'

'Good for him,' I said, though I wasn't entirely sure what a financial consultancy was. 'Would you like a cup of tea?'

'Tea would be most welcome.'

Bob ambled beside me as I made my slow progress into the kitchen. He didn't refer to my walking frame, for which I was grateful.

'Poppy and Alice are both at City of London Girls' now. Caroline off jet-setting as usual.'

'What is it she does again?' I unwrapped the tulips. 'Could you fetch that vase for me? From the shelf, there.'

'She's a headhunter, as in, finds the right person for the right job. Not like the pygmies of Borneo.'

Bob laughed again. He seemed nervous. I couldn't think why – we'd known each other for years. After he and Graham retired from the Ministry of Defence, the four of us used to play bridge together regularly. Graham sometimes poked fun at him. He was an earnest chap and I suspected he'd always had a bit of a soft spot for me, though he was far too loyal, to both our spouses, ever to act on it.

I placed the vase of tulips on the kitchen table.

'Joanna's come to stay.'

'Must be nice to have her here. Looking after you, is she?'

'Not exactly.'

I told him, over tea, all about Joanna; her drug addiction, her erratic behaviour, her pressuring me to sell the house. I didn't hold back out of pride, as I might have done when Heather was alive. Heather was always boasting about their multiplying grandchildren. She'd insist on bringing out photographs of the two girls from Richard and the three from Alistair. As though I wanted to know about their every achievement and each milestone they reached. But I had seen Bob in the depths of grief, as he had me, and it had created a bond between us.

It occurred to me suddenly that since Bob had been the executor of Graham's will, he was just the person to help me change mine. If Joanna kicked up a fuss he could explain it to her, prove that I was in my right mind. Not that she was supposed to care about money or possessions.

Bob took out a grubby-looking handkerchief and blew his nose. He rooted about in his nostrils before scrunching it up and shoving it back in his pocket. A glossy blob of congealed egg yolk stuck to his tie like a badge. Hopefully it was from that morning's breakfast and not yesterday's, or last week's.

'Downsizing isn't a bad idea though, Edith. You could move to my neck of the woods. Nice and peaceful there. I know all my neighbours. London isn't what it was. It's overcrowded and it isn't safe. I wouldn't risk taking the tube, not now.'

'Selborne may be delightful, but I've no intention of moving to Hampshire or anywhere else. I have decided however, to leave everything – the value of the house, all our assets – to charity.'

Bob's unkempt eyebrows drew together in what I knew to be an expression of concern.

'That's very generous, but, wouldn't it be better just to make a donation?'

I shook my head. I wasn't going to let him talk me out of it.

'It's a course I decided on recently, prompted by a friend, and

I feel very strongly it's the right thing to do. It would be a legacy from Graham and myself, a way of ensuring our name lives on. There's a small, independent charity I have a strong personal connection to. I can vouch for them and I know they'll honour my instructions.'

'Fair enough, you've obviously thought about it.' He brushed his fingertips over his moustache. 'Can't think what my lot would say if I cut them out of my will.'

I was pleased he understood. 'More tea?'

He held up a hand. 'Must visit your amenities. The old bladder's not what it used to be.'

He pushed himself up from the table, exiting the kitchen with large strides. He was surprisingly agile for his age and build. It was probably all the golf he played that kept him fit, and of course he was several years younger than Graham.

When he returned he sat down anxiously on the edge of his seat, pressing his hands between his knees.

'I've always been indebted to you, Edith, for the kindness you showed me during and after Heather's last illness.'

I waved a hand. 'You were a brick to me when Graham died. I couldn't have managed without you.'

He didn't respond. He just sat there looking awkward. For a horrible moment I thought he was about to propose. I'd spent enough years looking after an elderly man. I didn't want to acquire a new one.

'Why don't we have something a bit stronger?' He held up his teacup.

'All right,' I said cautiously. 'How about a Scotch?'

'That would be just the ticket.'

I was relieved he hadn't suggested champagne. Not that I had any. We moved into the sitting room and I fixed us each a drink.

'Since you're planning to change your will I imagine you'll want to look into your finances. Graham's will was straightforward because he left everything to you, and I don't recall you ever making any enquiries about his investments.' Bob cleared his throat. 'So, I don't want it to come as a shock if you discover that he cashed in a couple of ISAs. What I mean is, there may be a bit less there than you expect.'

'I'm sure it's all in order, Bob.'

I was about to explain that Paul, who was quite an expert in these matters, had been looking after my financial affairs, when Bob interrupted me.

'Graham made quite a considerable payment some years ago. He told me about it in confidence, late one night at the club. You know how it is, we'd both had a bit to drink. I would never have kept it from you otherwise. It's been weighing on my mind, and really, I think you ought to know.'

I tried to tell him that no, there was nothing I needed or wanted to know, but Bob ploughed on, as if now he'd released the brakes he couldn't stop.

'Must have been about eight years ago, Graham received a letter from some chap claiming to be his son. I thought the whole thing terribly far-fetched, but he knew enough to convince Graham. Turns out he was the result of a fling Graham had with a native girl in Kenya. Before he met you of course.'

He leant forward as if to take my hand. I pushed myself back in my chair, out of reach. None of what he was saying made any sense. Graham only had one child: Joanna.

Bob continued, speaking in a rapid, apologetic tone. 'It was all a bit tricky, not only because of the colour bar, but she'd been his prisoner, a detainee during the Mau Mau uprising. Graham was a young man at the time, out in the tropics. You know how it is. She seduced him in the hope of favours, an early release, then, when she discovered she was pregnant, accused him of rape. Went as far as making an official complaint. It was dismissed of course. Graham never expected to hear from her again. But then this man turns up. Graham didn't want him upsetting you. He had to make a few payments to resolve the situation.'

I'd drunk too much tea. I could feel the weight of it in my stomach, turning cold. I took another mouthful of Scotch.

'I thought of telling you after Graham passed away, but it seemed unnecessary, and unkind. Especially after all that unpleasant business with those complainants and lawyers and what not.' Bob studied the liquid at the bottom of his glass. 'But it's been preying on my mind that he might have seen the obituaries, or that feature on *Newsnight*, and decide to look you up; to call or write. What a terrible shock that would be for you.'

He looked up at me almost fearfully, as though he expected me to collapse in a fit of hysterics. He was wrong. It was as though his words were a wall of water cascading past me. If I kept very still and very quiet they would wash away into nothing. I closed my eyes for a moment. An inappropriate but overwhelming desire to sleep came over me.

Bob carried on regardless and I felt compelled to open my eyes again. 'Anyway, we used our contacts in the Home Office to get the chap deported. He'd first come into the UK as a child on his mother's passport. Never got himself a British passport, can you believe it? And she never renewed hers. Had nothing to prove his right to remain here.' Bob was breathing heavily. 'Graham made sure he'd never get clearance to re-enter the UK. That didn't come cheap. Had to grease a few palms.' He dabbed at the perspiration on his forehead with his dirty handkerchief. If he wasn't careful he'd end up with a smear of snot on his face. 'The mother was the chap's weak spot though. We told him we could get her deported as well if he didn't stay in Africa and keep a low profile. I've had a little poke around and discovered she's deceased now, died last year, so we can't hold that over him any longer. If he does try to contact you, let me know immediately. I can still make life difficult for him.'

I was still struggling to comprehend what Bob was telling me. 'But, if Graham really was his father then surely that makes him a British citizen?'

Bob looked a bit taken aback. 'He'd nothing to prove it. No birth certificate or any documentation like that, and Graham certainly wasn't going to endorse his claim.' Bob topped up both our glasses. 'Graham kept tabs on the fellow for the first few months. But he lost all contact with him after the Kenyan elections in 2007. You might recall the terrible violence that erupted after the president rigged the results. It ended up with well over a thousand dead. A lot of the bloodshed took place in the Rift Valley, which is where Graham's son was living. It was also initially directed against Kikuyus, which was his tribe.' Bob winced. 'It is possible he was killed.' He cleared his throat. 'On the other hand, he might have gone to ground. You know, chosen to disappear and start a new life somewhere else.'

It was a relief when Bob finally left. I was glad the girls were out too. I couldn't cope with company. I just needed to sit and think. The worst thing was the inevitability of it all. It was as if I'd been waiting for this revelation my entire married life. Anticipating the skeleton in the cupboard. I couldn't say why. I just knew there were things about himself Graham held back. Aspects of his life he didn't want to disclose.

I concentrated on the old school photograph of Joanna that stood on the mantelpiece, longing for it to bring me some comfort, some strength. Joanna was in her uniform, her long hair tied back in a ponytail, the school crest clearly visible on her blazer pocket. Her cheeks were round and rosy as apples and her beaming smile distracted one from noticing the spots on her nose. She looked happy and proud; her team had just won the school's hockey tournament. She must have been around fourteen. A year later she and her friend Ottie had chopped each other's hair off and pierced their ears. She stomped about in ripped jeans and those ugly Doctor Marten boots. I don't think I ever saw her smile so beautifully, so innocently, again.

I'd known white men in Kenya who thought African women fair game. Graham had never shown the slightest interest. Not in front of me, anyhow. I remembered the house parties my parents had hosted: the Europeans, smashed out of their minds, groping and fondling each other while our houseboys looked on. African men might have several wives and even mistresses, but I had never seen Africans behave with the sexual abandon of the settlers. That was one of the things that had drawn me to Graham – his self-control, his moral restraint. I suppose, after a while, I realised how hard he had to work to maintain it. He never let his guard down, not even with me.

I wondered if he'd ever seen the baby. Why hadn't he felt able to confide in me? Was it because of my miscarriages? I wouldn't have objected if he'd wanted to send money for its upkeep. Perhaps he never really considered the child his.

And then it came back to me. The stranger at the door.

We had been watching *Foyles War* on television one evening when the doorbell rang long and hard. Graham answered it. I could hear him talking to someone. He was gone so long I had to turn off the television. I remember being annoyed by the interruption.

I was about to investigate when Graham returned to the sitting room followed by a middle-aged coloured man. At first I assumed he'd come to read the meter, but then Graham said they had something to discuss and would be going into his study. I couldn't imagine what they had to talk about. The man didn't look like a civil servant and certainly wasn't a friend. He wore a thick grey anorak which hung open to reveal a very homely-looking fawn sweater, the sort of thing that might have been knitted for him. Funny the things that stick in one's mind. Now I wish I could remember him more clearly, but his face is just a blur. His skin was a caramel colour, I think. So it's feasible he was of mixed parentage.

After a while I heard raised voices. I went out to the hall to listen.

The man was talking. 'For her, it's a sin not to be able to forgive. It's a weight on her soul. Repent and she can forgive you.'

I thought the man must be a Jehovah's Witness or something. I was actually worried that after years of agnosticism Graham might be turning religious. Their conversation had continued in a low murmur.

Then the man shouted, 'I'll make sure you get done before you die. Expose you for what you are. You don't have immunity any more, we're not your colonial subjects. I know a law firm taking action against British officials like you – men who carried out acts of torture. I've been in contact with a journalist. She's very interested in my story.'

I'd felt quite sick. Perhaps he was a terrorist. He clearly had some sort of Marxist agenda. How quickly could I grab the poker from beside the fire? I might be able to hit him with enough force to knock him out. I still played tennis back then – I had a good backhand.

The door burst open and the man strode out of the room. I shrank back against the wall, but he didn't even look at me; just marched out of the house, slamming the front door behind him. Graham made his way slowly out into the hall. It was disturbing to see how bowed and frail he looked.

I put one hand on Graham's arm. 'Who on earth was that?'

Graham shuffled past me, back towards the sitting room, allowing my hand to slide off his arm. 'Just some misguided idiot blowing a lot of hot air.'

At the time, Graham said the man had claimed to be a journalist but was actually an activist with a vendetta against the British Army. I was so worried about Graham's health I didn't question him any further. But he had lied to me.

Graham was always very protective of me. As Bob said, he didn't want to upset me. That was all. I only wish he'd leant on me a little more. That he'd given me credit for being resilient enough to cope with knowing he had an illegitimate African child. If it hadn't been so acrimonious between them I would have liked to meet his son properly. But his mother must have turned him against Graham. Some women are bitter like that. If she was vindictive or mercenary enough to accuse Graham of rape she clearly had no moral scruples.

Graham must have taken his son's threats very seriously to have him deported. And I did remember the terrible violence that engulfed Kenya in around 2007 because Graham had taken such an interest in it. He got uncharacteristically worked up about it. Now I understood why.

I refused Joanna and Lauren's attempts to put me to bed that night. I told them I was more comfortable in my armchair. But the truth was I couldn't face my bedroom, couldn't face my bed, or waking up to whatever form Mary had decided to take that night. It was all very well telling myself they were just dreams; as soon as darkness fell and I faced the night alone my courage deserted me. Mary wouldn't give up, I remembered that much about her: she was stubborn. Now she'd found me, she'd hound me into my grave.

KENYA, 1957

IT WAS THE OTHER WOMEN who noticed Charity was pregnant. She refused to believe them at first. The thought of carrying Forbes' child was too disgusting to contemplate. She didn't expect the baby to survive the long days carrying slop buckets to the dump. Being made to run so the stinking brown liquid overflowed, dripping down her neck, into her eyes. The flies following, buzzing at the shit on her face.

Few babies survived in the camp. Their little bodies were tossed into the burial pits with the men who'd been hanged and the prisoners who'd died of disease, or beatings, or just exhaustion. Charity hoped Forbes' baby would end up there too. She wouldn't wail and beat her chest like the grieving mothers did. She just prayed it wouldn't kill her as well.

Sometimes she was seized with terror that she would die in childbirth and never see her parents or her brother again – never get home. She too would be tossed into the burial pit without absolution or funeral rites, her soul left to haunt the camp for eternity. If that happened she would haunt Forbes. She would make sure he suffered as she had done. Though she knew it was sinful, the prospect of revenge helped quell her fears. It was what kept her going through the daily torment.

When the pains in her belly started she thought at first it was going to be another bout of diarrhoea. She'd been sick so many times since being imprisoned it had become part of daily life. But by evening the cramps were squeezing her middle so tightly she dropped to her knees. She swayed on all fours, the surges of pain dictating her movements, making her bellow like a cow being slaughtered. She no longer cared if she died in childbirth, she just wanted to be released from the creature Forbes had forced on her. The creature was like a huge rock being driven through her bowels, splitting her body in two.

Charity was vaguely aware of the other women in their tent moving outside to give her some privacy, while Sarah and Wanjiku massaged her belly and back, singing to her to be strong; soon she would be delivered. Their voices carried her on through the surges of pain, encouraging, exhorting, as she kicked out in anger and cried for her mother. They held her up when she wanted to move, supporting her shoulders as she squatted. At last the rock was passed.

'It's a boy!' Wanjiku cried.

Charity heard the cry of a baby. But why wasn't the labour over? She was consumed by a mixture of anguish and outrage as the pains continued unabated.

'The placenta needs to come out,' Sarah told her, but she couldn't understand what the woman was saying. She tried to fight off Sarah's hands as they pressed down on her belly.

When the pains finally ceased she felt a gush of hot liquid between her thighs. In the dim light she saw it was blood seeping into the mud around her feet.

'Don't worry, that's normal.' Sarah lay her down on her bed, binding her up with strips of canvas ripped from the side of the tent. 'We'll bury the placenta correctly,' she whispered.

Charity didn't care what they did with it. There was no place in the camp free from evil.

They said she was fortunate – the labour only lasted a few hours. That didn't lessen the agony.

The women congratulated her on giving birth to a boy. They wanted to celebrate this new life. To remember what their old lives had been, when every safe delivery was a gift and motherhood a normal part of their existence. Sarah tried to place the baby on Charity's breast, but she turned her face away and refused to look at him.

'This baby is yours and yours only. Are you going to let him die?' Sarah asked her.

Wanjiku, kneeling beside her, scraped up a handful of earth from the dirt floor, smelt it and took a little into her mouth. 'The soil is ours,' she said, her dark brown eyes fixed on Charity's face. She pressed a little earth with the tip of her finger onto the baby's forehead. 'The soil is his, as he is yours.'

The baby's thin body was covered in blood. His red face wrinkled up and he let out a pitiful mewing. Charity watched as Sarah wrapped him in a torn corner of blanket. She understood what the women were telling her, that to abandon this child of her womb would be to let Forbes win. Here was a reason to survive, to speak. She should keep her son and teach him to fight for a free Kenya, but she didn't have the strength to care for him, or any mercy left to love him. All she could feel was the hot, sticky blood leaking out of her battered body.

Mrs Eastfield came into the tent carrying a torch. Her pink face went grey when she saw the baby's pale skin. Charity waited for her to ask which of the white officers had fathered this yellow child, but she just walked away from Charity's bed, her mouth a thin, straight line.

Charity was only half-conscious when she became aware of Forbes standing over her bed. She heard Mrs Eastfield behind him, her voice low and urgent. 'Number 6725 needs medical attention. She's losing so much blood, I think she's haemorrhaging.'

'All right.' Forbes voice hovered in the air above her. 'I'll call the hospital, get her and the child admitted. There's no reason why they shouldn't take her in. She doesn't pose a security risk to the other patients.'

When Charity woke up in a hospital bed with clean white sheets, she thought she'd been transported to heaven. The sun was coming in through a big glass window and the baby was sleeping in a cot by her side. A nurse was holding her wrist and counting.

'Welcome back,' the nurse said in Kiswahili.

Charity didn't remember being there before.

'I'm going to give you a bed bath,' the nurse smiled at her. 'And I've brought you in a nightdress.' She held up a buttercup yellow nightgown. Charity thought it was the prettiest thing she'd ever seen.

The nurse used carbolic soap and warm water to wash her; wiping away the dirt and blood of the camp with firm, steady strokes. Charity felt as though her body were being returned to her.

Afterwards, the nurse sat down on a chair by the bed, pulling it in close to Charity's pillow. 'I've told the commandant you are not well enough to be returned to prison,' she said quietly. 'How old are you?'

Charity could feel the milk leaking from her swollen breasts onto the yellow nightgown.

'Don't worry about that,' the nurse said, handing her a cloth. 'My name is Olerai. I'll be back later to check on you.' She patted Charity's arm before moving on to other patients.

Charity rolled onto her side to look at the baby. Damp curls of black hair framed his tiny face. Miniature fists were clenched beneath a round chin. He reminded her of her youngest cousin. He didn't look evil. He didn't look like Forbes. He looked fragile, delicate. A new-born soul in need of protection.

A week later she was sent to join her parents in the village they had been moved to. Nurse Olerai told her, with a questioning look, that the commandant had arranged for a taxi to drive her there. This news only alarmed her. Was he really going to let her go? Perhaps Forbes had paid to have her taken out into the forest and shot, or to some place where he could rape her again.

The driver was a fat, surly man who remained as resolutely silent as she was mute. He was probably a loyalist who assumed she was Mau Mau and hated her for it. Charity ignored the grizzling of the baby and stared anxiously out of the window, searching for familiar landmarks. Only after they had been driving for over an hour did she begin to relax a little, allowing herself to anticipate being reunited with her parents. Her longing to see them was diluted with fear at how they would react to the baby. Would they be disgusted by her for having a child? How could she explain to them what she had suffered, the horrors she had witnessed?

She let herself imagine the food her mother would cook for her; celebratory goat meat, roast sweet potatoes and black beans. Her tongue tingled at the thought of ripe green bananas, sugarcane and golden honey.

To access the village, they had to go through a fortified Home Guard post that looked little different to the prison. An armed guard looked down at them from a wooden watchtower. A British flag hung limply from a post. Once over the drawbridge, the taxi driver spoke briefly to one of the guards, showing his papers and hers. The gates were opened and the driver stopped the car just long enough for her to climb out, clutching the baby awkwardly to her chest. She was taken into the Chief's office.

Chief Githuku was a large, imposing-looking man. He wore a khaki jacket beneath the blanket tossed over his broad shoulders. He glanced at her papers, which the guard had placed on the desk in front of him. 'Ah yes, I had a phone call about you this morning.' He looked up her up and down. 'Your parents are decent people. I hope you've been sufficiently rehabilitated and won't cause any trouble here.'

Charity just nodded. The baby had started to cry and her breasts were leaking in response. Wet patches were spreading out across the blouse Olerai had given her.

The chief didn't appear to notice. 'Don't think that baby will get you out of the public works. Everyone around here has to pull their weight.' He turned to the guard. 'Take her through.'

Released into the enclosed village without any further directions, she walked hurriedly; too impatient to find her parents to stop and feed the screaming baby. The place seemed deserted. Only a few children, with swollen bellies and emaciated limbs, played unattended in the dirt outside small mud huts. There were no adults to be seen.

As she was approaching a group of larger huts with corrugated iron roofs, a woman emerged carrying an orange and red sisal basket. The woman's head, covered by a calico scarf, was turned away from her, but Charity recognised the forward tilt of her neck and the self-assured way she swung the *kiondo* over her shoulder in one deft movement.

'Mama!' Charity's voice forced its way back up and out of her constricted throat.

She ran to her mother, forgetting for a second the baby clamped to her chest, so that he slid down to her hip before she caught him up again. The shock stopped his crying for a moment.

Her mother staggered as she held out her arms, the empty basket dangling like an oversized sleeve. They clutched each other, weeping, the baby cocooned between them. Charity wasn't sure who was holding up who, she only knew she was home at last, safe in her mother's embrace. She pressed her face into her mother's soft neck, inhaling her familiar smell of wood smoke and castor oil.

'Nduta?' Charity's father called to his wife from within the hut. Then Charity felt his arms too, wrapped tightly round her and heard his broken voice repeating, 'My girl, my little girl, is it you?'

When they released each other, her father stared with ashy-faced horror at the baby.

Her mother wiped her wet cheeks with the palms of her hands. 'Let's go inside,' she said briskly. 'I was about to go to our farm to see what was ripe for picking, but there is some sour porridge to drink.' She pulled on her husband's arm as he stood, unable to move. 'Come on, Joshua.'

It was hardly the feast Charity had been anticipating. She followed her mother inside. It was strange to see the familiar objects from home in this new setting. The hut wasn't as spacious or pleasant as their old house, but it was palatial in comparison to the tent she'd spent the last year in.

'We thought they'd let us stay at home, but everyone in the area was forced to move here.' Her mother sounded apologetic.

'Even those of us who'd refused to have anything to do with the terrorists and their oaths.' She let out a heavy sigh. 'Some of the neighbours are suspicious of us. They're jealous because we got a better house.' She looked with concern at Charity, adding quickly, 'But, you know, we all get along as best we can.'

Charity was shocked by how much her parents, but especially her mother, had aged over the year they'd been apart. Mama's skin no longer glowed with silky plumpness. Knotted veins stood out on her legs and her feet and hands were as cracked and calloused as Charity's. Her beautiful face had gained lines, drawing the corners of her eyes and mouth down into uncharacteristic sombreness. Her eyelids drooped over eyes that had once shone with vivacity. But when she smiled at her, Charity caught a glimpse of the warmth and humour she treasured so much in her mother.

The baby still needed feeding but Charity felt embarrassed to let her father see the obvious maternal connection, even though it was clear he'd already assumed it. Her mother, picking up on her discomfort, draped a *kanga* over Charity's shoulders and placed herself as a screen between Charity and her father. At first the baby cried in frustration, twisting his head blindly from side to side as Charity struggled to latch him onto her breast. She was too tense for the milk to flow easily. With one arm around Charity's shoulders, her mother lifted the baby's head, angling it so that he could suck properly. Charity leant back into her mother's arms and they both watched with satisfaction the tiny red mouth sucking greedily, the little cheeks puffing in and out. Charity closed her eyes in relief as the pressure in her engorged breasts was finally alleviated.

Once the baby was sleeping contentedly, wrapped up out of sight, Baba leant forward impatiently. 'But you must tell us what happened to you.'

Her mother looked at her with a mixture of sorrow and encouragement.

So she explained to her parents how she'd been arrested on her way back to school. How she had tried to get letters to them. How all her protestations of innocence had fallen on deaf ears. She didn't tell them about Githii or Forbes or the horrors of the prison camp.

Her father said he too had tried desperately to find her, pleading for information at all the police stations and guard posts in Nairobi and Kiambu. He'd written several times to the District Commissioner. Her headmistress had also made numerous enquiries. There were too many people in detention. Charity had been lost in the pipeline.

None of them referred to the baby or how it had come into being.

Over the next few days, Charity discovered that, rather than coming to a safe haven, she had simply been sent into another form of incarceration. Only in this one she was protected by her parents and their acknowledged refusal to take the Mau Mau oath. Her father, who had been a teacher in the local primary school, was on friendly terms with Chief Githuku and was allowed into the Home Guard compound to teach the children of the loyalists. This earnt them certain favours.

When the Oxfam volunteers came to the camp with supplies for the starving women and children (for most of the men were in detention), only those known to be loyal to the British Crown were given the powdered milk, sugar and tea that was handed out.

Charity was even invited to come to childcare classes.

'You can enter our cleanest baby competition,' a white Homecraft officer told her, smiling eagerly.

When Charity declined the woman looked affronted. 'I see

what you mean,' she said to her companion. 'They lack the three Ps.' She turned back to Charity, continuing pointedly, 'pride in yourself, your home and your children.'

Charity didn't bother trying to explain that she couldn't attend the class because her days were spent on enforced communal labour. This was similar to the work she'd first had to do in prison, only this time they were building an actual road. She wasn't given any exemption for having a new-born baby; he had to be carried with her and fed as she worked. If they paused at all the guards beat them with sticks. Once they'd finished the day's work, the women hurried to their small plots of land to salvage the vegetables and fruit they'd planted, before nightfall and curfew sent them rushing home again. Everyone was permanently exhausted.

Charity noticed another woman with a *nusu-nusu* baby. She handled the baby roughly, leaving it mostly to the care of its brothers and sisters. Charity, on the other hand, was growing increasingly attached to her child. It was as though she had given birth to that innocent part of her that had been destroyed by Forbes. A part so fragile and tender she must protect and watch over it constantly to keep it from harm. Her mother, too, was taken with the baby, cradling him in her arms and singing to him whenever Charity would let her. This wasn't often, as Charity panicked, becoming unable to speak or breathe whenever she was separated from him.

Mama followed her gaze, alighting on the half-blood child. 'A lot of women here have been abused by the Johnnies and by the Home Guard.' She traced a circle in the dust with her foot. 'Some mothers tried smearing their daughters with soot and animal dung to make them unattractive, but they took them anyway. If the girls refuse, they do such terrible things to them, many die.' She stared at the pattern she had made in the earth.

'It's as if these men have lost their minds. They can do whatever they want and they've turned into monsters.' Tears ran down Mama's face. 'I can't bear to think of what's been done to you.'

Charity looked down at the baby. She'd wondered why Forbes hadn't let them die to hide the evidence of his crimes. Once he'd told her it was a government decision, to impregnate her with a white child and make the Mau Mau turn against her. She hadn't believed him, but now she wondered if it might be true. She shook her head. She wasn't going to think about him again, wasn't going to let him have that power over her life. As Sarah had told her, what good did remembering do when all it brought you was suffering?

Charity's father came home even later than the women one evening. He'd been to Nyeri to see the nuns at the Consolata Hospital. They'd agreed to take the baby. He'd also been to see Mother Winifride at Charity's former school. He'd made the mistake of telling her about the child and the headmistress wasn't sure about letting Charity resume her place. She thought Charity would no longer fit in with the other students. It would be difficult for her to return to being a schoolgirl after her recent experiences.

Charity clutched the baby so tightly he began to cry.

'Whose is he?' Baba demanded. 'Whose baby is he, that he means so much to you?'

So Charity told her parents, it wasn't because of the father that she loved the child; quite the opposite. She didn't care if she couldn't go back to school, she wouldn't give up her baby.

Although Charity and Nduta pleaded with him not to, Joshua insisted on going back to the police. He didn't care if he was arrested and tortured, he wanted to bring charges against Forbes. He even found a lawyer in Nairobi to take on the case, but after many months of waiting they were told there was insufficient evidence. The case had been dismissed by the military court.

Charity's brother was still studying for his degree in London. Joseph wrote to his parents suggesting Charity joined him there. He had a part-time job and it would be easy for her to find work too. He'd benefited from the fundraising efforts of their local women's church group; now he wanted to help his sister. He'd saved some money and a wealthy English friend was happy to lend the rest that was needed for her fare. Charity could start a new life, safe from the violence in Kenya.

'This is the perfect solution,' Baba said. 'The nuns will take the baby and you can make a good life for yourself in England. I'm sure I can persuade Chief Githuku to authorise a passport for you.'

Charity would rather have gone to America, but they had no connections there and she was desperate to get out of the miserable conditions in the village. Sometimes she felt bitter towards her old headmistress for refusing to admit her back to school, but she couldn't let go of her baby.

'I'll take the baby with me to England,' she declared.

Mama took her hand, stroking it gently. 'Charity, you know that isn't possible. Who will look after him while you're at work? How will you feed and clothe him?' Her mother looked defiantly at her father. 'I will care for the child until Charity is able to send for him.'

Baba was reluctant, but eventually Mama's reasoning won father and daughter over. Charity could not stay in the village. The current chief was better than the last one and kept his guards under control, but who knew what might happen to him? He might be shot by the Mau Mau or replaced on a whim by the administration. Did they want Charity gang-raped by soldiers or taken into the guard post and tortured? Charity didn't have to stay in England. Life would return to normal again eventually and her child would be waiting for her. She had survived the prison camp, she could survive without her child for a year or two.

Charity thought of Nurse Olerai who had saved her life. She would like to become a nurse like her. The prospect of travelling to Britain on her own was terrifying, but not as terrifying as staying in the village. As soon as she was trained she'd return to Kenya. The violence couldn't continue forever and they might even have independence by then.

Before she left they named the baby. Naming him after his father's father, as was the custom with firstborn sons, was out of the question, so the women decided he would be called Kariuki after his maternal great-grandfather. Charity hoped this would ensure he grew up to be kind and gentle like her grandfather. That he would feel a part of and follow in the traditions of her family.

'Don't forget me,' she whispered into his tiny ear. 'I will come back for you.'

LAUREN

'DID YOU APPLY THAT fake tan yourself or was it inflicted on you?' Mum pulled a stupid face at me. 'You look like you've been rolling around in a bag of Cheesy Wotsits.'

'You think you're so funny. It was my partner at college actually, we have to spray-tan each other for our assessment, don't we?'

We'd got Amber and Leo to bed and were sitting at the kitchen table, having a cup of tea. At least the kids hadn't noticed my new Oompa Loompa skin shade.

'Don't you want to know how my assessment went then?'

'Were they judging your work or your appearance?' Mum raised her eyebrows.

'I got a distinction.'

'In spray tan – well done.' She blew on her tea.

'You don't have to be so sarcastic. It actually takes some skill to do it properly. Only three of us in the class got distinctions.'

'I take it your friend wasn't one of them.'

I grabbed my bag off the floor. I only wanted my phone, but Mum seemed to think I was leaving.

'I'm only joking with you.' She reached into the back of the cupboard for her secret stash of chocolate. Like I was still a kid and she could win me over with a treat.

'You shouldn't make comments about the way I look. It's very undermining.' I tugged at the hangnail on my thumb. I needed to moisturise my cuticles.

'Everything you're doing right now is about appearances, isn't it?'

For a scary moment I thought she was talking about the double life I was leading with Edith and Jo.

'Not everything. Most of what I do is about making people feel good.' I ripped the hangnail off. A spot of blood pushed its way up through the nicked skin.

'The beauty classes are only part-time – you didn't have to jack in your A-Levels.' She threw her hands up in the air. 'Every second shop round here is a nail spa or waxing salon. God knows how they keep going – they're usually empty.' Mum gave me a sad look. 'You always seemed so bright at school.' Shaking her head, she sent a strand of her hair, like a coppery-gold ribbon, over my sleeve. 'You should at least do a course in business admin – open up your options.'

I leant forward to break off a couple of squares of Galaxy and her hair fell away from my arm. 'How would I pay Mike rent if I was doing A-levels?'

'He wouldn't expect you to pay rent if you were still at school.' She took a noisy gulp of tea. 'It was for your own good – make you see what the real world's like.'

I stared down at the table. I knew if I said anything about the way Mike treated me she'd just accuse me of being jealous or resentful. I hardly ever got any time alone with Mum, I didn't want to argue with her.

She gathered up the felt pens Amber had left scattered over the table and stuffed them into a pencil case. 'He may not always show it, but he really cares about you too. It's not easy being a step-parent, but he does his best.'

I turned to Mum. This was my chance to admit something that had been disturbing me for the past two years. 'Makes me feel weird, knowing I'm only here because Nan was raped.'

She choked on a mouthful of tea, spitting half of it back into her mug. 'That's not true. You're here because me and your dad loved each other.'

'Did you?' I pushed at a crumb of chocolate on the table and it melted under my finger. 'I thought it was just lust.'

'Lauren! I adored your dad, and he did me.'

'Why didn't you stay together then?'

She looked at me like I was being childish. 'We were at different stages in our lives. He'd already been married, had a kid. He didn't want to tie himself down again. We grew apart.'

'So he didn't want me?'

'Of course he wanted you. He doted on you. You were his baby girl.' She stated it like it was a fact – that was that, question answered, conversation closed.

But I couldn't let it go now. 'Paul said Dad and his mum were still together when she found out about you, and me.'

Mum's mouth narrowed. 'Their marriage was over long before me and Kari got together.'

Sounded like a bit of a cliché to me – the 'my wife doesn't understand me' sort. Dad never actually bothered to get a divorce or marry my mum.

'If I meant so much to Dad, how come he didn't stay in touch?'

It took a while for Mum to answer. When she did, her voice had softened, become thoughtful. 'Him disappearing like that is something I will never understand. You've got to believe me, Lauren, your Dad loved you. If Nan was here she'd tell you the same thing.' She broke off and stared at the wall, her eyes unfocused.

'Do you think he might have killed himself?' My voice came out in a croaky whisper.

I'd never dared ask Mum this before. When I was younger, I'd convinced myself he'd gone to Africa. That he'd found out he was the king of some long-forgotten land – somewhere so remote he couldn't phone or even send a letter – but that one day he'd show up with a chest full of treasure, ready to take me back as a princess. But since Nan had told me about how he was conceived, I thought maybe the trauma could've sent him off the rails. He might've felt so dirty and contaminated he didn't want to exist any more.

Mum looked stricken. 'No, I don't. He wasn't that sort of person. And if he'd died, surely we'd have been informed. Your nan, or Paul's mum as the next-of-kin – the police would have told them at least.' She shifted uncomfortably in her chair, reminding me for a second of Edith. Then she rolled her shoulders back, putting on her receptionist voice. 'Kariuki wasn't some baby daddy. He was so proud of his kids.' She got up and refilled the kettle. 'You know he never had a father, he didn't grow up with that relationship, but that just made him all the more determined to have one with you.' She had to raise her voice above the noise of the kettle. 'Sometimes I think, maybe he had an accident and lost his memory. That he got mugged – all his ID, everything was stolen, so he's no way of knowing who he is. It's the only way I can make sense of him vanishing without a trace.'

She swept our mugs up off the table, rinsed them out and dropped another teabag in each. Then stood with her back to me, watching the kettle.

'I still expect him to appear at the door.' She spoke so quietly I had to strain to hear, but I got the note of longing in her voice.

'How would he know where you are?'

I had this permanent anxiety at the back of my mind that, if Dad was still alive, he might turn up at our old flat looking for us and no one would know where we'd gone. He'd go to Nan's and find she wasn't there either. He'd be totally gutted.

Mum plonked the refilled mugs down firmly on the table, setting the tea swirling, but not quite spilling over the sides. She'd given me Leo's mug. It had his name on it and a picture of a dinosaur.

'Paul's mum hasn't moved. She's got my details – she'd tell him where we are.'

'Are you two in contact then?'

'Not recently, but obviously when Kari went missing we got in touch. We're both adults – we can work together when we need to.'

Why hadn't I thought of that? All this time worrying over something so unnecessary.

The front door slammed. Mike strode into the kitchen, dropping his keys on the table.

'All right?' He kissed Mum on the cheek, then nodded at me.

'Hi love, how was the match?' She smiled at him.

We never talked about my dad in front of Mike. It wasn't that he was a taboo subject or anything, but it wasn't encouraged either. Anytime he did get mentioned, Mike would make some sarcastic comment about men who couldn't face up to their responsibilities. Hearing Mum's voice go soft like that, it occurred to me that maybe he was jealous. All those put-downs.

242

I used to take them to heart, feel bad about my dad, now it just pissed me off. What right did he have to judge someone he'd never even met? I'd never say anything mean about Mike in front of Leo or Amber.

He grabbed a beer out of the fridge. 'You look tired, Orla, you should get to bed.' He patted Mum on the shoulder. 'We need to make an early start tomorrow, I told my sister we'd be at hers by lunchtime.'

They were going camping with his sister's family in Devon. I hadn't been invited. Not that I'd want to go in a million years, but it's always nice to be asked.

I glanced at the clock. It was only half nine. 'Better get going,' I said.

Mum and Mike exchanged an awkward look.

'Would you mind leaving your key? It's just we've got a plumber coming in to do some work on the bathroom while we're away and I had to give him mine.' Mum said.

'Can't you just get it back off him when you come home?'

'We need a spare,' Mike said, holding out his hand.

I was going to ask why they didn't get another key cut, but what was the point? It was obvious they didn't want me having access while they were away. Did they think I'd have another house party and trash the place? Broadcast it on Facebook? Had they even noticed how I was always cleaning up after Amber and Leo?

I peeled their house keys off the keyring Nan had given me and dropped them on the table, avoiding Mike's outstretched palm. The little felt terrier looked at me sadly. Now there were just two keys left – the keys to Gainsford Square.

The first time I met Paul was on my sixth birthday. Dad was taking me out for a special treat. He wouldn't tell me or Mum what it was – it was going to be a surprise. I was so excited I woke Mum up as soon as it was light with a cup of cold tea. She wouldn't let me use the kettle so I just poured water from the hot tap onto a tea bag. Only the water hadn't heated up yet. Mum made me get into bed with her and I fell back asleep snuggled up against the soft warmth of her body. I used to love our morning cuddles.

I woke in a panic, sure that Dad must've been and gone. I imagined him waiting on the landing outside our flat, ringing on the doorbell while we were sleeping. His happy birthday smile turning to a sad frown as he walked away, shoulders drooping.

'When has your dad ever turned up before ten?' Mum gave me a squeeze. 'Come on, I'll make you pancakes.'

Of course Nan arrived first. She'd brought me a new dress. It had a lot of ruffles and bows. The best thing about it was she way the skirt spun out as I twirled round for her. She'd never had a daughter so she liked to dress me up, do my hair. She'd make me sit for hours, combing out and cornrowing my hair, because Mum didn't know how to do it properly and Nan couldn't let me go to school looking like a wild thing. She didn't believe in all this 'natural hair' business. At least she let me watch TV while she did it.

Trouble was I was a leggings-and-t-shirts kind of girl. When I looked in the mirror I wanted to cry. The neck of the dress was too tight, the sleeves too short and it was yellow like mustard. I wanted to take it off before Dad arrived, but Mum wouldn't let me.

'You look beautiful, darling.' Nan beamed and held out her arms.

The minutes ticked by and still no sign of Dad. After lunch

Nan settled herself on the sofa and her eyes began to close. I sneaked my coat out of the cupboard. It was a warm August day, but I thought I could get away with wearing it over the outfit I'd planned on, without Nan or Mum noticing my change of clothes. The doorbell rang. I dropped the coat and ran, skidding down the corridor.

'Hello Princess.' Dad swung me up into his arms.

'Kariuki?' Nan called from the sitting-room. 'Are you going to come in and have a piece of cake?'

'Thanks Mum, but we need to get going. Don't want to miss the film.' Dad winked at me.

'What film are you taking her to?' Mum asked.

'Just some kid's movie at the Odeon.'

Dad always seemed a bit awkward when Mum and Nan were together. Maybe it was because they were always telling him off. Mum did it in a jokey way, but she meant it seriously. Nan did it in a cross way, but she meant it lovingly. Sometimes I wished they'd both just be nice to him.

There was no time to get out of the dress, but I didn't really care any more. Dad carried me on his shoulders all the way from the bus stop to the cinema. I had to duck my head as we went through the glass doors. Dad set me down on the ground and the smell of popcorn and sweets hit my nose.

'Lauren, there's someone I want you to meet.'

I looked up and standing over me was the handsomest man I'd ever seen. Tall and slender, his short hair was shaped into the neatest, straightest lines. Any boy in my school would've been impressed. He held out his hand.

'So this is the birthday girl. Hello sis. Nice to meet you at long last.'

I turned to Dad in confusion.

'I thought it was about time you two met. This is your brother,

Paul.'

This wasn't the surprise I'd been expecting.

'How can I have a brother?'

Dad crouched down beside me. 'You're my special girl, yeah, and Paul is my son.' He glanced up at Paul. 'He's eighteen now, can you believe it?'

Paul rolled his eyes. He looked bored.

'Is he my surprise?'

They both laughed.

'Well I'm sorry I couldn't wrap him up and put him in a box for you.'

I burst into tears. This was not what I wanted for my birthday. Dad looked baffled, and then annoyed.

'D'you like popcorn?' Paul asked.

I nodded.

'Come on,' he held out his hand. 'Salty or sweet? Coke or 7-Up?'

'I'm only allowed a little drink of Coke.'

I took Paul's hand. His skin was much browner than mine, more like Dad's. Did that mean Dad loved him more?

'I'll get you a small one. What about M&Ms, shall we get a bag of them too?'

'I suppose I'm paying for all this.' Dad followed us to the counter.

Inside I sat between Paul and Dad with my own bag of popcorn and a huge drink with a straw. They didn't even make me share the M&Ms. Paul said he'd pick me up after school one day and we could hang out in the park together. I imagined the kids in my class staring up at Paul in awe and hoped he was good at football.

'Nice dress.'

'You think?'

'Nan got it for you, didn't she?' Paul grinned.

'How did you know that?'

'She showed me when I was round at hers.'

'Is she your nan too?' I never knew I'd been sharing her all this time.

'Course.'

'Why didn't you and Nan tell me about Paul?' I whispered to Dad.

'We were waiting for the right time. It's complicated, with his mum.'

I was about to ask why, when the lights grew dark and the film began. *Pirates of the Caribbean: the Curse of the Black Pearl.* It was the most exciting and the scariest thing I'd ever seen.

Mum was furious when she found out. Said it was typical of my dad, to take me to a film much too old for me. I'd have nightmares for weeks and she was the one who'd be kept up every night.

'But Paul wanted to see it,' I told her. 'Did you know I have a big brother?'

I wanted to ask her about Paul's mummy. Who was she? Why was it complicated? Was she brown like Nan? Was that why Paul's skin was browner than mine? Because my mum only had pink skin? But Mum's mouth had disappeared into a thin line, which meant she was upset about something.

'Get ready for bed. I need to talk to your father.'

I was too tired to argue, even though it was my birthday.

I stared out of the smeary bus window at the betting shops, the fried chicken take-aways and pound stores. A drunk couple were having a row outside the Wetherspoons. She was shoving him in the chest, but the bus moved before I had time to see how he reacted. Downstairs I could hear some crazy person ranting. I was glad I was on the top deck.

Jo hadn't brought up the cigarette case or selling stuff again, but she'd been uptight round me lately. I was sure things had been moved about in my bedroom, reckoned she might have been looking through them. My Shu Uemura eyelash curlers had gone missing, which I was really pissed off about, but I didn't dare ask her about them.

At least Paul hadn't said anything, so she can't of told him. I'd cleared the browsing history on Edith's iPad and I'd used a separate email with a fake name on eBay, but I kept thinking, what if Jo got the police involved? They'd be able to trace my details, wouldn't they?

Maybe moving out of London wasn't such a bad option. It was about time I saw a bit more of the world. I didn't have to stay here any more, didn't have to wait for Dad to come back. If he was still alive he'd find us – one day, he'd find me and Paul.

I thought Edith would be in bed by the time I got back, but a light was on in the sitting room and I could hear the TV, so I poked my head round the door to check if anyone was in there. Edith was asleep in her armchair, a blanket over her knees. She slept downstairs a lot now – said she preferred it. I switched off the TV and was about to take the half-drunk bottle of wine and empty glass from the little table beside her, when she opened her eyes.

'Lauren, is that you?' She sounded alarmed.

'Yeah, just me.' I bent down next to her. 'Shall I help you upstairs?'

'Is it very late?'

I checked my phone. 'Just gone ten.'

'Would you sit up with me for a little?'

'Sure.' I nestled into the other armchair, tucking my legs underneath my bum.

'Help yourself to a nightcap if you want one.' She waved a hand at the drinks cabinet. It was full of dusty old bottles of syrupy looking liquids. Jo had finished all the gin.

'I'm all right, thanks.'

Edith leant forwards. 'The older one gets, the more one lives in the past.' She gripped her blanket, stopping it from sliding off her knees. 'There are things I regret, Lauren – regret deeply. I've made plenty of mistakes in my life, some worse than others.'

The glow from the floor lamp highlighted the shadows under her eyes and the grey hollows of her cheeks. She looked a bit like an old lady off a horror film. My heart was racing. Did she know about Forbes? Did she regret marrying him?

'I've done some despicable things.'

'What kind of things?' I tried to keep my voice calm and encouraging.

'I strived always to do what was right, to protect my nearest and dearest, and yet, people have lost their lives because of me.'

Bloody hell, this wasn't about Nan then. What worse things could the Forbes have done?

'How, Edith? What people?'

I was asking too many questions. I should've just waited for her to tell me. She shook her head.

'I didn't mean to alarm you. I must sound terribly melodramatic.' She pushed herself up out of her chair. 'I'm going to have a drink. Are you sure you won't join me?'

'Go on then.' I hoped this might encourage her to keep talking. 'What about your wine?'

I nodded at the side table, but she'd pulled a round brown bottle out of the cabinet and was trying to read the label. Her hand was shaking so much I thought she might drop it. I got up to take it from her.

'I think this is a brandy. You fetch the glasses. The little ones from the shelf there.'

I took two crystal glasses out of the cabinet. They needed a wash – there were smudgy fingerprints all over them.

'That's it, put them down there.' Edith tapped the top of the cabinet.

She slopped amber liquid into and over the glasses. I was going to get a cloth when she shoved one of them into my hand.

'Cheers,' she said grimly.

The brandy was like petrol, burning my throat as it went down. Wished I could've added some Coke at least. I tried not to cough. I pulled a tissue out of the box on the side table, but it stuck to the gluey drops on my glass.

'That's a good Cognac.' Edith managed to top up her glass before sitting down again. 'I want to make amends. To pay off an old debt.' She nodded determinedly. 'I've always put family first, but I've come to realise that doesn't always bring about the best results. It isn't always best for those involved.' She knocked back the rest of her brandy.

It flashed into my mind that this was the time to tell her the truth. She must've done some really bad shit to feel so guilty. She was admitting she'd been in the wrong, so she might understand that me and Paul had had to use some dirty tricks to put things right.

She suddenly reached a hand out towards my face, like she wanted to stroke my cheek. It gave me a bit of a fright – Edith wasn't the touchy-feely type.

'Sometimes I think you care more about me than my own daughter does.' Her voice was slurry.

My heart was beating hard. If this was the time, I had to say it right – there'd be no going back after.

'I always do my best for you, Edith, treat you like I would if you were my own nan.'

I really was on the point of telling Edith everything, but I was too slow getting my words together and she jumped in with a question.

'Can you keep a secret?'

'Yes,' I said, nodding maybe a bit too enthusiastically.

'This is in the strictest confidence, you understand?'

'Of course.'

'I'm leaving everything I have to charity.'

My whole body flopped with disappointment. That wasn't a revelation, not to me anyway.

'To Paul's charity?'

'You're not surprised?' Edith gave me one of her nit-picking looks. She wasn't as drunk as I'd thought.

Shit, I kept fucking this conversation up. 'It just makes sense, that's all. If you're thinking about charities, why not his one?'

Maybe I should've told her then that Paul's charity was just a front. That the money would be going to me and him, not to any disabled vets or anything like that. But when it came down to it I just couldn't bring myself to ruin all our plans. Not just for our sake, but for Edith. She worshipped Paul. It could literally kill her, knowing he'd been scamming her, that nothing he'd said about the army was true. I couldn't be responsible for shocking her like that. She was too frail.

'Of course, I've discussed it with him. It's exactly the sort of charity Graham would have approved of – focused and effective, no money wasted on admin.'

Jesus, so she was still focused on what Graham would want. Just as well I hadn't opened my big mouth. Edith wasn't ready to hear the truth. Maybe she never would be.

I was annoyed with myself afterwards though. I should've got more out of her. I'd blown my chance and I might not get another one. I stuck my head out of my bedroom window. I could still taste the brandy burning the back of my throat, even after brushing my teeth. People were laughing in one of the gardens below – young voices – maybe it was those students. At least someone was having a good time.

OK, so Edith had her secrets and I had mine. I guess that evened things out. The main thing was she was leaving her money to Nan's descendants, whether she knew it or not. Forbes wasn't going to win. I just wished I could feel more chilled about the whole thing, like the way Paul was. I had this permanent fear at the back of my mind that we'd get done for taking the money, even if it was rightfully ours.

It wasn't like I was planning on splurging it all though. I'd honour Nan's memory by doing something proper with it, something worthy of her. Mum would expect me to blow it all on beauty treatments or something shallow like that. Well she was wrong about me. I'd show her and Mike and all the rest of them. I didn't exactly know how yet, but I was going to do something important with my life, to make a difference, to change things for the better. Not just people's appearance – their minds as well.

EDITH

WHEN I SAW THE DOOR opening, I thought it must be Joanna coming in to me, that she was having one of her bad dreams and wanted to get into bed with me.

'Jo-Jo?' My voice hardly escaped my mouth, it was so feeble, so old.

Whoever it was didn't respond. They stood, a black silhouette, at the foot of my bed, watching.

There were days when I wished I could die, when life seemed too much of a struggle and I just wanted to give up. What was the point in crawling through the hours with no future, no purpose? But now, in the dark, my heart beat more strongly than ever and I would have done anything to make that figure disappear.

Instead it only grew more present, taking shape in the light from the open door. Gradually I made out a handsome young man, lithe and muscular, wearing a white shirt open at the neck and khaki trousers, leaning forward over the bedstead towards me, his blue eyes filled with laughter, his red lips parted to reveal an even row of white teeth. His skin was tanned, but not burnt, his fair hair neatly cut and slicked back with Brylcreem. He reminded me of an actor from the Nairobi Players.

'Teddy?' I called out hesitantly.

My body ached with desire, there was a heat between my legs I hadn't known in years. I stretched my arms out towards him, welcoming him into my bed.

With one hop he was over the brass rail and crouching beside me. As he moved, I was sure I spied more than two legs, but he leapt so fast I couldn't count them.

'Edith,' he purred. 'How beautiful you look.'

I reached my right hand out to stroke his cheek. He turned his head and I caught a glimpse of a second mouth gaping open as the base of his skull, a flash of teeth, the flick of a tongue.

'Edie,' the second mouth chastised, and the voice that emerged was Mary's. 'Have you forgotten Mama's stories? The ones we let you listen to, sitting with us on the floor of our hut? Remember the ogre who lured young girls into the forest to eat them. As they walked, each girl saw through his disguise and slipped away between the trees – all except one foolish female, so overcome with longing she ignored the tell-tale signs and followed him, deeper and deeper into the forest.'

I tried to get out of the bed, but the ogre caught me fast by the wrist. No longer a handsome young man, the creature squatting beside me looked more like a giant toad – its skin black and warty, its yellow eyes darting from side to side. It belched a terrible sulphurous miasma, the gas filling my mouth and nose so that I could hardly breathe.

'Open your mouth, my friend Hyena, and taste this special meat. Swallow it at once while I get you another, even more tender than the first,' the toad rasped.

I tried to cry out that I was not a hyena, the monster was mistaken, but hands squeezed my sides, tickling me under the ribs so that I was forced to open my mouth and laugh, painful, hysterical laughter.

Something hot was thrown into my mouth, I could feel it burning my throat as it forced its way through my body, corroding my insides, turning my stomach into a cauldron. I reached for the glass of water on my bedside table, desperate to put out the fire consuming my belly, but the groping, tickling hands pulled me away.

'Now will you leave me in peace, Hyena? Now I've fed you full?' The toad bellowed in my ear. 'Leave me my goats and my chickens, greedy Hyena.'

'She who commits a crime cannot be helped,' Mary's voice sang out. 'She must pay the price.'

'I'm innocent,' I gasped. 'Forgive me, Mary, it wasn't a crime, I was doing my duty.'

'Where is Graham's son, Edith? What did you do with him?'

The toad's head had swivelled round, its second mouth flapping at me, a gaping, green-lipped hole.

'I don't know! I didn't do anything.'

'Edie never does anything. She's a good girl, obeys the rules.'

The toad was bouncing slowly up and down on its back legs, rocking the bed, making everything spin. 'The hyena who closes her eyes as she tramples the chicks must still be punished. The mother bird does not forget.'

I could hear wings whirring around my head, feel the brush of feathers against my face. Needles jabbed at my skin, piercing my flesh. I held my arms up, but it darted round and through them, pecking, pecking with its sharp little beak.

'Give me my child,' it seemed to chirrup. 'Give me my child.'

I threw myself out of the bed, just managing to land on my feet, my knees cracked and my legs almost gave way beneath me. Bent double, I shuffled forwards, reaching my hands out for the wall, feeling for the light switch. If I could just turn it on, flood the room with light, return it to normality. Still the bird kept pecking at my back with its vicious little beak.

'Where's my child? Where's my child?' It whined in my ear.

Which child it meant – Mary or Graham's son – I didn't know or care. I batted at it, wishing I could crush it against the wall. My hand caught the dressing-gown hanging on the back of the door. I pulled it on for protection, holding myself up by the door handle. Clinging to the open door I hauled myself out onto the landing, towards the light.

LAUREN

IT WAS ME WHO FOUND HER. I was coming downstairs, thinking 'do I have time for breakfast? Is the manager going to be in today?' when I saw Edith's dressing-gown lying crumpled up on the hall floor. 'What the hell's that doing there?' I thought. Then I saw the swollen purple feet sticking out below the flowery material, the wisps of white hair above the collar.

I ran down fast as I could and turned her carefully over on her back. She was heavier than I expected. Her head rolled towards me, eyes wide open, staring. Her mouth was twisted to one side, her tongue hung out of it, swollen and bloody, like maybe she'd bitten it. I kept saying her name as I tried to find a pulse, on her neck, at her wrist. I couldn't feel anything but thought it must be me not doing it right. I knelt beside her, trying to slow down my breathing, to stop myself from panicking.

Half-remembering the first aid course I'd done at school, I filled my cheeks with air and blew gently into Edith's mouth.

Dunno how long I did that for. Then I tried pumping my hands down on her chest. I knew there was a tune you were supposed to do it in time to, only I couldn't remember what the fuck it was – some disco from the Seventies. I could feel her ribs under my palms, even through the quilted material of her dressing-gown. I was scared they'd crack, but her body was as limp as a ragdoll's and it was obvious she couldn't feel anything. My bag was hanging up on a hook. I fished my compact out and held the mirror in front of her mouth. Nothing, no misting over.

It seemed to take an age for Jo to get downstairs. She gave out a horrible cry when she saw Edith. Sinking to her knees, she lifted Edith's body into her arms and cradled her like a baby, rocking back and forwards, making a funny moaning sound. I cried too then. I didn't know if I should try to comfort her or leave her alone with her mum.

I kept thinking of Nan. Is that what she'd looked like when she died? Was her face twisted like that when the neighbour found her? If only I'd been there, to hold her, to tell her how much she'd meant to me, to all of us. Instead, here I was with the wife of her torturer. It was all so fucked up.

I had to step over them to let the paramedics in. I put my hands on Jo's shoulders, steering her out of the way while they checked Edith over. They asked us if she'd signed a Do Not Resuscitate order, but we didn't know. One of them got a defibrillator and shocked her. It was horrible, watching her body jerk about like a puppet. Then the lady paramedic looked up at us and said she was very sorry but Edith was gone. I nearly said, 'What d'you mean? She's lying right there'. Stupid. I suppose it was the shock. The paramedics – they said I'd done everything I could. No one could've done more, they said.

They must've got in touch with the surgery because Edith's doctor turned up on the doorstep. I thought she might've shown a bit more emotion, but I guess she had to be professional. She was very calm and efficient, talking quietly to the paramedics while me and Jo sat on the stairs. Jo was breathing very loudly.

Dr Morahan stared at us both for a minute, like she was weighing us up, then she asked Jo if she was Edith's daughter. Jo just nodded.

'Are you feeling OK, Joanna?'

She took Jo's pulse and I noticed her checking out Jo's arms. Then I remembered what Paul had said, about Edith telling her doctor Jo was a drug addict.

'She'll be fine, won't you Jo?' I said, rubbing Jo's back.

Jo leant against me and I felt so bad I wanted to howl. I could feel the tears trickling down my cheeks and dripping off my chin onto my neck.

'It's very distressing when someone dies.' Dr Morahan nodded briskly. 'Especially when it's unexpected.'

Talk about stating the fucking obvious. Was that her idea of comfort?

She crouched down to examine Edith's body, pulling her dressing-gown open to look at her skin. I didn't like the way she did that – seemed disrespectful. Then I saw the bruises on Edith's arms and legs.

'That must be from her falling downstairs,' I said. 'They weren't there yesterday.'

'You live here too, do you?'

'Yes. I brought Mrs Forbes in to see you once, about a month ago.' It was like talking to my old headmistress. I felt guilty even though I hadn't done anything.

'I do have a lot of patients – can't remember everyone I'm afraid.'

Dr Morahan was searching around Edith's body. What was she looking for? Did she think we'd clobbered Edith? Was she looking for the murder weapon?

She sighed and pushed herself up slowly with her hands on her knees. She had dark circles under her eyes and her greying hair was a bit of a mess. To be fair to her, she might've been working all night.

She looked at Jo. 'Your mother probably had a stroke, but we'll have to get a coroner's report because I can't establish the exact cause of death here. I don't think they'll need to do a post-mortem though, as it's almost certainly due to natural causes.'

Almost certainly? What did she mean by that?

She said she'd arrange for a funeral director acting for the coroner to take Edith away. Once the exact cause of death had been established and the death was registered, Jo could choose whatever sort of funeral she wanted.

'I want a green burial. With one of those wickerwork coffins.' Jo pushed the damp hair away from her face and wiped her nose on the back of her hand.

I remembered Edith saying she wanted her ashes buried with Graham's. They'd bought a plot in Barnet cemetery for all three of them – Jo as well – but it didn't feel like the right time to bring that up.

Before they left, the paramedics carried Edith into the sitting room and laid her down on the sofa. They closed her eyes and pushed her tongue back inside her mouth. Jo put a cushion under her head and straightened her dressing-gown. Her white hair puffed out in a little halo behind her.

The only dead body I'd seen before was Nan's, in the funeral parlour. I went with Mum. She stroked Nan's face, but I hung back. I didn't want to touch her. It didn't feel like that body was Nan. Her spirit was gone for sure – to heaven, if there is one.

I don't think Edith believed in heaven. At least she never talked about it – not to me. She'd probably prefer extinction anyway, not to have to think about anything any more. She definitely didn't deserve to go the same place as Nan, though I kind of liked to imagine it. What a surprise Edith would get meeting Nelson Mandela up there.

I got Jo to come into the kitchen and made a pot of tea. I forgot to give her herbal, but she drank it anyway, milk and all. I even put a spoonful of sugar in, for the shock. We just sat there, stunned. I said, should I call Paul, and Jo nodded.

She'd been really narky with Edith the night before. Wanted Edith to go to the theatre with her. Said they could get taxis there and back, but Edith didn't feel up to it.

'Take Lauren,' she'd said.

'Are you going to pay for us then, Mum?' Jo said. 'Because we certainly can't afford London theatre tickets.'

Edith just harrumphed and asked me to switch on the TV. Jo was always trying to get her mum to pay for things. Never succeeded, though. She was using the wrong strategies, but I couldn't exactly tell her that. Not that it made any difference now. I just couldn't get my head around the idea that Edith was dead. I'd never sit watching the news with her again.

I must've been sleeping very heavily not to hear her fall. Then again, she was so light she probably didn't make much noise. Maybe she got up to go to the toilet and went the wrong way. If she was half-asleep and groggy from the sleeping pills, she might've got confused, lost her bearings, walked right off the top of the stairs. Or maybe she wanted to go down to the kitchen for a glass of water or something. Had a stroke on the landing and went tumbling down. I just keep hoping she wasn't having one of her nightmares. I'm sure I'd have heard her if she'd cried out or called for me.

Paul had to hold Jo up when the undertakers took Edith's body away, she was crying so hard. She kept saying how Edith had wanted to stay in the house and she should never have tried to get her to move. It was all her fault, she shouldn't have put pressure on her mum – maybe that's why she'd had a stroke. She should have taken better care of her.

'Don't. You mustn't blame yourself.' I couldn't stop myself from saying it, even though I did think Jo could've been nicer to her mum.

Paul looked at me over Jo's shoulder and shook his head. His mouth was in a tight line. I could see the muscles in his jaw were clenched. Was he wondering if he'd got everything sorted in time? His expression was warning me not to give anything away to Jo. He'd be working out the best way to handle her. He was probably upset about Edith dying so suddenly, too.

Jo pulled herself together enough to stagger into the sitting room and grab a bottle from the drinks cabinet.

'We must all toast Mum.' She waved the bottle in the air.

It was only eleven and I was feeling a bit sick, but we trooped back into the kitchen and let her pour us each a glass of brandy. We sat around the kitchen table exchanging memories about Edith, while Jo worked her way through the bottle. I made us all sandwiches and more tea.

Jo's friend Ottie came over. She was a lot more conventional-looking than Jo. Her highlighted hair was cut in a layered bob and she wore an expensive-looking white shirt over her skinny jeans. She threw her arms round Jo, holding her tight while Jo cried. Me and Paul left them to it.

'I've got to get back to work. You OK, Lauri?'

We were standing in the hall, right where Edith's body had been. I didn't realise until Paul put his arms round me that I was shivering. I pressed my face into his chest, inhaling the familiar smell of his aftershave.

'What about the coroner and the post-mortem? I didn't like the way that doctor was looking at me.'

'It's just procedure. Don't sweat it.' Paul tilted my chin so that I was looking into his eyes. 'Doctor Morahan's covering herself. She's the one who prescribed the sleeping tablets, and she knew Edith slept upstairs. I made sure to tell her that last visit.'

'What about the charity? What if they trace it back to us?'

Paul glanced back at the kitchen door, but Jo was talking too loudly to hear anything we said. 'They won't. It's airtight. Wouldn't occur to Jo anyway. She can't think past herself.'

'She'll go apeshit when she finds out Edith hasn't left her anything,' I whispered.

Paul just shrugged and gave me a little smile. 'So let her. All you have to do is sit tight and hold your nerve. We're nearly there, Lauri. Just be patient.'

I didn't feel like I was nearly anywhere. I felt completely wrung out, like there was nothing left inside of me. I went upstairs and sat on my bed. I couldn't face going into work. I tried calling Mum, but her phone went straight to voicemail. Maybe there was no signal where she was camping.

I must've fallen asleep because suddenly the room was in shadow and the windows of the house opposite were glowing yellow across the gardens. A bird was singing in the walnut tree. I pushed my window open and leant out. The scents of jasmine, honeysuckle and roses were all rising up out of Edith's garden, blending in the air into one, rich, sweet perfume. I breathed in deeply. It seemed like years since I first moved in, though really it was only a few months.

'Thanks Edith,' I whispered. 'I'm glad I got to know you.'

Maybe it was for the best I'd never managed to confront her, to tell her everything. Then I thought of Jo. Me and Paul might be the only relatives she had now. Shouldn't we tell her?

I stuck my head round the kitchen door. Jo and Ottie had moved onto wine. Looked like they were halfway through their second bottle. Jo was leaning over the table, swaying slightly.

'Erm, you OK if I go over to my friend's?'

I'd texted Ash and he'd told me to get an Uber straight over to his.

'Don't worry, I'll look after Jo.' Ottie smiled at me. She had a kind face.

'You go and be with your friend.' Jo's speech was slurred and her eyes were half-closed. 'Friends are precious. Cherish them while you've got 'em.' She pointed at Ottie. 'This woman here – she's my oldest and bestest friend.'

Ottie patted her hand. 'That's right, darling, and I'm here for you.' She nodded at me and mouthed, 'You go.'

It was a relief, took a bit of the pressure off, knowing Jo had a friend in London to look after her. It was the house we were supposed to end up with, not some crazy, drunk auntie.

It's the look on Edith's face I can't get out of my mind. The doctor said it was the stroke made her expression go like that, but I swear it was terror. There was something weird going on in that house. Sometimes I think maybe we brought it out – me and Paul – playing games on Edith with the lights and the radio. That we drew something out – or somethings, plural. I can never make up for doing that. I'll always feel bad about it even though it was only a couple of times.

We hadn't done any of that stuff for weeks though – didn't have to – Edith was being haunted without our input. Plus, she was already having nightmares when I first moved in. Before I'd even done anything, she woke me up, screaming in the night. So it wasn't my fault – not really. I mean, me and Paul, we actually made Edith's life better – we both worked really hard to keep her happy.

Jo was in the house too, and she never heard her mum fall, even though she claimed to be such a light sleeper. And she went to bed after me.

Like the doctor said, it was probably Edith's age. Could've happened anywhere, at any time.

LONDON, 2008

Charity sat on the sofa, her granddaughter nestled against her, watching a Disney film and eating popcorn. The warm little body beside her brought her such a sense of contentment, of safety. There was really nowhere else she'd rather be.

So many times she'd told herself she'd go home to Kenya: once she'd saved enough money; once Kariuki was through school; once she could persuade him to come with her; once her grandchildren were grown; once she retired. It remained always a dream.

She'd only been back once – when her father was dying and she went to fetch Kariuki. That was forty-five years ago. She couldn't leave England now; not until Kariuki came back. Not until she found out what had happened to him. Paul would be fine. He was at university in Nottingham, studying business. He took after his uncle, had a good head on him. Of course, it was mostly down to his mother. Esther had always pushed him hard.

Charity had done her best to stay on good terms with Esther after Kariuki left her, but Esther was very angry about the separation. She seemed to blame Charity for Kariuki's shortcomings.

Charity had always been a little in awe of Esther, a British-Nigerian businesswoman who'd made a huge success out of her interior design company. Charity never quite understood why Esther had agreed to marry Kariuki, an unambitious accountant for a small stationery company. Though she, of course, was very proud of him and all he'd achieved.

Esther had changed her and Paul's second name from Mathu to Matthews. She said an English name was better for business, but Charity was sad Paul no longer shared her Kenyan surname. Neither of her grandchildren had African names.

Charity stroked Lauren's head. After Kariuki, it was her granddaughter she worried about most. Lauren's mother was a sweet girl, always very friendly. She had an Irish background and had been brought up Catholic. She leant heavily on Charity for childcare, which Charity was only too happy to provide. Now Charity was pleased for Orla that she'd got married and it was wonderful she was expecting another baby. She just wasn't so sure about her choice of husband. Michael reminded Charity of some of the surgeons she'd worked with: brilliant at their job but emotionally cold. He had a good job in advertising and would provide for his new family, but he wouldn't love Lauren like her daddy had.

Kariuki was twelve years old when Charity finally told him who his father was. She'd been avoiding it for so long it was actually a relief. From the day he landed in England at six years old he kept asking. He'd been expecting to meet his baba and was bitterly disappointed to discover he only had a mama in London. She palmed him off with excuses for years, until she finally snapped and told him the truth. To her surprise his behaviour improved afterwards – he stopped getting into trouble at school, became kinder, more respectful towards her. Started to do his homework, wash the dishes; it was as if he was trying to make up for his existence, to prove he wasn't like the man who had forced him on her.

By this time Charity was a qualified nurse. Not the State Registered Nurse she'd have liked to be – that took three years' training and none of the black nurses got to do that, not even the ones who'd already trained in the West Indies. They were all expected to do the two-year course and become SENs. The work was harder: it was all sluicing out and bed baths and none of the doctors so much as looked at you, let alone talked to you. You couldn't become a matron if you were a SEN. There was no hope of promotion, but it was work and it paid, just about.

Charity was the only African nurse at training school. All the others had been recruited from the West Indies. She was also the youngest, and they took her under their wing. She liked the other women, but kept her distance. She let them straighten her hair, but she never slipped out of the dormitory window for a night on the town, never confided in them. How could she? How could she begin to explain what she had experienced? They must have guessed at something though, because she woke them up sometimes with her nightmares.

The closest she got to a friend was Gladys, an eighteen-year-old from St Lucia who was as homesick as she was, though the home Charity missed had been destroyed in 1956. Years later she and Gladys still worked together at the North Middlesex. They'd stop for a chat whenever they got the chance. They weren't allowed tea breaks like the state registered nurses, but they'd have a laugh as they made beds and emptied catheter bags, doing their best to avoid a scolding from the sister in charge.

No one in England knew she had a child – not even Gladys.

She had to change her shifts when he arrived, working nights so that she could pick him up from school. Her brother was back in Kenya and she couldn't afford a babysitter. Sometimes, despite her anguish at leaving him as a baby, she thought it would have been better if Kariuki had stayed in Kenya with her parents, but her mother had been struggling with the little boy. He kept getting into fights with other children and their mothers complained about him.

It was Gladys who noticed how exhausted she was. 'You look half-dead, girl! What's the matter with you?'

After she opened up to Gladys, they became true friends. When Gladys married a bus driver from Trinidad, the couple would have Charity and Kariuki over every Sunday they weren't working. Kariuki worshipped Sam, who took him to the park and to football matches.

Charity's feelings for her son veered between a fierce protective love and a fearful loathing. She knew she smacked him too hard when he misbehaved, then she'd be overcome with guilt and remorse. Sometimes she had to wrap her arms around him and hug him tightly to stop herself from beating him.

As he grew older, she was constantly relieved not to see the commandant in him. Kariuki's skin was dark honey brown, his eyes a warm chestnut, his lips soft and full. He had a kind smile and, when he wasn't acting up, could be very sweet-natured. It was hard for him, she knew. He missed his grandparents and the farm they had moved back to. He got angry when the kids at school called him names. He needed a father. Sam was great, but soon he and Gladys had children of their own, taking up their time and energy.

Charity started going to church with Gladys. At first it was the familiarity of the prayers, the smell of incense and flowers, that were a comfort, but after a while it became the mainstay of her life. She'd drag Kariuki along with her, hoping it would improve him, but he never took to it the way she did. She found a new family in the congregation, solace in the teachings. The generosity and love that were an intrinsic part of her nature found expression in the practice of religion. This gave her enough fulfilment to laugh off Gladys' exhortations to get herself a nice man. Like a lay sister, she led a spiritual existence. Even when patients were insulting and objected to being cared for by a black woman, she found strength and meaning in the service of God, whose own son suffered and died for her salvation.

Despite being in the country that was the origin of so much pain, despite the hostility of many of the white residents, it seemed easier to put the past behind her in the fast-paced capital. At Christmas time she'd take Kariuki to the West End to see the lights and in the summer they'd walk along the embankment and look at the Thames or take in the sights around Trafalgar Square and Piccadilly Circus. She also loved the church outings to the seaside. She'd never been to Kenya's coastal province, never seen the Indian Ocean. Her first encounter with the sea was in England.

Next year, she kept telling herself, next year I'll take the boy home. But both she and Kariuki became increasingly embedded as Londoners.

It was her faith that kept her going after Kariuki disappeared. She'd never stopped worrying about him. When his marriage fell apart and he took up with a girl almost half his age, what could she do but be there for her grandchildren and their mothers? Often she wished she'd never burdened him with the knowledge of his origins, but he had always been a good son to her and a loving father, never got in trouble with the law, kept a steady job. One day she knew they'd be reunited, if not in this life then in the next.

Charity was delighted Lauren spent so much time with her. The greatest joy in her life came in the form of her granddaughter. There was nothing of Forbes in this little girl, who was sweetness through-and-through. Loving and optimistic, Lauren reminded Charity of both the girl she'd once been and her mother, Nduta. Lauren's presence lifted her heart and made her feel her life had been worthwhile.

LAUREN

'COULD YOU ANSWER the door, Lauren?' Jo looked up at me.

She and Paul were sitting in the armchairs on either side of the fireplace. I felt a bit weird about her sitting in Edith's chair. It was stupid really, but it seemed disrespectful somehow. I felt like we should leave the chair empty, to show who was missing. Not like I expected Edith to come in and take her place or anything, though in this house you never knew. The thought made me shiver. I turned quickly and walked down the hall. Mustn't think about ghosts or I'd never sleep at night.

Bob shook my hand. His palm was all sticky. He smelt like a charity shop, of musty old clothes and BO. When he passed me his jacket I could see a wet patch spreading out across his back.

'Hello, Bob.' Jo got up, smiling sadly as she reached her arms out towards him.

As Bob got nearer she obviously changed her mind about giving him one of her usual hugs, holding him at arms' length and squeezing his shoulders instead. They stood in the middle of the room looking awkward, then they both spoke at once – Bob to say how sorry he was about Edith, Jo to ask him if he'd like a drink. 'Tea, coffee, or something stronger.'

'Just a glass of water, thanks.'

'Is tap OK?' Jo turned to me. 'Could you get Bob some water? Put some ice in it.'

I got that she was grieving, but that didn't give her the right to treat me like a servant. Almost made me look forward to seeing her expression when Bob told her about the house. She thought she was doing me a favour letting me stay here. She'd soon find out she didn't have any more of a right to be here than I did.

'I'm glad you're all here,' Bob said when I handed him the glass. 'As you are all beneficiaries of Edith's will.' He was trying to put on a cheery front, but I could tell he was nervous. His hand trembled as he took a sip of water. 'I realise I could have just written to you, but I wanted to see Joanna, and it's better to do these things in person, isn't it?'

Jo raised her eyebrows when he said about us all being beneficiaries, but she didn't say anything – just smiled and nodded at us all, like she was the queen or something.

I had to sit next to Bob on the sofa. It was that or the floor. Once I was sat down, I realised the floor might've been the better option, but it was too late to move.

Paul kept his face neutral. He was sitting back in his armchair, legs crossed, his right ankle resting on his left knee, his hands loosely curled over the armrests. He looked like a bit of a don –chilled, but in command.

Bob had pulled a stack of papers out of his briefcase. He twisted round towards me. 'So, Lauren, let's start with you, shall we?'

I hoped she hadn't given me the snake necklace. Not that

it made any difference now, seeing as I'd already sold it. She might've left shares or something to us – she was always fretting about her investments.

'Edith has left you the grandmother clock.'

And I swear to God, as he said that the clock went and chimed the half hour. It was so weird we all laughed, which broke the tension.

'And the clock agrees,' Bob said.

What the hell was I going to do with that clock? Maybe Mum would like it. Wasn't sure I wanted to see it in her house though. It might be jinxed, bring bad luck. Was that how Edith wanted me to remember her, as a granny? My eyes fuzzed over.

Jo was dabbing at her eyes too. 'That is such a sweet legacy. A bit bonkers, giving you that old clock, but what a lovely gesture.'

'Yeah,' I shrugged. 'Dunno where I'll put it.'

'Well, you can always leave it here for the time being.'

I glanced over at Paul. His face was calm, his eyes half-closed. He wasn't giving anything away, but then he knew he was holding the ace.

'Mr Paul Matthews.' Bob cleared his throat. 'Edith wanted you to have her late husband's medals, his regimental sword, his hunting rifle and his golf clubs and accessories.'

I felt a bit sick. That's who Edith saw in Paul. That's why she was so in love with him – he reminded her of Forbes. Not enough for her to twig who he was – the colour of his skin would stop her going there – but enough for her to trust him.

I looked up at the face I'd been avoiding for all this time. The framed black-and-white photo of a man in uniform, his square jaw, the dent in his chin, the way he was staring, his eyes fixed on the camera, no fear, no uncertainty. I'd always thought Paul looked like Dad (only younger and less gentle), but now I could see the fit with the face in the photo, like one image had been slid on top of another. Did I take after Forbes too? The thought made me want a total blood transplant.

'What a relief!' Jo tossed her hair back over her shoulders. 'Rather you than me, Paul, but I'm sure you can put them to good use. Sell the lot if you want, I won't mind.'

Jo trying to chirpse Paul was sickening too. I wished I could tell her how they were related.

Paul gave her a relaxed, open smile. 'I'm not really the hunting, shooting or golfing type, but it was nice of Edith to think of me.' He sounded kind of humble.

Bob frowned and shuffled his papers. 'Joanna, your mother has bequeathed you all her jewellery. She has also left you the watercolour paintings of Mount Kenya executed by your late grandmother.'

Shit. She was bound to remember the snake necklace – how was I going to explain that?

Sweat was trickling down the sides of Bob's face. He fumbled in his pockets, looking for something, but they seemed to be empty. I grabbed the box of tissues off the side table and passed them to him. He held one against his face. When he pulled it away, shreds of white paper were left stuck to his skin like flakes of dandruff or eczema. Paul and Jo were watching him like they were two hungry cats staring at a fat little robin.

After a silence that seemed to go on forever, Jo said, 'Well, it was sweet of her to want to name specific items. That means a lot.' She nodded. 'I suppose the house and everything else comes to me automatically.'

Bob coughed. The loose skin under his chin wobbled like jelly.

'I can understand that this might come as something of a shock. I did question your mother over it.' He held up one hand, palm out, like he was taking an oath, or stopping traffic.

'But she was absolutely adamant that this is how she wanted her estate disposed of.' He took another sip of water. 'The rest of her estate, the house, her savings, shares and bonds, have all been left to a charitable organisation.'

So we'd done it. Edith had left us the lot. I didn't have to play the nice little helper any more. I felt like I ought to be more excited, but I couldn't get rid of this sense of dread that we'd get found out and end up in prison. Mum would be so disgusted with me.

'She can't do that.' Jo twisted the rings round on her fingers, her voice had gone all squeaky. 'I'm her next-of-kin, her daughter. She can't just disinherit me.'

'I'm afraid she could. I did check with her solicitor and she said that in this country, unlike France, for example, people can leave their assets to whoever they like. As you know, your father left everything to your mother. There were no stipulations about who was next in line.'

'This is un-fucking-believable.' Jo shook her head wildly. 'She never said anything to me about leaving her money to charity. What about the house? I live here. That must give me some rights.'

'If you'd been living here for two years or more it would, but you've only been back for a few weeks. I think Edith viewed it more as a visit than anything permanent.'

'She knew I had nowhere else to go.' Jo was shouting now, leaning forward out of her chair like she was gonna pounce on poor old Bob. 'What the fuck am I supposed to do? And you let her do this? You and the solicitor?'

'We did question her, as I explained, but Edith was very clear on this matter. She felt she had to be cruel in order to be kind. She thought it would be better for you this way.' Bob's voice went a bit softer. 'This is a very emotional time, of course – it's all very upsetting – but your mother did love you, Joanna, she only wanted what was best for you.'

'How the hell can leaving me penniless be what's best for me?' Jo shook her hands in the air so that her bangles clanked up and down on her arms.

Bob glanced over at Paul like he hoped Paul would come to his rescue, but Paul just sat there, palms together, his chin resting on his fingertips, like he was deep in thought. The corners of his mouth were turning up just a tiny bit – not enough for anyone else but me to notice the smile.

I'd of felt sorry for Jo if she'd been sad, but all this indignation just reminded me of how entitled she was. She assumed the house was coming her way and it wasn't even like she wanted to live in it. She just wanted to make money off it.

'What is this charity, anyway?' Jo got up and started pacing round the room. 'Don't tell me it's a bloody cats' home.'

'No, no, nothing like that.' Bob shook his head. 'I don't think your mother even liked cats.'

'Well what was it then? Some chugger must have got to her, conned her into leaving them her money. Why didn't you investigate?'

I felt like I might wet myself, but it was too late to run off to the toilet. Paul knew what he was doing and he'd said the plan was airtight. I just had to play it cool like him and everything'd be fine.

Paul finally spoke. 'With all respect, Jo, and I totally get how you feel, but Edith was nobody's fool. She might have been elderly, but no one was going to pull the wool over her eyes.'

'I don't agree.' Never mind wool over eyes, Jo sounded like a wax strip was being pulled off her pubes. 'Mum could be very susceptible to the opinions of others.' She gave a little snort. 'I think I know my own mother better than anyone else in this room.'

Paul had said Jo would get nasty. I'd thought she fancied him so much she'd never point the finger at him. Maybe I was wrong.

Bob coughed. 'A childhood friend of Edith's was an unfortunate victim of the Mau Mau uprising. Apparently, she was shot and killed by British soldiers. I can only imagine she was caught in crossfire. Edith said the girl was very bright; that she would have gone on to do great things if her life hadn't been cut short so tragically. I think, in a strange way, Edith wanted to make amends. She felt guilty about the girl's death, seemed to think she might have done something to prevent it. Anyway, the school her friend went to is the beneficiary. Edith wanted to provide the opportunity for Kenyan girls from poor rural backgrounds to have a decent education. I'm sure you'll share my admiration for your mother in promoting such an excellent cause – one that really will have long term benefits for the country of her birth.'

We all stared at Bob. Paul let out a long low whistle.

'Wow,' I said. 'I never saw that coming.'

Maybe I was getting as hysterical as Jo, but I had to fight the urge to burst out laughing. It was weird but I actually felt kind of relieved, like I'd just been lifted off this massive meat hook I'd been dangling off for the last few weeks. I pressed my feet into the floor. There it was – solid ground – I'd forgotten what that felt like.

Bob gave me a funny look, then turned to Jo. 'I'm sure you'll be proud to know that the school will be changing its name to the Graham Forbes Academy for Girls.'

Then I really did feel like I might chuck my breakfast up all over the sofa.

'This is ridiculous. Mum never mentioned any schoolfriend who was killed in Kenya to me.' Jo had got a bottle out of the cabinet and was pouring herself a big glass of red wine. 'Did she ever refer to this girl to either of you?' She looked accusingly at me and then Paul.

We both shook our heads. Paul's face had gone an ashy colour. He went over to the window and forced the heavy frame up. A warm breeze drifted in, pushing the hot air in the room around.

'Never heard of her,' I said.

Then I remembered Edith's nightmares.

'She wasn't called Mary, was she?'

Bob checked through his papers. 'Yes, yes she was. 'In memory of Mary Mwangi,' he read out slowly. 'Died 1953.'

They all looked at me expectantly. My hands had gone clammy. I only realised I was gripping them together in my lap when they started to slide apart. It was stupid really, to feel disloyal to Edith, considering everything. Bit late in the day for all that, I told myself, but the morning she asked me not to tell Jo about her wetting the bed came into my mind and tears started up in my eyes again.

'Edith used to call her name out in her sleep. One time, she said Mary was coming to get her. And the other night, she said there was stuff she regretted – bad stuff.'

'Why didn't you tell me?' Paul and Jo said in stereo.

'That certainly suggests she wasn't in her sound mind,' Paul added carefully. 'If she thought she was being pursued by ghosts.'

'That's right!' Jo jerked her glass, showering drops of red wine onto the carpet. The burgundy spots sank into the grey pile, spreading out like blood stains in a TV crime scene.

'Edith was entirely lucid when she explained her wishes to me.' Bob was sounding pissed off now. 'We went through it all with the solicitor.'

What had Edith done, that she got her friend killed? I shifted to face Bob. 'Edith was completely together when she told me she wanted to leave her money to charity, to make up for people she'd got killed.' I couldn't bring myself to look at Paul. 'I didn't know she meant a girls' school, but…' I swallowed. 'Sounds like a good cause. The sort of thing my nan would approve of. The name seems all wrong though. Wouldn't an African name be better?'

Bob smiled patronisingly at me. 'Well I think that's up to the school, but well done for confirming Edith's wishes, young lady.' He patted my hands. 'I know this isn't easy.'

I wiped my hands on my jeans. If it was up to the school I hoped they'd come up with a better name.

'Well done?' Jo snarled. 'My mother didn't get people killed. What a ridiculous thing to say. 1953 – she'd only have been fifteen then. What do you think she was? A child solider?'

She was shouting at me, her voice dripping with sarcasm. I could feel my heart thumping, the blood pounding in my ears.

'OK, OK, no one's accusing Edith of anything like that.' Paul jumped in. 'I think we all need to take a step back here. Obviously this is a big shock for Jo. And, I have to say, the choice of charity seems a bit dubious. Can you leave us with a copy of the will, Bob?'

'I don't know, I'll have to contact the solicitor.' Bob sounded annoyed.

'Don't bother. I'll be contacting the solicitor myself.' Jo re-filled her glass. 'I'll be contesting this will. There's no way it's valid, whatever little missy here thinks.' She flicked her fingers at me. 'This house is mine.'

I jumped off the sofa and faced up to Jo. Every cell in my body was fizzing with adrenaline. All the thoughts and feelings, about Nan, my dad, Edith – everything I'd been holding down for so long, forced their way up, out of my mouth.

'No, I don't think your mum was a child soldier, but I know

exactly what your dad was.'

'Lauren!' Paul called my name, quietly, urgently, but it was too late.

'He was a rapist. That's what he was, and do you know how I know that? Because he raped my nan.' I jabbed a finger at her. 'Yes, Jo, who thinks she's so hard done by, not inheriting mummy's house, well, guess what? Your dad left my nan with a child to raise on her own, a child he forced on her.'

Jo stared at me like I was completely crazy.

'And your mum didn't trust you – she thought you was a drug addict, and the way you behave I don't blame her.' I was shouting myself now.

'What the fuck are you talking about?' Jo shook her head.

'Lauren, you're over-excited.' Paul's voice was as sharp as a knife, but at least I'd kept him out of it. It was up to him to tell his truth. 'Lauren was very distressed by Edith's death, finding the body, you understand, it was a traumatic experience for a young girl. I think she's transferring her grief about her grandmother onto Edith.' He came over and put his arm around my shoulders, sitting me back down on the sofa.

'Wait a minute.' Bob laid a hand on my elbow. 'Where did you get hold of that story? About your grandmother being raped by Colonel Forbes?'

'It's not a story, my nan told me herself. After we saw Forbes on *Newsnight*. She was arrested in Kenya and taken to a detention camp where he was the officer in charge, and he raped her.' I looked Bob straight in the eyes, daring him to doubt me. 'She never wanted to tell me, but she couldn't help it when she saw his face on the telly – it brought it all back. The torment he put her through. She had to give birth in prison. She said it was a miracle she and my dad survived.'

It was me who got Nan to watch *Newsnight*. I was doing

Media Studies GCSE and it was part of my homework. She'd never have seen it otherwise. Me and Paul, we wouldn't even be here.

Bob's cheeks were red. The sweat was pouring down his face. I was scared he might be having a heart attack.

'So you're Graham's granddaughter? Is that why Edith had you living with her? I thought it was just a professional arrangement.'

I was about to answer when Paul cut in. Keeping a grip on my arm, he leant towards Bob.

'So, let me get this straight. You're saying that Lauren's accusation, about Forbes, is correct and that you knew about it?'

'No, no,' Bob spoke quickly. 'I'm not saying anything of the kind.' He looked at Jo like he was scared and worried at the same time.

Jo had sunk back down onto Edith's armchair. 'Don't spare me, Bob. I might as well know the worst.' She shook her head and muttered, 'If it can get any worse.'

Bob hunched over, clamping his hands flat between his knees. 'Graham did have a youthful indiscretion with an African woman which resulted in a son. This was before he married your mother.'

I could feel Paul's hand heavy on my shoulder, warning me not to speak.

'And the son – that's your dad?' Jo stared at me.

'Yes, but it wasn't an affair – it was rape, in prison.' I turned to Bob. 'And my nan was only sixteen, which made her technically a child.'

At least Jo looked sick when I said that.

'We only have her word for that. Graham was certainly not aware of her young age. I agree some boundaries were crossed, but things were different back then. And you have to remember it was a war situation, the army were operating under a great deal of pressure. I can assure you, Joanna, no case was ever found against your father.'

'So, there was a case?' Paul asked.

'There was an accusation, but it was dismissed.' Bob looked at me. 'And when your father turned up, he received a very generous pay-out from Graham. What I don't understand is why Edith never said anything about you to me.'

'Or to me.' Jo sounded outraged. 'It seems like everyone knew except me.'

'What do you mean, my dad turned up?'

Bob looked startled. 'Didn't Edith tell you? Your father contacted Graham.' He nodded over at Jo. 'Graham felt he owed his son some sort of financial support, gave him £10,000. Told him not to come back.'

I couldn't believe it – my dad had actually met Graham Forbes. I just stopped myself from twisting round to grab Paul.

'Can I just clarify something?' Paul held up one hand, keeping the other one clamped to my shoulder. 'This pay-out, was that settled in court and when was it made?'

'No, it was a private arrangement, about eight years ago. Why?'

'Dad disappeared eight years ago,' I said. 'When I was ten.'

'I'm sorry to hear that.' Bob sounded disapproving. 'He might have used the money to go abroad – back to Africa, perhaps.'

'Like father, like son.' Jo pulled a sour face. 'Didn't want to share the money with his daughter.'

'My dad wasn't like that. He'd never leave his family short.' Fuckers, they didn't know anything about my dad. He was better than all of them put together. 'My nan was broke when she died. There's no way Dad would've let that happen. If he'd had money, he would've sent it to her. And to my mum and all.'

'But you were only ten. How well did you know him, really?'

Jo raised her eyebrows at me.

'Well enough.' I felt like slapping her.

I could see Dad now: kissing Nan on the cheek, tucking a blanket over her knees, the love in his eyes when he asked her if she'd got everything she needed. Nan telling him not to fuss. Dad calling round with flowers for Mum and sweets for me. I could almost feel his hand in mine as we skipped down the street, hopping from one paving stone to another, arms swinging. He never cared what other people thought, just so long as I was having fun.

Paul sat beside me on the armrest of the sofa, his arm pressing lightly against mine. It was like having a wolf breathing down my neck, waiting for its moment to pounce, only I wasn't sure who was going to get it.

'Just asking on Lauren's behalf – this payment, could it be traceable?' I was amazed how calm his voice sounded.

'I believe it was made in cash.' Bob's face went red.

'Did you make the payment, on Graham's behalf?'

'I had nothing to do with it. Graham told me about it afterwards,' Bob said indignantly.

'How come he told you?'

Paul's tone was relaxed, curious, like he was chatting to someone in a pub. Only I could feel how much effort it was costing him, the tension was pulsing out of him like electricity, crackling from his arm to mine, discharging out into my chest until I felt like my heart would explode.

'And why did nobody tell me?' Jo's bracelets jangled on her wrists. 'I have a half-brother out there somewhere. I've been living with a niece and nobody thought to mention it.'

After a long pause, Bob said, 'Perhaps Edith was worried about how you might react.'

'Why, for God's sake? Did she think I'm so immature I'd be

jealous or something? I could have supported Mum emotionally through all of this.' Jo shook her head sadly. 'My mother really didn't know me at all.' She got up and poured herself another glass of wine. 'I thought we were friends, Lauren.' She gave me an evil look. I suddenly felt quite thankful to be sandwiched between Bob and Paul.

'I swear, it's been a nightmare having to keep this secret, but I promised not to tell anyone.' At least that was all true.

'How typical of Mum not to want anyone to know the Forbes' dirty little secret, Dad's black love-child.' She narrowed her eyes, examining my face. 'You don't look anything like him.'

'Good,' I couldn't help saying. 'And my dad wasn't a love-child.'

'My father was not a rapist.' Jo sank down on the floor in front of us, crossing her legs and cradling her glass of wine in both hands. She looked like she was going to cry. 'Let's face it, none of us really know what happened between my dad and Lauren's grandmother. I mean, she might have lied about her age – a lot of women do. And what was she doing in prison if she was only sixteen?'

I could feel Paul's hand curling into a fist against my back.

'Well, exactly,' Bob said.

And I'd actually felt sorry for the sweaty bastard.

'Nan said there was a twelve-year-old girl in there with her who'd been given life for hanging out with armed men – life! Because her brothers and cousins were carrying. My nan was picked up for being out on the street after curfew. She'd no reason to lie about her age, but whatever age she was it was still rape. It was British Government policy – that's what Forbes told her. To make the Mau Mau turn against her for having a white man's child.'

'That's nonsense,' Bob spluttered. 'Rape has never been

endorsed by the British Government.'

'Happened though, didn't it?' Paul said. 'Torture, sexual assault. That's why those Kenyans won their court case. British Government had to apologise, pay them compensation.'

Someone in the square was bouncing a football. The regular thud as it hit the ground was coming in through the open window.

'Dad wasn't implicated in any of that.' Jo looked up at Bob.

'You were in Italy at the time. Your parents thought it unnecessary to trouble you with it.' He pushed his hands along his thighs, like he was trying to press out the creases in his trousers. 'There were some rather unpleasant accusations, as aired, very irresponsibly, on that particular *Newsnight* programme. Of course Graham denied them all. It was all just hearsay, rumour. There was absolutely no evidence.'

'I'm evidence.' Well it was true, whatever Mum said. It was in my DNA, like a genetic disease.

Paul rubbed my back, his hand making circles over my spine.

'It would have been extremely difficult for your grandmother to admit to an affair with a European, being forced might have been something she convinced herself of, to save her honour.' Bob spoke hesitantly.

If he could've witnessed Nan's pain when she told me, felt her suffering, then he'd know what complete crap he was spouting.

'Perhaps Forbes convinced himself that it wasn't rape, to save his honour,' Paul said.

Jo shot him a wounded look. 'Anyway, all this secrecy and subterfuge just proves Mum's will can't be trusted.' She nodded vigorously. 'We'll contest this will together, Lauren. It's our birthright that's been given away to strangers. There's no way it'll stand up in court.'

I didn't know whether to laugh or cry.

After Bob had gone Jo had a change of mind.

'Pack up your stuff and get out of my house.' She spoke more quietly than I'd ever heard her before and she couldn't bring herself to look me in the face.

'It isn't your house though.' I tried to catch her bloodshot blue eyes.

She really lost it then. 'It is my fucking house and I don't want liars living here. I don't know what you and Mum were up to, sneaking around behind my back, but I won't have it.' She grabbed me by the shoulders and pushed me towards the hall.

I turned to Paul, expecting him to intervene, but he just jerked his chin at me, like I should go along with what Jo wanted. She was shoving me out the room.

'Get your fucking hands off me,' I yelled, the anger rising up like smoke through my body.

I ran up the stairs, Jo following me. I tried to push my bedroom door shut, but she forced her way in. She started pulling my stuff off the shelves and dumping everything on the bed.

'Edith would hate you doing this to me.'

'Don't you dare talk about my mother or what she'd want.'

'She said I cared more about her than you did.' Well, she had said that.

Jo looked like she might throttle me. Her eyes narrowed and her mouth twisted into a tight line. 'My mother didn't even want you here any more, didn't see the point of you once I was home.'

Paul turned up in the doorway looking worried. He was probably scared I'd spill the beans on him.

'Lauren, love, I think, given everyone's high tension right now, it is best you leave.' He held a fist up to his ear and mouthed 'I'll call you' behind Jo's back.

Where exactly did he expect me to go? Just because his mum

still kept his old bedroom for him, he assumed mine'd do the same for me.

'Jo,' he said, like he was talking to a hyperactive five-year-old about to kick off in the supermarket. 'Let Lauren get herself sorted. We can sit in the garden until she's gone.'

Why was he sucking up to her still? He put an arm round Jo and tried to lead her out of the room, but she wasn't budging. She stuck her hand out, her arm trembling.

'I want the front door keys back.'

Paul nodded at me and winked. Faced with the two of them I didn't feel like I had much choice. I didn't fancy sleeping in that house with Jo anyway. There was no lock on my bedroom door – she might try and murder me in the night. I could imagine waking up with her hands round my neck. The bitch was batshit crazy.

When I came downstairs with my bags, Jo was waiting in the hall. She literally escorted me off the premises like a security guard with a shoplifter.

I stood on the doorstep feeling completely stunned. My hands were shaking so much I could hardly get my phone out. I was tempted to march back up the steps and hold my finger to the bell until they let me back in. Why the fuck was I covering for Paul? Let's see Jo's face when she found out he was her nephew. Was she going to chuck him out as well?

He was standing at the living-room window watching me. Why didn't he stand up for me? Was he angry with me for what I'd said?

'What the fuck?' I mouthed at him.

'Be patient,' he mouthed back, waving his mobile.

Then Jo walked back in the room and he turned away to talk to her.

I pulled my empty keyring out of my pocket. All I had left

was the little felt dog. Now I had no keys to anywhere. I was homeless.

❂

'You off on holiday?' Sam's mum stood in the doorway looking at my suitcase, pretending she couldn't see the bulging binbag under my arm.

'Sam said I could stay for a bit.'

I stared down at the doormat. It had 'Home' printed in big black letters across the middle of it, more like a warning than a welcome. It was a relief when Sam came rushing down the hallway. She squeezed past her mum and grabbed my things.

'Come straight up to my room,' she said, leading me up the stairs.

I was scared Paul might hate me for telling Jo and Bob about Nan, but he texted me later that night to check I was OK. He said to sit tight and not to worry. He was sure he could get the earlier will – where Edith left everything to his charity – endorsed and overturn this new one. He still wouldn't tell Jo about being her nephew.

Sam's parents agreed I could stay for two weeks. After that I guessed I'd be on the sofa at Mum's until I could find a room to rent. I didn't want to get my hopes up about Paul's plans. Couldn't find the enthusiasm for them any more, to be honest. I just felt done in by the whole thing. All that tension, worrying about getting caught out – I didn't need it.

At first it was great hanging out with someone my own age again. A proper friend I could have a laugh with. I hadn't realised how much I'd missed that. But having to get up for work got harder and harder – heading out into the rush-hour crush, leaving Sam sleeping off our nights' out. And then having to traipse all the way up to Colindale for my courses.

Sam was up for going out every night and I didn't want to be left at home with her parents, watching box sets on TV. Also, being out was better than the two of us squashed up on her single bed together. But I was getting so tired I was finding it hard to concentrate at work and on my course. I missed having my own bedroom.

It was weird being back in a family home again too, being treated like a kid by Sam's parents. At least with Edith I'd felt like I had a right to be there – not just because of Forbes being my grandad, but also because she needed me. We had our routine and I had a job to do, which I suppose made me feel kind of grown-up and important. Jo was spouting shit about Edith not wanting me there.

I started to get really depressed. Everyone else seemed to be having more fun than me. I was sick of serving snotty customers and getting grief for not hitting the sales targets. Then a client complained I hadn't done her nails properly. She wouldn't let me near her to redo them. No, my manager – also my tutor – had to do it. So I got an earful from her as well. I suddenly thought, is this going to be my life from now on? Sucking up to bitches? Is this what I really want to do? The thought of going back to Mum's and being lectured by her as well just about did my head in.

The thing about renaming that Kenyan school kept niggling away at the back of my mind as well. It was like spitting on Nan's grave, giving it Forbes' name. What was the point of all the stress and heartache of the last few months if that was the end result?

It took me a while, but eventually I got up the balls to ring the school and ask to speak to the head. I told them I was Graham Forbes' granddaughter, saying that felt so weird, but it got me a conversation with Mrs Ochanda. She was so nice, listened to everything I had to say, about Nan, what Forbes had done, all of it. She was totally unfazed, already knew about the other allegations against Forbes.

She had this calm, assured way of talking, like she could handle anything. I pictured her sitting behind a big wooden desk, wearing a smart wax-print dress in purple and green, with a matching head wrap. But she might have been in a trouser suit for all I knew.

She said of course she was delighted with the donation. It was very generous of Mrs Forbes and would make a huge difference in enabling Kenyan girls from rural backgrounds to attain an education. The school was all about empowering girls to achieve their potential, to go out and make a difference to the world. It had a proud history of notable alumni. The name Graham Forbes did not sit easily with that mission. She paused for a moment.

'The wording of the will expresses a desire, not a stipulation. I doubt it would stand up in a Kenyan court if someone were to insist that the wish to rename the school was upheld. Is anyone likely to insist on that, anyone you know?'

I told her about Jo's plan to challenge the will. She sighed. Said she wouldn't rely on the money in that case. I didn't say anything about Paul.

'Thank you for taking the trouble to speak with me, Lauren. It was a courageous thing to do. I'm sure your grandmother would be proud of you.'

That made me choke up a bit. I mumbled something random.

'So, you're eighteen, you said. Are you at school? What are you studying?'

'Beauty.'

'Is that a subject? You sound like a very intelligent young woman. Don't waste the opportunities you have in Britain.

Education is a gift. Use it.'

That was a bit of a put-down. What made me feel really shit though, was the thought that if Paul's plan worked we'd be taking money from that school. That couldn't be right.

I needed to see him, to talk him out of challenging the will and to get him to stop Jo too. I didn't understand why he was still so fixated on the house and the money when basically his whole project was sorted. He just needed to tell Jo who he really was. Make that spoilt cow see what a monster her dad was. Her and stupid old Bob and everyone else like them.

I picked a time when I knew Jo would be out at her yoga training and texted Paul to check he was in.

Even though it was only a week since I'd left, it still felt strange walking across Gainsford Square. 'Hello House, how've you been without me?' I looked up at the glossy black front door. The bay tree on the doorstep was looking a bit yellow and the red geraniums in the window box were wilting. 'Bet you're not as clean as when I was living inside you. You're probably all choked up with dust. Can't see lazy old Jo doing any polishing.'

I was just about to walk up the front steps when the door opened and a white guy in a pinstriped suit and hot pink socks came out. He was talking to Paul. When he saw me, Paul came bouncing down the steps and pressed his key into my hand.

'Go down to the basement and wait for me. Jo's in,' he muttered, before heading straight back inside.

I stood in front of the pinstriped gent – he was wide enough to hide me from view in case Jo was looking out the window. 'So, were you visiting Mrs Forbes' daughter then?' I said in my most chatty tone.

He tried to walk away without answering, but I was blocking him so he ended up telling me Miss Forbes had asked him to evaluate the contents of the house. She'd told him she wanted to sell the lot, but then her partner said they'd changed their minds. He sounded really pissed off. I guess by 'partner' he meant Paul, which was a bit weird.

'The grandmother clock's mine,' I said quickly, in case Jo asked him back. 'Mrs Forbes left it me in her will.'

'The miniature longcase in the hall?'

'If you mean the clock, then yes.'

He perked up then. His bushy eyebrows popped up to meet his receding hairline. 'Beautiful piece.' He carried on, talking to himself like I wasn't there, 'Seventeenth century, very unusual brass dial with those foliate scroll spandrels, and the inscription. I'd need to take another look, but I think it might be a John Wise piece.' He looked at me like he'd just remembered I was standing right in front of him. 'I could sell it for you if you like, get you at least a thousand for it.'

'A grand? You serious?' I stared at him, wide-eyed.

'I could get someone to collect it tomorrow, give you cash for it.'

'Hmmm, it's the sentimental value though, innit?' I looked him up and down. 'I'll have a think about it.'

He smiled. His teeth were bleached so white I wished I was wearing sunnies to cut out the glare.

'Of course, completely understand. I'll give you my card, and if you change your mind just give me a call. Tell you what, why don't I take your number? I can give you a ring next week – see how you're feeling then.'

I took his card. 'That's OK. I'll call you.' Made me feel kind of smug, being able to say that.

He nodded. 'Just don't go selling it on eBay, or Gumtree. You won't get anything like what it's worth. Come to us first – if you change your mind, that is.'

'Thanks for the tip.' I winked.

Paul would be keeping Jo away from the windows, I could sneak down to his now without her seeing me.

While I waited for Paul I checked my phone to see if I had any pictures of my clock. I was sure I'd taken some for Insta. I'd been planning on making some clever comment about time flying – because of the *tempus fugit* inscription – but never got round to it.

When I finally found the photos, I saw for the first time how beautiful it was. The gold face with the delicate swirls round it and the way the dark brown wood picked up the light. Mind you, that was thanks to all my polishing. It'd been dusty as anything when I first arrived. You could see how warm the wood was. It was glowing from the sunlight shining in through the glass panels in the front door. Made me feel sad I couldn't go up there and put my hand against its side. I wanted to lean against it and feel the pendulum knocking against my ribs, hear its loud ticking and its bright chiming in of the hour.

'What're you really worth then, Granny?'

After a lot of searches, I sent a photo of the clock to this auctioneer named Bonhams. I liked the name cos it reminded me of the actress that played Bellatrix Lestrange in the Harry Potter films. She looked like she'd know all about old stuff.

Paul wouldn't give up on Edith's will, even after I told him what a good cause the school was. He said I was as bad as the Forbes, spouting their patronising middle-class ideas about charity. Couldn't I see? Charitable donations were just a sop to the establishment, a way of making sure things stayed the same. The rich could throw their crumbs to the poor and get slapped on the back for it, just so long as they didn't have to pay what they owed in tax or change their lifestyles in any way. If he got the money he'd use it for campaigning, for making a real difference.

It didn't matter what I said about Kenyan girls being able to get an education. I even asked him to talk to Mrs Ochanda, but he wouldn't listen. I said, why wasn't he campaigning now if that's what he wanted to do, but he claimed he needed funds for that. I'd thought it was the principle that was important to him, but it seemed like the money had started to stand in for everything else so he couldn't see past it. Instead of freeing him up, that house was not just tying Paul down, it was tying him up in knots – him and Jo together. I didn't want to get trapped with them.

I'd always looked up to Paul, thought everything about him was perfect. Now I wondered if I really knew him at all. I'd seen him how I wanted him to be, just like Edith and Jo did. He was our ideal man in three different ways, but none of them was real.

Jo was surprisingly friendly when I texted to ask if someone could come round to take my clock away. She called me back, saying she had a favour to ask me too. Typical Jo. She went on about how hard it was being all alone in the world and feeling like her mum must've hated her not to leave her anything. Why would she choose strangers over her own child? I did my best to make her believe Edith did really love her, but I'm not a bloody therapist. Then she said she'd talked it through with Paul and he'd made her see how having me as a relative might be a comfort. OK, I thought, I know where this is leading. Then Jo asked me to do a DNA test. I wasn't worried. To be honest, I'd be relieved if it told me I wasn't related to Forbes, but I knew in my heart what the result would be. Nan recognised Forbes the second she saw his picture, and the way she reacted, I knew she wasn't mistaken.

As it turns out, my clock wasn't really a granny. The man from the Bonhams place – who wasn't anything like Bellatrix Lestrange, which was a bit of a let down to be honest – said grandmother clocks are more like a modern invention and don't fetch half so much as grandfather clocks. No, my clock was an ebony miniature longcase and it went for £110,000 at auction.

I offered half to Paul, but he wouldn't take it. Said it was mine fair and square, which was sound of him. I'd hoped the money would stop him going after Edith's will, but no chance. Then I tried to give Mum some of it, but she said I should invest the money. Buy myself a flat, or use it to further my education. That was the kind of investment Nan would've approved of.

Me and the clock man from Bonham's got on pretty well as it happens. I asked him about some of the other stuff of Edith's – didn't tell him I'd sold them of course. I just wanted to know more about those pretty plates and the weird snake necklace and how you can tell if something's valuable and how old it is. He said if I was interested in antiques I should study history of art. He liked my descriptions – said I had an eye for detail. I said he should see some of my nail art. He invited me to a lecture at the Victoria and Albert Museum.

I only went because it was free and he said there'd be drinks. I took Ash with me for back-up, thought it was the kind of thing he might like. We got a bit bored in the lecture so we sneaked out the back and went off round the museum. We had such a laugh. Some of the fashion stuff was amazing, especially the jewellery. Like these creepy brooches that had a close-up painting of somebody's eye with a tiny diamond teardrop. The pictures were so small you could hardly see them but there was so much detail in there. They must've used the tiniest brush ever – like a mini eyeliner brush.

I was trying to read the little card underneath when Ash said, 'You really get off on this shit, don't you?'

'Yeah,' I said. 'I guess I do.'

As we were leaving he put an arm round me. 'You know,

sweets, it's obvious you're not happy in Selfridges. I'm not saying you should give up on the beauty industry, but I don't think it's where you want to be and it shows. I've never seen you so fired up about make-up as you were in there looking at those jewellery collections.'

We were walking past the Science Museum, heading for the tube. I thought of what Mrs Ochanda said, about all the opportunities over here. Didn't always feel that way, but I guess she was right – there was a lot going on.

'D'you think I should ask for a transfer to the jewellery counter?'

Ash laughed. 'Maybe, then work your way up to become a buyer. I think you need a business degree for that though.'

'I suppose I could switch courses. Take some A-levels – see what I want to do after.'

'Yeah, I mean, you've got all this money now. The world's your oyster.' We paused at the entrance to the tube. 'You know Stacey's looking for someone to flatshare. She's finally moving out of her mum's.'

'Stacey? Oh my God, I couldn't live with her!'

Ash shrugged. 'She's all right you know. She's smarter than she lets on.'

'What the hell is that?' I pointed at the mess on my plate.

'Lentil spag bol.' Stacey rolled her eyes like it was obvious.

'Where's the spaghetti?'

'We've run out so I used rice noodles, only they've gone a bit mushy.' She stirred her fork round her plate.

I was so hungry I took a mouthful. It actually tasted OK. I just had to shut my eyes while I ate it.

Stacey laughed. 'Oh babe, you do look funny. Watch you don't miss your mouth.'

That was the nice thing about Stacey – she never took offence. She was surprisingly easy to live with. Maybe staying with Edith and Jo had lowered my standards, but Ash was right – there was more to Stacey than you might think. Also, she was really tidy and I liked that.

She nearly wet herself when I said I'd move in with her. I never even knew she liked me that much. To be fair, it was also because she'd found this really cool flat in Whitechapel and needed someone to share the rent. It looked a bit rough on the outside but inside was amazing. Really modern. It was about as different from Edith's place as you could get. There was an open-plan kitchen-living area with smooth, glossy grey cupboards that opened like magic when you pressed them, and sparkly black flooring – no carpets. Long windows opened out onto a little balcony.

'Estate agent called it a Juliet balcony – ain't that romantic?' Stacey told me when she showed me round. She leant over the edge and shouted, 'Romeo, Romeo, where the fuck are you?'

On the street below, a man in a *salwar kameez* looked up with a startled expression. Then a pigeon landed on the railings and Stacey quickly pulled the windows shut. We collapsed on the sofa giggling.

There was even a walk-in shower.

Turns out Stacey was a bit of a Beautuber star, with half a million followers on Instagram. She got sent so much stuff to promote she gave half of it to me. People liked her because she said what she really thought about the products. Also, her make-up style looked a lot better on a screen than it did in reality.

Stacey said she'd hated working in Selfridges – that's why she came across as a bit stroppy. A mate of hers had opened this trendy hairdresser's in Shoreditch and said she could have her own room at the back for giving beauty treatments. She's only going to use vegan products on her clients. She'd watched this video called *Cowspiracy* and said she couldn't take part in animal cruelty no more. Hence why we had to eat weird lentil mush. Her blogs were going more and more towards all-natural cosmetics but she wasn't there yet. And she said she didn't want to do the blogging full-time because she's a Taurus and needs financial stability.

If it takes off she said I can work in her little salon too. I don't mind doing Saturdays, but I need to focus on the 'A' levels. I enrolled in a college in Hackney. I didn't find anywhere offering history of art, but I've signed up for history, politics and English and they said I could go on to do history of art at uni if I wanted. We'll see.

Paul always said you had to know your history if you wanted to put things right. If I understood the hows and whys of the way the world is, maybe I could do my bit to change it. Show him I wasn't just sucking up to the establishment and swallowing all their lies. And no one like Edith could ever assume I didn't understand or tell me I was ignorant or uneducated.

I was definitely going to write Nan's story. Set the record straight. Everything she'd been through, everything she overcame – I'd put it all out there on my own blog. Or even better, in a book – the kind you see on *Oprah's Book Club*. Maybe it'd get made into a movie. I even started imagining who'd play Nan as a young girl till I told myself to get a grip. My God, though, when I thought about what she went through and how it'd all been covered up and forgotten about… I couldn't give her justice, but I'd make sure she finally got the recognition she was owed.

I'd been on the point of telling Mum everything, couldn't stand keeping it to myself any longer. But when I went round there Amber was sick and Mike came home early. Mum was busy with them and I got cold feet. Maybe I'll tell her one day –

just not now. Think she might turn her back on me if she knew what me and Paul had been up to. I'm the golden girl right now and to be honest, I just want to enjoy basking in all that appreciation for a bit.

Sometimes I wonder if Edith knew what the clock was worth. I hope she did and that was why she left it me. Out of all the antiques in the house, why leave a clock to an eighteen-year-old? It wasn't exactly portable – wasn't like a Fitbit or a piece of jewellery I could wear.

I didn't feel guilty about selling it – I'm not sentimental about things. It's people and what they do that matters. '*Tempus fugit*', as the clock said. Time flies – better grab it while you can. I'm sure Edith would approve of what I'm doing with the money, especially seeing as she wanted everything else left to a school. I'm just carrying on that legacy.

It was so weird to think she might've met my dad, and that Graham definitely had. If I'd fessed up to her, told her everything, she might've been able to give me some clues about what happened to him, where he went.

I'd told Paul about all those papers in the attic. He was going to go through them – said he'd let me know if he found anything. Paul thought there was something very dodgy about the way Dad disappeared straight after meeting the Forbes, as well as this payment Forbes was supposed to have made. He even suspected they might've had him bumped off. I took that as another sign Paul was losing it – he seemed to think he was living in some sort of thriller. No, what made sense to me was Mum's idea – that Dad had had an accident or been mugged and lost his memory. He definitely wouldn't've killed himself, not after finding Forbes. I mean, why would he? Especially after being given all that money.

Dad always made me feel I could do anything, be anything

I wanted. Even though I was only little he always listened seriously to me, like I was another adult. We'd have such cool conversations as he pushed me on the swings or we walked through the park. He was brilliant at distracting me when the lifts were broken and we had to take the stairs to the flat.

If I made a name for myself by, like, writing books and ending up on TV, Dad might recognise me. It'd jolt his memory – like when Nan saw Forbes on *Newsnight*, only in a good way. I smiled to myself as I pictured the scene – being reunited with my Dad after so many missing years, how he'd wrap his arms around me and we'd cry with happiness. Dad always gave the best hugs.

That was the other thing I was thinking about doing with the money, hiring a private detective to look for Dad. That's what Stacey said she'd do. Also, me and Paul might take a trip out to Kenya – see what we can find. For now, though, here I am back in E1, sliding round the lino in my socks.

ACKNOWLEDGEMENTS

Charity is a work of fiction which was partly inspired by the landmark case brought against the British government by Leigh Day & Co on behalf of five elderly Kenyans who were detained during the Mau Mau independence movement of the 1950s. A settlement was finally reached in 2013 and the then foreign secretary, William Hague, expressed regret that thousands of Kenyans had been subjected to torture and other forms of ill-treatment at the hands of the British colonial administration.

Research for the novel included recently released documents at The National Archives, Kew (many colonial era documents remain locked); pamphlets and documents at the Archives & Special Collections, SOAS Library; the work of historians Caroline Elkins, David Anderson, and Huw Bennett; the writing and memoirs of Ngũgĩ Wa Thiong'o; Josiah Mwangi Kariuki; Jomo Kenyatta; Muthoni Likimani, Wangari Muta Maathai and Wanbui Waiyaki Otieno, among others.

I'm hugely grateful to all the readers of early drafts, in particular; Lily Teevan and the members of my Royal Holloway, University of London writing group for their insights and encouragement.

My thanks to all at Lightning Books: Dan Hiscocks, Clio Mitchell for copyediting and typesetting, Ifan Bates for the wonderful cover design and especially my editor, Simon Edge, for his excellent guidance.

With thanks always to my husband, Colin Teevan, for his constant support, love and inspiration.

ABOUT THE AUTHOR

Madeline Dewhurst studied English at Queen's University Belfast and went on to complete an MA in Research and a PhD at Queen Mary, University of London. She also has an MA in Creative Writing from Royal Holloway. She is an academic in English and Creative Writing at the Open University.

Her previous writing includes fiction, journalism and drama. *Charity*, which was longlisted for the Bath Novel Award, is her first novel.

She now lives in Kent.

If you have enjoyed *Charity*, do please help us spread the word – by posting a review on Amazon (you don't need to have bought the book there) or Goodreads; by posting something on social media; or in the old-fashioned way by simply telling your friends or family about it.

Book publishing is a very competitive business these days, in a saturated market, and small independent publishers such as ourselves are often crowded out by the big houses. Support from readers like you can make all the difference to a book's success.

Many thanks.

Dan Hiscocks
Publisher
Lightning Books